THE HEART OF
THE SYNDICATE

THE HEART OF THE SYNDICATE

S.M. STILES

Queer Space

New Orleans & New York

Published in the United States of America by
Rebel Satori Press
www.rebelsatoripress.com

Cover illustration: S.M. Stiles

ISBN: 978-1-60864-389-9

*This book is dedicated to the part of my heart
that is now sleeping in stardust . . .
the DAVE to my BLAINE,
SARA-JANE
This book exists because of your transcendent support—
and because you took so fucking long to peer read my other shit,
I wrote this one while I waited.
(Ha! But seriously—thank you.)*

*I know all of your universes are connected to mine.
But you left this one far too soon.
I'll be looking for you in the next one.*

*You and I will meet again, my friend in the stardust.
— the BLAINE to your DAVE*

Y/OUR FUTURE IS Y/OURS . . . . . .

To the outside world doing business with the Thornwryght crime syndicate, the words could be interpreted in more than one way.

OUR FUTURE IS YOURS . . . (We are here to serve you and do what we can to get you what you need. Sacrifices might be made to get that done if the price is right.)

YOUR FUTURE IS YOURS . . . (We are here to protect you and keep you from harm. We will help you become what you wish to become. If the price is right, you are untouchable.)

OUR FUTURE IS OURS . . . (We mind our own business and won't take anyone else down with us if we are ever exposed. We are proud and resilient and will share it with you if the price is right.)

But there was only one true way for a Thornwryght to canonise it—

.   . . . . . **YOUR FUTURE IS OURS**

Those words were the core of the family secret.

I.

"Father has summoned The Twenty-One."

HE WAS BORN TO ACCEPT that he was destined to one day burn in Hell with the rest of his family—but burning on Earth first seemed really fucking unfair.

Especially getting burned twenty times and being left with twenty scars.

They were small enough to potentially become insignificant, but there were constant reminders surrounding him that the scars were still there. Even if he refused to ever look into a mirror or look directly at his bare skin, a day never went by that he forgot to care that they were there.

Cigarettes were everywhere on the large private peninsula. It was the sticks, the smoke, the rubbish left behind or expensive accessories. All of his spoiled siblings smoked.

Synclare Thornwryght had twenty of those, too.

He had seven years for the pain of a fresh cigarette burn to finally dull into just a vague detail of unforgettable memories, but now he had new reminders on his hands—defensive wounds. He was now twenty years old with a sibling and a burn for each year of life. It was an unpleasant tally.

After being held down and branded—albeit with a sumptuous brand—Synclare had retreated into his room to hide. He wanted to leave his current world and play one of his virtual consoles, a gift his family had received from the yakuza. He blamed how poorly he was doing on his pain—and how much he sucked at everything, anyway. He found out that he may even suck at just being related to his family.

Somehow, he fucked that up, too.

The reason that Synclare had been burned again was because of a fresh rumour spreading on the Thornwryght peninsula. It was possible that not all of the infamous Ephraym Thornwryght's twenty-one children were actually his.

Because he looked the least like his father—red-haired and covered in freckles—everyone suspected he was not actually related to the dark-haired rest of them. His family had dark siren eyes throwing judgement, but he had green doe eyes drowning in consternation.

His siblings were inspired to start bullying him again by trying to burn off more of his freckles with cigarettes. He feared his eyes were also on the agenda.

The only thing that kept him alive in such a bloodthirsty family was blood—and he might not have that anymore.

He was small and thin and not a good fit in a crime syndicate, anyway. He wasn't a fighter—he was just angry. He had to be. He was angry and he kept to himself.

He was often just left to be angry at himself.

Synclare's room in the mansion was the smallest. It was practically a closet, but he liked it. He was in an unused wine cellar which gave his room a post-apocalyptic look. It looked like the room of a typical young adult in the enhanced 1983▶▶—they were all wild about the latest technology and neon wrapped around tenebrous imagery. The only light available in his windowless room was an enormous glowing tapestry that hung from the wall—it looked like a rainy, neon city street that he could just walk right through to a place he'd rather be.

The young redhead hoped his father wouldn't hire anyone to actively run the kitchen above him so that his room could remain a secret.

Only one sibling knew where his room was.

His sister Brayden knocked and entered Synclare's room when she didn't hear him yell at her to go away.

Synclare wasn't the only one in the family who was pale, red-haired and freckled. Brayden was also born a fair-skinned ginger, but she was not small and thin, nor was she weak.

She was the second oldest of the Thornwryght children and the oldest daughter. She had long braids that were always wrapped around her head and laying across her shoulders in unique and attractive ways. She had crimped bangs and her strawberry hair was dyed black. She wore concealer to hide the freckles on any exposed skin. She didn't have as many freckles as her little brother, but she still wanted to hide them.

Her eyes were green like Synclare's, but she wore dark gold contacts with a braided pattern around the iris. Her eyes were not the same large doe eyes as her brother, though. They were upturned and almond-shaped like most of the Thornwryghts.

Synclare admired his sister. She was "cursed" with the same looks as him, but she didn't let that keep her from her destiny. It also helped that no one but Synclare knew that she was a redhead. Their mother had successfully hidden this fact—but failed to be able to do so with Synclare. There were more suspicious, watchful eyes in the family by the time he was born.

But Synclare had a feeling that her true appearance would be excused at this point because she had already proven herself to be a Thornwryght worth keeping.

At age twelve, she had choked three burglars to death. They had broken into the mansion—she had lured them there herself. She used her long braids to kill them, one by one. She had grown out her hair and planned it all from a very early age, inspired by her nickname—Brayd.

Synclare had his own nickname that only she ever used—Sync. His name inspired nothing. If anything, the rest of his family would want to hear his nickname as Sink. It may inspire them to find him a place at the bottom of the sea.

At least he couldn't be burned anymore down there.

Before Sync acknowledged his sister, she saw his freshly burned hands. Brayd quickly snuffed out her cigarette and hid it.

"Who was it?" she angrily asked.

Sync pretended not to know what she meant as she sat down next to him on his bed and touched his hands.

"I painted them myself. I don't need a servant to do it for me." His nails were now painted five neon colours instead of his usual black with just a neon middle finger.

"Who burned you, Sync?"

Annoyed that she wasn't taking the hint that he didn't want to talk about it, he threw off his virtual helmet and tucked his hands into his pinstripe jacket.

"Doesn't fucking matter. All of them. What do you want?"

"Father has summoned The Twenty-One. We have to go." She stood up to show the urgency of her message.

Sync realized then what the message on his vidphone was that he had just recently ignored.

[3]

"Do you think he has chosen his heir?" he asked.

"I doubt it. He'd throw a party for that. I haven't seen any preparations for something that grand. Your room is right under the pastry kitchen and it's silent as a cemetery. They'd definitely be using it. He also wouldn't make such a momentous decision on a Thursday."

Sync gingerly swallowed and felt his chest ache with uncertainty. He never liked being summoned, especially when it was for an unknown reason. If it was to announce the chosen heir, he wouldn't even have to be awake for it if he felt inclined to try to prop himself up in a corner to zone out. He'd sneak in earphones and listen to something else until it was over.

It would *never* be him that was chosen.

If anything, he hoped it would be Brayd. He probably wouldn't be banished—or executed—if it was Brayd.

Brayd helped straighten up Sync's usual attire—a custom black three-piece suit with subtle neon pinstripes of every colour of the rainbow. She checked him over to make sure he wouldn't be an eyesore to the rest of the family.

She gave an exasperated sigh seeing the checkered fluro lining inside the jacket again, but appreciated the plain white buttoned shirt and sea green sweater underneath it all—this time.

He didn't care when she started plucking off the pins on his jacket lapel. They were pins he had collected over the years, typically finding them on the ground in the nearby city. The default focus his eyes had were usually down near his shoes.

Brayd first removed the one that was checkered green with the word "whatever" written in cursive—their father hated that word.

The others were just as tasteless, though—Sync intended for them to be.

Same SHIT, Different DAY

This Place . . . SUCKS

Question Authority

DANGER HIGH VOLTAGE

Do You Get The Point

God's On A Mission From Me

Born 2 Die

I'VE GOT A HARD ON

YOUR MOVE!

I'm A Clover ♣ Not A Fighter

Watch Your Step

Fuck Off & DIE!

I ♥ Daddy's Money

Eat the Rich

Reach Out & Suck Someone

Creature of the Night

OUT RAGE OUS

Just Pretend It's Candy

ASK ABOUT OUR MYSTERY ITEM

BE A PROBLEM SOLVER

He'd put them back on later.

She flipped the switches on his checkered slip-on shoes that stopped them from glowing. While down there, she tried to rub off the "FUCK YOU" he had written on the edge of one of the midsoles, until he defiantly stepped away.

Brayd always ignored his pants being purposely too short in an attempt to make himself feel taller and to show off his fluro orange socks.

She also sadly ignored the pin on his right shoe that said "*non smoking*," wondering where he got it—she thought it was the most depressing one of all. It looked cheap and dirty like his other pins. This was the opposite of the expensive black diamond stud earrings he always wore. She knew those had been their mother's.

She tried to tame his unkempt crew cut. It was overgrown and sticking up in the front. He had not shown up when the barber came to the peninsula.

Brayd finished her fussing by tugging on the rope he always wore around his neck.

"I know you have ties, Sync."

"They're fucking nooses, too," he growled.

Sync was tired of wearing the Thornwryght syndicate logo that was on every tie available to him. As wicked as the syndicate was, he thought the symbol looked like a sad, stupid ankh moth. He was sick of looking at it. It was all over the peninsula and impossible to avoid—but at least he could avoid it in the mirror. Everywhere else he tried to squint and see something much more wicked, like a spaceship or a tiger.

He yanked himself away from her touches and headed out his wine cellar bedroom door with slumped posture, stomping up the stairs.

Together with his sister, they went to the main ballroom on the ground floor. Just before Sync would be seen by their father standing at the top of the grand staircase, Brayd jabbed on her brother's lower back to make him stand up straight. She then spotted the pin on his back shoulder—DON'T FOLLOW ME. I'M LOST.

She reached out to snatch it, but then let it be.

Sync groaned, but appreciated the reminder about his posture. He also appreciated that she let him physically brood all the way until the last possible moment. Brayd was the only one who understood him.

One of the first eyes that he felt land on him was his father's personal bodyguard and driver.

Sync glared back. "He's staring at me again, Brayd," he growled through gritted teeth.

Brayd leaned in closer to her younger brother, but still kept her eyes on all of their other siblings gathering around to make sure none were targeting her little brother.

"Who? Oh." She spotted the tall man at their father's side.

She liked his magenta hair and thought his scarred face was impressively valorous, especially the intense bruising that looked like a patchy eye mask around his anisocoria.

"You know he had a brain injury. You see his pupils? They don't match. He's allowed to stare," she whispered as she headed to the front of the line. "He can't hurt you."

Sync tried his best to ignore him, but a strange mechanical glint in his eyes always drew his attention back—and he was always still looking at him.

Once all of his children had arrived and were standing in the order they were born, Ephraym Thornwryght took a moment to analyze them—The Twenty-One.

1. Tobyas Edwyn — 36M
2. Brayden Alyce — 35F
3. Benjamyn Mylo — 34M
4. Amelya Brynda — 33F

5. Davyd Austyn — 32M
6. Adalyne Natalya — 32F
7. Jannyce Sofya — 31F
8. Maryo Kennyth — 30M
9. Sebastyan Blayne — 30M
10. Annalyse Marye — 29F
11. Krystyn Mychele — 28F
12. Danyel Alvyn — 26M
13. Jokym Crayg— 25M
14. Mycah Colyn — 24M
15. Julya Patryce — 23F
16. Elyzabeth Jyll — 23F
17. Olyver Kyrklyn — 22M
18. Synclare Tymotheos — 20M
19. Lakeyth Jaymyeson — 20M
20. Fyrene Valentyne — 19F
21. Eryc Valentyno — 19M

All of his children analyzed him back—but more in admiration.

He was a man with a very strong silhouette. He had bronze skin and long crimped black hair that reached his hips. His almond-shaped eyes were copper and striking. He was immensely intelligent and courageously conniving and he looked trustworthy and untrustworthy all at once. He took care of himself above all other things—and all other people.

Ephraym dressed to kill—and killed. He always wore the Thornwryght signet ring on his pinky finger, often leaving marks on bodies he left behind.

He made sure all of his children wore expensive suits. Even the servants' uniforms were expensive. If they wore their own cheap loungewear, they had to stay out of sight. He allowed personal touches if they were requested in writing. Brayd cut the end of her sleeves into strips and braided them, as well as across her shoulders and knees.

Sync was ignored enough that he figured he could get away with all of his—but also Brayd secretly requested Sync's to keep him out of trouble.

"I'm going to put an end to all these fucking rumours," Ephraym announced. "I am tired of the bullshit that has been going on around here."

Sync wondered if being burnt was part of the bullshit he was calling out, but he doubted it. His father never paid much attention to him—unless one of the family sacraments was due.

According to Brayd, Ephraym didn't even care when some of the oldest siblings had added old writing ink to his baby bottle and made him drink it. He had barely survived being poisoned—and often starved himself from the rooted fear of it happening again. Brayd suggested that incident was why Sync was often malnourished as a child and it stunted his growth, leaving him the shortest of The Twenty-One, even though he was not the youngest.

Sync still just thought he was cursed. He was told that after that event, his eyes actually grew. They were more green-eyed—fearful, envious and pathetic. Only something like a curse could make eyes swell in size and change in colour.

Ephraym descended the stairs gracefully. His bodyguard followed.

"My solution is simple. Every child who claims to be mine is going to willingly give a blood sample. We're going to test to see who is related to me and who isn't. The technology to do this has advanced so much, as you know, thanks to our family."

He wandered over to the decorative throne and checked its cleanliness with his white gloves. The grand piece of furniture was embedded with the company logo as well as their syndicate slogan—**Y/OUR FUTURE IS** Y/**OURS**.

To the outside world doing business with the Thornwryght crime syndicate, the words could be interpreted in more than one way.

OUR FUTURE IS YOURS . . . (We are here to serve you and do what we can to get you what you need. Sacrifices might be made to get that done if the price is right.)

YOUR FUTURE IS YOURS . . . (We are here to protect you and keep you from harm. We will help you become what you wish to become. If the price is right, you are untouchable.)

OUR FUTURE IS OURS . . . (We mind our own business and won't take anyone else down with us if we are ever exposed. We are proud and resilient and will share it with you if the price is right.)

But there was only one true way for a Thornwryght to canonize it—

YOUR FUTURE IS OURS.

Those words were the core of the family secret.

Sync was just as sick of seeing the slogan everywhere as much as he was the stupid logo.

"The heir to this family *must* be blood related and I will not choose anyone who isn't to take my throne. We've done so much for so many generations and it must continue to be a Thornwryght who stands at the top of this enhanced timeline to keep our secret. I don't want to have anything to do with anyone who isn't a true Thornwryght. They would have no business here. The secret would have to *die* with them."

This was the moment that all other eyes were on Sync. Now the bodyguard's eyes were not.

Synclare wanted to fall through the marble floor.

Ephraym Thornwryght summoned three servants with a snap of his fingers—a forensic scientist, a medic, and a DNA expert. Sync was annoyed with all of the choices.

The medic was a young woman named Yenvieve who had pursued Sync romantically when they were younger. He had been stoked about it at first—she had pretty blue eyes, long black hair and an adorable French accent that stereotypically complimented the fact she was a maid at that time. He had quickly realized that she was probably acting on an order from his father and cold shouldered her.

The forensic scientist was a man named ███████ who had collected and purposely lost all of the evidence from Sync's mother's murder. Sync wanted him to purposely lose himself. There was nothing remarkable about his presence, so Sync thought that would be easy enough for him to disappear with no proof that he ever existed.

The third person was just as unremarkable—a Japanese Scot that was all triangle shapes and ears. He was a DNA expert that was less a servant and more a consultant. He was an obnoxious and chatty man named Marx Thespot that Sync thought needed a good kick in the knob.

"Tacyturn will observe every one of you getting your blood taken," the father said as his personal driver stepped forward towards the oldest son, Tobyas. "If you object to the needle from the medic, he'll get your blood some *other* way," Ephraym warned. "He may get too much. Any attempts to get yourself away from him will be in . . . vein," he said with a laugh.

"No need for your pet. If you can't get any blood, I can tell ya just by lookin'," Marx whispered eagerly to Ephraym—who promptly shushed him.

Sync knew it was in his best interest not to refuse the blood draw. He stared at the marble floor until it was done. By the way he was treated with the needle and spoken to, he could tell Yenvieve was still angry with him. He was fine with it—he was worth hating.

After each Thornwryght gave a sample of blood, each vial was carefully labeled.

Ephraym told the room, "It will be about fourteen days, possibly more because there are so many of you. I will call upon The Twenty-One again when the results are in. It will be interesting to see what number The Twenty-One becomes then." He made sure to look at each of his children right in the eyes as he strolled along their perfect line. "I am certain you will no longer be . . ."—he gestured as if he didn't know what he was going to say—"*be . . . intyuno*," he finished with a dry chuckle.

Then Ephraym and his servants left the room.

Sync immediately disappeared before any of his other siblings could decide to cut him off—or even just cut him. He was no longer safe now that their father was gone and they no longer had to behave.

Brayd caught up to him cowering in a corner.

"I don't think I'm his real son," he whimpered into a ficus.

"Don't say that! If you're not, then I'm not!" Brayd barked, yanking him away from the plant. "We look the same, don't we?"

"No, because *you* hide your freckles with shit and put shit in your hair."

"That doesn't change my blood, Sync."

Sync scoffed. "It may as well. You're amazing, Brayd. Father isn't going to cast you aside if you're not related to him. I don't think it matters. This is just an excuse to throw out the weak links." He jabbed a finger at himself, then started to shuffle off in a hurry.

"Then don't be a weak link!" Brayd called after him.

Sync rolled his eyes. "You want me to fucking dye my hair, then, too? It's too late for that."

Brayd grabbed Sync's shoulder and squeezed. "I just don't want you to fucking *die*, Sync."

Sync sighed. "I won't die, Brayd," he mumbled. "I'm at least coward enough to know how to run away."

"Where would you even go?" she asked.

"Who fucking cares? Nothing will change." He retreated to his basement room.

Sync felt the pin that she purposely left on his shoulder. He knew she left it because she knew it was the truth however anyone looked at it.

"I'm always lost. If I scored a trip to the fuckin' kingdom in the sky, I'd still stumble stupidly into Hell."

He knew that even if he did somehow find a way into Heaven, he would probably just burn there, too.

11.

"You got the wrong redhead!"

H AVING A LIFESTYLE WHERE DAYS and nights blurred together, Sync went back to losing track of time. He had decided to lay low until the DNA results were in.

A few days into that and he realized that his life wasn't changing much at all.

He kept his distance from his family and spoke to no one in person. He once spoke to Brayd via their vidphones, but that was it.

"That looks like your room, Sync. I haven't seen you in days. I thought you ran away. Turns out you're just avoiding me. That's nice."

Sync had said nothing and continued flipping through his vidkeys to find a movie to watch.

Brayd had sighed. "Are you eating? You haven't been to the dining hall."

"Sure."

"Those needle meals don't count."

They both knew that they were for servants or emergencies.

"Then no, I'm not eating."

He had then found a vidkey he liked—a 1978▶▶ German film called *Neonsein*—and plugged it into a screen slab he had perched precariously on a shelf.

Brayd had sighed again. "What are you going to do with yourself? The results are soon. You should leave now and come back when I call to tell you that we *are* related to father."

"What, so I can re-enter the mansion like a badass with a couple of middle fingers pointed at our other siblings, right?" His voice had been seething with sarcasm.

"I'd rather you do something that makes the other siblings *like* you, Sync."

"In that case, I'd re-enter the mansion as a fucking corpse. They'd be happy to see me then." His voice had been flat, but serious. "Maybe I'll just stay here and hide for the rest of my life even if I am somehow related."

"That's what you already do, Sync, and it's not working."

"Imagine their joy when they come down here looking for wine and find my dead body instead. Hope they bring a screwpull so they can celebrate right away."

She ignored him and continued trying to offer advice. "You've got to do *something*. Getting out of here would be good for you. No one in the world knows what you really want in life."

"Good."

"Maybe you should go all the way to the new Mars settlement. It's less risky now. They're looking for more people. If you don't want anyone in the world to know what you want, maybe you'll find it *there* in another world entirely."

"I'll do something that drastic once I learn to become fucking bulletproof," he had sarcastically said, clearly not entirely listening to her. "How about that?"

Then Sync had tossed his vidphone onto the floor. He drowned out anything his sister was trying to say by playing his movie and turning the volume up. At some point, she had hung up. Sync thought it may have been during a very loud and very messy car crash in the film. His own ear drums were throbbing.

Several hours after the call, Sync wandered up to the empty kitchen above his room hoping to find some pastry dough in the freezer that he could gnaw on. Luckily, there were plenty.

He grabbed one of the boxes and opened the fridge to check on what he could wrap up with it and found an entire plate of dinner waiting for him—steak, potatoes, a bottle of rose water, and a yogurt cucumber salad.

There was also a note attached with a braided piece of ribbon.

Put that freezer dough away and eat this instead, you fluro heathen. —

Brayd

For the next several days, Sync found a meal waiting for him in the refrigerator. He was relieved he was able to enjoy the grand dining hall meals without having to actually go. He liked to eat late at night when meals

[13]

weren't being served.

He also enjoyed Brayd's notes, which just got sillier and sillier. It reminded him of the days when he had lost his childhood friend—her level of silliness to snap him out of it had been inimitable.

Then she had abruptly misplaced her sense of humour again. Sync had a feeling that pressure by the siblings closer to her age had influenced her to stop.

As time was getting closer to when Brayd was likely to call him with the results, Sync decided to pack a bag. He was certain he was going to have to go, but he continued to delay actually leaving. He only ever went as far as planning it in his head. He wasn't one to jump to action—unless he was playing a video game.

He would sneak out late at night, steal one of the family's many cars and drive off the peninsula as fast as he could. He had even decided what car he liked best—the 1975►► Drofton Aphotic Coupé. Though he wanted to drive one of the brighter coloured ones, he would go for a darker colour to hide in the night.

Sync also considered a vintage midnight purple 1965►► Joßerand Tinqkov solely because it was his brother Tobyas' favourite car. Tobyas' verbal abuse had been the reason that Sync was too afraid to learn to drive—so he'd be laughing triumphantly as he drove unsteadily off with it.

After packing, Sync saw that it was midnight. He headed up to the kitchen to retrieve his usual meal, but there was none. He stared for a moment at the empty fridge, then shrugged.

He returned to his room and took out a meal syringe and injected it into his side. It was unsatisfying, but it would satiate him enough so that his growling stomach wouldn't keep him awake.

Sync lay back on his bed—a cot inside a small tent. He had an expensive bed in his original bedroom, but he couldn't move it discreetly. It likely wouldn't fit, either. It was the same with the rest of his high-priced furniture.

He sighed and stared up at the nothing all around him inside of the tent that blocked out the neon light—he was trying to let his mind get that way, too. He waited for his brain to shut down and relax.

From the corner of his eye through the mesh tent door he thought he saw some tiny glinting lights. He turned his head to look, but still saw darkness in that corner of the room where the neon lights of the tapestry didn't reach.

Then he thought he heard footsteps near the wine cellar door—not just near the door, but on the inside. He felt like he would have known if someone had opened the door, but the sounds were definitely inside the wine cellar. He knew the sound of sneaking around—that was all he ever did. He could not see anything through the thicker fabric of the tent in that direction. Whoever was there was also strategically staying out of the light of the tapestry.

He held his breath, feeling around for his shoes beside the cot.

Once he found one, he slowly unzipped the tent door and triggered the glowing neon checkers and threw it across the room towards the hallway leading to the door.

Suddenly shadows were looming over him, backlit by bright ever-changing colours.

People were approaching his bed.

Before he could react, there were three gunshots.

The first gunshot hit his neon tapestry, causing it to spark, malfunction and flicker out.

The second caused a splatter of blood to hit the tent.

The third gunshot resulted in a body falling across his legs, causing the tent to collapse on him.

Sync flailed out of his bed, wrenching himself through the unzipped portion and backed up as far as he could away from the cellar door. He felt sick to his stomach with fear. He could see that the dead men were armed with guns, but that's not where the bullets had come from.

He yelped when a hand grabbed him firmly around his upper arm.

Tacyturn stepped out of the shadows, standing in front of Sync.

The young man gawked up at him, having never been that close to him before. He was at least a foot taller than him, and Sync really felt small. The bodyguard was in his usual asymmetrical navy-blue suit, magenta polo shirt and magenta tie. His angular buttons were gold and his shoes were black penny loafers.

Keeping his gun pointed at the door, Tacyturn moved forward and picked up the shoe, turning its light off. He tossed it behind him and Sync scooped it up.

Just as the redhead put both of his shoes on, Tacyturn shoved the nearby packed bag into the young man's arms and yanked him to his feet.

Sync wanted to speak, but Tacyturn put his finger to his lips and yanked the fragmented tapestry off of the wall. The detrimental bullet had hit the shape of a heart on the neon sign of a strip club. Behind the tapestry, Sync saw what looked like a deep, clean scratch in a perfect rectangular shape.

As he was peering at it and wondering how long it had been there, Tacyturn tugged a metal wine rack rod from another wall and stabbed it into the clean groove, prying out the rectangular portion of the wall into a broken heap of materials on the floor. Sync was shocked at the mess it made, but also the ease that it had all come out—he had no idea that wine cellar walls were so many different layers.

When he looked into the hole, he realized he was looking directly into the slightly elevated maids' bathroom that he had been using for himself. He was annoyed when he realized that all this time, he could have just dug through the wall instead of having to sneak around a long way just to use it.

Just as he was going to verbalize his annoyance, Tacyturn put his hand over his mouth. He did so just long enough for Sync to take the hint—not long enough for him to get pissed about it. Then the driver grabbed Sync's arm and pulled him through the makeshift door.

He kept his arm around Sync's waist and leaned against the bathroom door, listening. Fervent footsteps were going down the stairs into the cellar.

Tacyturn quietly pulled Sync along through the narrow servant hallways. Every move that the bodyguard made was strategic and logical, knowing exactly where he was going.

Sync's mind was going blank and he just let the man lead him where he needed to be.

He wasn't sure why he was putting his trust in him—but he had just killed two people for him.

In a hallway just before the front doors, Sync saw a plate of food broken on the floor.

He stared at it.

Without thinking, he shoved away from the driver and went to it, scooping up the letter that was amongst the broken glass.

Before he had time to look at it, Tacyturn tugged him out the door, around the corner and down nearby stairs that looked like they were headed into a city's subway station.

Down below was the vast underground garage where all of the Thornwryght vehicles were parked. After the driver swiped his wrist across a digital pad, the gates opened.

Tacyturn led Sync to the very car that he had wanted to take. It wasn't even the dark coloured one he was going to settle with for the sake of being discreet—it was the fluro orange one that Sync liked best.

Wasting no time, he shoved the young redhead into the back seat of the 1975▸▸ Drofton Aphotic Coupé and sat in the driver's seat. He waited for a moment before starting the car.

As he did so, he heard three other vehicles start their engines. Sync didn't hear them and lifted his head up to look out the window.

"Stay down and do not move or make a sound," Tacyturn said, tugging Sync away from the window.

It was the first time that Sync had ever heard him speak. Even though it wasn't much, he could tell his accent was just like a Southern accent right out of a film he had recently watched.

He had always thought that the Hollywood version of an accent from the South sounded fake—but now he was hearing it in real life.

His own accent was from the region where the peninsula was located. He thought he sounded just like everyone else speaking New England English—like he had no accent at all.

Sync decided it was wise to listen to this man. His voice was like a silvery engine with a steely edge and he felt like he had to trust it. It was much better than his own way of talking—often just a brittle attempt at a stentorian voice.

The frightened young man clutched his bag and wedged himself down onto the floor.

All he could do was brace himself and listen.

Tacyturn remained still for a long time, listening beyond the cool hum of the Aphotic.

Sync was about tempted to speak, but then the car suddenly lurched ahead and they sped towards the garage's exit.

After a few strange twists and turns and small collisions and scrapes, they were back on the surface.

The young man could see nothing, but he could hear everything and feel a lot. He heard other cars following close behind. He felt every turn, sudden brake, sudden acceleration and even when the car lifted off of the ground or went in reverse.

He heard shots being fired and could feel them hitting their car. When a bullet hit the window above him, glass showered down on him.

When he leaned forward, he could see Tacyturn. He looked calm even though it felt like he was accomplishing amazing techniques and showing great skill under pressure. This was the moment that Sync's mind cleared enough to realize that he was in a movie-esque car chase—and missing all of it. He whimpered with disappointment that he didn't have a front row seat—just a rear floor nook.

Sync clutched his bag tighter when he felt the other car scrape alongside their vehicle and get stuck somehow. He heard the Aphotic go into automatic pilot mode and saw the sunroof open. He then saw Tacyturn disappear upwards. Bullets destroyed the front seat windows just as his black penny loafers disappeared.

After the sound of a few precise gunshots, Tacyturn dropped back into his seat and turned the wheel. He bucked the enemy vehicle—which was now being driven by a corpse—off of the side of their car.

Not long after that, Tacyturn whipped the car around towards where they had come from and floored it.

After hearing a car crash, Sync decided that he had just played a game of chicken with whoever the other driver was—the other driver lost. Tacyturn turned the car around again and gently nosed the loser vehicle off of the nearby cliff.

Then, they were back on the main road again.

Seeing the light poles, Sync knew they were heading directly to the gate and were no longer off-roading. But before they hit the gate, Tacyturn tucked the Aphotic into a dark corner and turned off the engine.

They waited. Sync could only hear his own breathing.

After just a minute, several cars sped by, heading towards the Thornwryght mansion.

Tacyturn waited a bit longer for a straggler vehicle.

Once he felt it was safe, Tacyturn took their battered vehicle through the main gate and headed towards the nearest city.

Even though the ride had become normal and peaceful, Sync said nothing—because Tacyturn said nothing. The young man was starting to feel stupid being pointlessly wedged onto the floor, but his fear kept him there.

There was a bullet hole in the headrest where his head would have been.

Sync analyzed Tacyturn as best as he could in his position. He could see the gnarly scar on the side of his head, standing out because his dark brown hair was shaved down on both sides. The surgical parts of the scar spiraled out, reaching his right eye. The back of his head was also shaved down, leaving just the hair on the top of his head. That hair was long and magenta and pulled back into a flowy ponytail. Sync would not have that hairstyle if he had a scar like that. He would want to always wear a hat or have his hair down.

As long as Sync had seen him around his father, the driver always had what looked like perpetual black eyes that were connected by bruising across the bridge of his nose that was normally accompanied by a severely damaged nasal structure. Sync thought it made him look wicked cool—like a boxer healing from an intense match—but wondered what caused it all to stay put and never fully heal. It tried, though, because the contused raccoon mask always looked a bit different every time anyone saw him.

Then, out of nowhere, Tacyturn tersely asked, "Coffee?"

"*What?*" Sync huffed, "Is that the fucking code for everything being safe now?"

"It's the code for coffee," he responded flatly.

Sync sat up straighter, feeling like everything might be safer, regardless of the bodyguard being unclear. The man's emotion also never changed—between killing two men, driving extremely dangerously, and now driving calmly into an unknown future.

"Isn't it too late for coffee?" Sync asked.

"Up to you."

". . . Coffee sounds good."

Sync slowly pulled himself off of the floor and sat in the seat proper, buckling his seatbelt.

He could see that they were in the city and that Tacyturn was already heading to a late-night drive-thru coffee shop.

They didn't even have time to order before a drink was delivered to them on a tray.

Without looking back, Tacyturn offered him the coffee. Sync took it and sipped it. It was his father's favourite—an iced ube macchiato with an extra shot. The family logo was on the cup where the customer name usually was laser etched.

They pulled away before a second drink arrived. Sync was not surprised. He doubted his father ever bought Tacyturn—or any of their servants—any sort of treat. Ephraym would never allow servants coffee. His father worshipped coffee and the servants were to only worship him.

"Are you going to tell me what's going on?" Sync asked, intending to sound like he was demanding an answer, but only sounded like he was pleading. "Is this drink supposed to distract me? I can drink and talk just fine. The results came in, did they? I'm probably not his fucking son. I don't know why you'd be helping me, of all people. Are you acting on father's orders? You must be. That's your fucking purpose. Unless you've gone fucking rogue, but you've gone fucking rogue for the worst person ever. Where the fuck are we going?"

Sync continued ranting and Tacyturn remained silent. Sync only became angrier—he had to hide how worried he was getting. He felt his heart sinking into his shoes as he saw the city lights fading.

They were now on a road less traveled and heading into what was probably the middle of nowhere.

"Are you just going to keep driving until I finish my drink? Then where we are is where I'll dig my own fucking grave? Will I use the cup as a shovel?"

Tacyturn's eyes finally glanced up to the rearview mirror and looked at Sync.

"Sounds like a movie," he said.

"Yes, it fucking does," Sync whined angrily. "But this isn't a fucking movie! This is my real fucking life we're talking about here! Movies aren't fucking real! There's no movie magic. YOU DIE FOR FUCKING REAL!"

Tacyturn went silent again and Sync became more agitated.

Then he remembered the note from the broken plate of food. He pulled it out of his pocket and opened it up.

It looked like it had been re-written several times.

I accidentally burned myself with my cigarette earlier.
The way I flinched was familiar.

I have decided to stop smoking.
I should have stopped the first time I lit up a
cigarette near you . . . and you flinched.
. . . At least I now know it won't be what kills me! ☺
—*Brayd*

Sync ripped off his seatbelt and lunged forward, barking at Tacyturn.

"I think you fucked up! You got the wrong redhead! You were supposed to get Brayd! She's definitely my real sister. If I'm not related to father, she's not either. She'd never let herself get killed and father would never let her die, so you were probably supposed to get her! What the fuck is wrong with you? That's a huge fucking mistake! You're going to be so fucking done! You probably didn't know she had red hair, but the test results should have clued you in tha—"

"Brayden Thornwryght is dead."

Sync's jaw dropped and he tried to speak again, but it only came out as a whimper. He fell back against the seat and slid down, clutching his note from his sister.

After a moment, he finally uttered, "That can't be true." Then his anger rose, trying to suffocate his sadness. "YOU FUCKED UP! HOW COULD YOU LET HER DIE LIKE THAT? HOW COULD YOU? WHY THE FUCK DID YOU SAVE ME INSTEAD?"

"Her death warned us about your danger."

Sync wasn't sure what to think. He was stunned into silence. He allowed himself to be overcome with sadness. If he spoke again, he might reveal that he was crying. Tears quietly stained his freckled cheeks.

He cowered in the backseat and remained quiet for the rest of the car ride. He didn't want to know any more for the time being. He knew too much. The only person in the world who cared about him was gone and he couldn't shake the feeling that it was his fault.

He was the weak link. The rumours definitely started because of that. If he had just acted like he fit in like his sister, there would never have been any question, there never would have been any DNA tests, and Brayd would still be alive.

It was all absolutely his fault.

By the time Tacyturn had stopped at a gas station, Sync had fallen asleep—despite having finished his caffeinated drink.

The driver reached back and took the cup from his limp hand. He exited the vehicle and went to toss the cup into the trash bin. He hesitated.

Then he quickly finished the rest of the drink—just a few mildly coated ice cubes. He then threw the empty cup away, gently brushing his thumb across his wet lips.

As the tank filled up, Tacyturn leaned his back against the broken window near Sync's head and stared up at the stars.

Once the tank was full, he examined the damage to the Aphotic on the way back into the driver's seat and turned the vehicle on. He sat there for a moment, adjusting his rearview mirror so he could see Sync.

He then stepped out of the car and took his jacket off, revealing his short-sleeved magenta polo shirt underneath and his gun tucked away neatly in its holster. He emptied his jacket pockets and transferred items to his trouser pockets before sitting back down.

The driver then twisted around, stepped on his seat, leaned across the center console and draped the jacket over the sleeping young man before turning back to a driving position.

Then he continued driving into the cold forested night, away from all enhanced electric light.

III.

"Ikaw lang ang isa."

SYNC WAS QUICKLY BECOMING AWARE of the morning light hitting his eyelids. He didn't want to open his eyes, but he knew he had to.

He wished that night's car ride had lasted forever. If he never had to get up again, he would never have to face what was going on. Before he opened his eyes, he still held on to the possibility that everything was a dream.

The young redhead blinked and confirmed he was still alive and still inside of the Aphotic. There were still bullet holes and broken glass around him.

He wasn't sure when he had gotten the driver's navy-blue jacket, but he was happy to have it, now very aware of the cold and moist early morning air coming in through the broken windows. He only liked the morning after he had been up all night—it was a nice time to bundle up and sleep and hide from the sun.

He snuggled into the jacket as he sat up, noticing that it smelled like Hoppe's No. 9 and something else he couldn't quite pinpoint.

Sync peeked out of his broken window. They were now at an old remote cabin and Tacyturn was talking to an old couple.

The driver was thumbing through a stack of bills. After settling on an amount, he offered it to the couple.

"Take everything you value and leave."

"The day is finally here!" the old woman exclaimed. "I can't wait to get out of this unenhanced shithole!"

Her husband reassured the crime syndicate bodyguard and tried to reel in his wife's inappropriate excitement as he said, "It wasn't that bad. We enjoyed our humble duties here."

"I'm going to the cyber casino!" she cheered, waving the bills around like pom-poms.

"Is that really the best way to spend our first day of freedom, darlin'?" the husband asked as he pulled her aside.

Tacyturn turned towards the car to see that Sync was awake. He also saw an extremely fluffy dilute calico cat sitting on the hood of the Aphotic.

It was staring at him.

As the couple bantered, the cat and driver stared at each other. Tacyturn thumbed through another small amount of money.

Interrupting the old couple, Tacyturn offered them the bills. "Take your cat, too."

The old woman stopped her happy jig to ogle the money.

The husband said, "We don't have a cat."

The driver turned back to the car. The cat was gone.

He pondered for a moment, then slowly turned back to the couple and offered the money again.

"Leave a chess pie in the oven."

The old woman agreed as she eagerly took the extra two hundred dollars.

Tacyturn returned to the car and drove into the woods, just out of view of the cabin.

Once parked, the driver stepped out and told Sync to remain in the car. Sync didn't object—he wanted to stay in his warm and nice-smelling jacket cocoon.

Remaining next to the car, Tacyturn kept an eye on the woods. He subconsciously took out a cigarette and went to light it, but very abruptly changed his mind and tucked the electric lighter and gold cigarette case back into his pocket.

To distract himself from wanting to smoke, he walked around the Aphotic and examined all of the damage, now in the sunlight. He could remember what caused what.

He caught sight of the barn cat a few times. He thought it might be circling them—until he witnessed it catching a rabbit for breakfast. The driver thought about doing the same.

After an hour, Tacyturn drove them back to the cabin. The couple had just left.

The driver parked the car inside an old barn, then opened the door for Sync.

The young redhead mechanically exited the vehicle, hugging the oversized jacket and dragging his bag along the ground. Tacyturn scooped up the bag and carried it for him, leading him to the front door of the cabin.

The key was in the door. Its keychain had the Thornwryght symbol on it. The wooden door had their syndicate slogan burned into it.

Sync wrinkled his nose. "An actual fucking key? This place hasn't been enhanced?"

When Tacyturn opened the door and beckoned Sync in first, the young man groaned as he looked around the old dirty cabin. The only thing that stopped him from being entirely disappointed was the smell of the pie baking in the oven.

After settling in and eating pie, Sync sat near the old wood fireplace that Tacyturn had prepared whilst the young man ate. The driver then offered to exchange his jacket for a warmer blanket.

"I can't remember your fucking name," Sync finally said to the driver without looking him in the eye, handing him the jacket while happily taking the blanket. "I do remember you've been my father's driver for five years now. I even remember the name of the previous driver, Teena. I even remember she has a nice ass.

"Now she's married to my brother Tobyas because he gets everything he wants. Though, she probably has been assuming that he's the heir because he's the first-born son, but I don't think she realizes we're not in fucking medieval fantasy times. Now it's too late and once father chooses an heir, she won't be able to jump ship, but she'll sure as fucking hell try. She was father's bodyguard for ten years. Five years is not a lot of time. I don't know if I'd trust someone with my life after even just five fucking years."

Tacyturn stood by the fireplace in silence.

After Sync stopped talking, he waited a moment. Then he looked impatiently up at the driver.

"I *said* I can't remember your fucking name!" he huffed.

The driver took one of his master Thornwryght keydiscs out of the thick black band on his wrist and handed it to Sync.

The young man snatched it and read the name on it—TACYTURN▶▶

It was a special disc that was marked with several colours, indicating that he had access to almost anything.

"What the fuck kind of name is that? No last name?"

Tacyturn said nothing.

"Fucking perfect," the young redhead spat as he tossed the keydisc away.

[25]

The bodyguard deftly caught it.

The driver watched as the high of his anger dwindled and the sadness came over him again.

"So, what happens now? The cup is gone. Should I grab a shovel? Can I bathe myself and just go back to sleep in a bed? At least that way I'll be nice and fucking clean and comfortable when I die peacefully in my sleep. It's the coward's way. You'll have a nice pretty corpse to present to my father. You could even dress me up in whatever you want. Won't that be nice? Hide me back in the wine cellar so that everyone can start drinking right there with my corpse to celebrate!"

He covered his head with the blanket and groaned, hiding his anxious expression, trying not to think about all the ways his sister could have been murdered. He hoped it was quick, but doubted it. His family was cruel.

"Seriously, what the fuck are we waiting for?" he moaned.

Tacyturn turned his head slightly for a moment, then took out his vidphone.

After checking a message, Tacyturn crossed his arms and said, "Ikaw lang ang isa."

There was a long pause before Sync peeled the blanket off his head. "Fucking what?"

The driver picked Sync's vidphone up from the coffee table and handed it to the young man.

"That sounds like the nonsense my father says to confu—"

Just as Sync touched his vidphone, a message arrived. It was from his father, indicated by the name and gold colours that lit up on the edge of the cube.

He unfolded his vidphone to its largest size and read the digitally scanned letter.

To The One (Ang Isa):

Out of all of my children, Brayden Alyce was my only true daughter and you, Synclare Tymotheos, are my only true son. Your mother was the only woman who didn't lie to me. It's a

[26]

shame that she is no longer with us, but she had twice failed to produce a child that looked like me.

Now there are nineteen outsiders living in my home who I no longer acknowledge as my children. Unfortunately, Brayden has been killed by one, a few, or all of them. The Nineteen had eyes and ears inside of the laboratory and the results leaked before even I was able to know them. Brayden was the best choice for heir and, therefore, the bigger threat, so they put a priority hit on her. Upon finding out about her death, I sent Tacyturn to protect you.

I believe The Nineteen figured out that if the only two true children were dead, I would have to choose from a non-blood child.

They are absolutely right.

To The Nineteen, they are still my children and I have agreed to choose one of them if they manage to find and kill you. I have sent them all letters like this one. I have implied that whoever is the one to snuff out my bloodline is the one who gains the company. I would have to respect that.

I have suggested that it must be done by their hand and there must be proof. This will hopefully reveal those who will be severely punished when they hopefully fail. It should also gain you extra time when a deadlier hired hand has to deliver you alive. This is one of the only two ways I can help you.

I will not kill The Nineteen myself. I have raised them and they are my last resorts if you stay the way you are. I need them to continue to trust me.

Fate has chosen you. Our family has had control of fate for so long now, but not this time. I would have never chosen you to be my heir. You know this.

You do not act like a Thornwryght, but you are one.

I pray that you learn to act like one.

You are The One, so act like you are the one and only.

Lending you Tacyturn is the other way I can help you.

Just remember that he only obeys the commands of a true Thornwryght.

Simply TELL HIM WHAT YOU WANT. Use him well.

Then come back and prove yourself worthy of my name and we'll protect our family secret against The Nineteen side by side.

DO NOT FUCK UP MY LEGACY, SYNCLARE TYMOTHEOS.

Signed⋯⋯Ephraym Sylas Thornwryght

The young man gaped at the letter. His insides twisted up when he read the last line—he could hear his father yelling. He rarely raised his voice—but when he did, it was terrifying.

"So . . . you *are* protecting me? I'm . . . *I'm* the fucking heir?" He ruffled his red hair in disbelief, not knowing what to do with his hands. Tears filled his eyes. "That's fucking RIDICULOUS! What rotten fucking luck for the Thornwryght bloodline!"

He dropped his vidphone and put the blanket back up over his head.

"Fate fucking sucks and this blanket smells fucking weird. I'm going to remember its fucking smell fucking forever!"

"Speculoos."

"Ugh, more fucking nonsense words?"

Sync confusedly peeked out from his blanket to see that Tacyturn was holding out a hot cup of tea. Sync took it and retreated back into hiding. It smelled amazing, like a spiced biscuit. He realized it was the other faint scent on his jacket.

He also realized that he had been so focused on reading the alarming note from his father, he hadn't noticed Tacyturn making tea. He didn't even know enough time had gone by to steep it properly.

"I don't know what the fuck you said," Sync grumbled as he sipped the tea to find out that it tasted just as amazing as it smelled.

As Sync glanced down to the message from his father, he watched as it glitched off of his vidphone. He figured his father must have remotely deleted it or weaved a self-destruct program into the file.

The only words that remained were the ones in all capital letters.

Sync kicked his phone away, spooked by the lingering message. He tugged worriedly on the noose around his neck, tightening it.

"So . . . what now?" Sync asked, sounding drained and feeling lost.

"You tell me," Tacyturn said, clearly waiting for some sort of command.

". . . *Fuck*."

IV.

"I want you to stay by his side."

THE DRIVER STOOD NEARBY AND waited patiently as Synclare Thornwryght angrily ranted and sadly moaned throughout the entire day. Tacyturn said nothing—the heir never asked him a direct question.

Sync also never made anything clear about what he wanted. The driver had to make assumptions based on commands that were already in place by his father.

He tried to offer to feed him—even hunt for him—but Sync just quietly inhaled the rest of the pie that first day.

Tacyturn had also meticulously removed the charging hub from the Aphotic so that Sync could charge his vidphone he was constantly playing video games on.

Sync usually tried to hide what he was playing—especially when it was a virtual piano simulator. Even though he played so many games, none seemed to make him very happy.

The only time Sync seemed happier was when the barn cat had followed Tacyturn back into the cabin. He had thought the young man was happy to see him—then the cat had emerged from between his legs, yowling loudly for attention.

She was very friendly and trotted up to Sync's open arms and accepted all of his affectionate touches. After that moment, Tacyturn always saw her somewhere nearby the young man.

When night finally arrived, the driver kept an eye on all the doors as Sync showered, moving a chair to be in the optimum place to do so.

Clearly anxious to sleep, the young redhead said nothing when he left the bathroom and collapsed into the bed, covering his entire body with blankets that he hoped were clean.

The cat curled up nearby the cocoon he made for himself. She blocked the one air hole that Sync had and he was too depressed to care. He briefly found comfort through an amusing thought when he went over how it could be documented if he died that way—death by pussy suffocation.

Tacyturn waited a significant amount of time before moving again. He listened until he could no longer hear Sync crying himself to sleep.

After giving Sync another air hole, the driver stepped outside of the cabin and walked a good distance away to an old phone booth. He kept his eye on the cabin and surrounding areas at all times.

He visually called Ephraym Thornwryght using his vidphone.

His boss spoke first. "You were supposed to call hours ago."

Ephraym stared at the driver, pausing to let his disappointment sink in. He didn't expect any response.

"I'm going to be brief. That is all that I have time for. The Nineteen are going to continue to hunt Synclare down to prove themselves, but Synclare better be the one who proves himself. He's the only option for an heir and he's not the best option. He's weak and not worth bowing down to. No one respects him. He doesn't respect himself. He needs to tap into the Thornwryght blood in his body and stop being an embarrassment. My genes are in there and will be the only thing that can save him."

He was briefly interrupted by a servant bringing him his late night coffee. He took a few sips before continuing, purposely making Tacyturn wait.

Fortunately, Tacyturn's patience was unmatched. Ephraym knew this and always tested it when he could to make sure the bodyguard was functioning properly.

After a few smacks of his lips, Ephraym decided that the coffee was made incorrectly and sent the unseen servant off to get him another.

When he continued, he said, "I want you to do whatever is necessary to toughen that little shit up. Keep him out of sight until he is ready to fight back and take the throne. He has a very small attention span before he starts feeling bad for himself. I want you to do what you can to gain his trust. No more calls unless I call you."

Ephraym squinted, trying to see where he was. Once he realized, he was angry.

"Why are you outside? Get your ass back to the cabin! I want you to keep him unharmed. I want you to stay by his side."

Tacyturn gave a curt nod.

"I want you to tell me his status right at this moment."

"Asleep."

"And his emotional state?"

"Morose."

"What did he do when you told him about Brayden?"

"Cried."

"And when he read my message?"

"Cried."

Ephraym groaned. "Pathetic."

The servant returned in record time, out of breath.

The boss sipped the coffee.

"You've got a lot of work to do," he stated as he thought about how the second coffee tasted.

Tacyturn could tell that it was worse—he still felt a twinge in his subconscious that he should be reaching for his gun to take care of the person responsible.

Instead, Ephraym took a gun out of his drawer and handed it to whoever was there beside him.

"Kill the person responsible for this coffee. Even if it's you," he matter-of-factly told the offscreen servant. "I suggest a far better shot than the one you just gave me."

Then he turned back to Tacyturn as if they had never been interrupted.

"Don't fucking fail me, Tacyturn. You know what will happen if you do."

There was a moment of silence until both of them heard a faint gunshot.

Ephraym smiled. "To both of you as one."

Then his boss hung up on him.

Tacyturn folded up his vidphone and tucked it into his trouser pocket while reaching his other hand into his jacket. When he pulled his hand from his jacket pocket, he had his cigarette case and his lighter. He popped a cigarette out and lit it.

He quickly smoked it as he scanned the cabin. He took deeper breaths and forced longer exhales than he usually did, pointing the smoke towards the sky.

Once he was done, he put out the cigarette butt into the coin dispenser. He unceremoniously tossed the rest of his encased unsmoked cigarettes, then dropped his lighter on top of the gold cigarette case where it landed on the floor.

He left the phone booth and briskly returned to the cabin.

Outside, he used an old water pump and wiped off his face and underneath his shirt quickly with a broken piece of soap. He left his navy-blue jacket hanging on an old rocking chair on the covered deck.

Then he went inside and stationed himself in his strategically placed chair and did not move until morning.

V.

"Lucky."

$\mathbf{F}$OR THE NEXT WEEK, SYNC was continuously feeling harassed by Tacyturn.

At first, the driver asked him several times if he wanted to learn to fight or learn to shoot.

Sync avoided answering directly each time.

After that, it felt like the driver was trying to start fights by physically getting in his way.

Tacyturn no longer had to say anything—Sync knew he was asking the same questions over and over again with just a look or a physical gesture. He was always nearby and never let Sync out of his sight entirely. The young man craved the isolation of his wine cellar and the comfortable simplicity of his neon tapestry.

Wanting to stay out of the driver's way, Sync used his needle meals in private when the chess pie ran out. Eventually, he ran out of them, as well.

Tacyturn began serving him meals, using whatever was in the cabin—Sync was concerned with the lack of expiration dates.

The young redhead thought he was purposely serving him meals he didn't like, hoping for Sync to tell him what he actually wanted.

He didn't. He ate what was given to him—but complained the entire time.

Most of the food came from jars that he recognized as being canned at the Thornwryght peninsula, straight from their garden. He wondered why this cabin only had his least favourites. He always hoped for dragon fruit, lychee or strawberries, but he never got any.

He never saw Tacyturn eat, but he also never really saw servants eat—they weren't supposed to when their masters were around, unless they were invited. They were rarely invited—especially not even for just a cup of coffee.

Tea was okay. Tea was for peasants, according to Ephraym. It was just

[34]

dirty water.

Needle meals were sometimes all they were allowed to have if their jobs required their attention around-the-clock or if they had too much work to do. It was similar to the instant teeth brushing capsules. Sync liked to hoard both for the convenience and effectiveness. Sync assumed Tacyturn was using everything meant for servants who were not allowed much time to care for themselves—they were to spend most of their time caring about what their masters wanted.

The only thing that Sync ever made clear to Tacyturn was that he was miserable, but offered nothing to fix it. He felt like he deserved to be miserable.

After the several days went by, the physical confrontations escalated. Sync didn't know this man even after a week and he wasn't sure what he was up to. He thought he was safe, but then he wondered if Tacyturn would ever go rogue in retaliation for being a Thornwryght servant.

It had happened before.

When Sync walked over to the charging hub to get his vidphone, Tacyturn none-too-gently shoved him away.

"Seriously, what the fuck is wrong with you?" Sync growled, stumbling into the fireplace. The tip of his neck rope was singed in the fire. "I wish you'd at least answer that question."

The young man had paused even though he knew Tacyturn wasn't going to say anything back. It seemed like he had said less than thirty words that entire week.

"Why the fuck do you want me to fight so bad? Isn't that what you're here for? That's your fucking job. What do you need me for? You'd be better off leaving me the fuck alone!"

Tacyturn moved threateningly closer to him and Sync cowered backwards, stumbling onto the couch. He raised his hands to protect his face.

The cat, who was on the back of the couch, hissed at Tacyturn.

"What do you want, Synclare?"

"Why does it matter?" the young man whined, tired of being asked.

"You can't get what you want if you don't speak up."

"Or *you* don't get what you want if I don't speak up, is that it? Don't fucking make this psychological shit about me if it's just something you

[35]

want as some obsessed servant. This family doesn't want me and neither do you. You're just trying to set me up so that this shit can come to a quick end. I'm better off dead and you're better off getting away from this family while you can, too."

Sync kept his eyes shut and never moved his arms away from his face.

Tacyturn dropped his fist and took his hand off his holstered gun.

"If I'm not told what to do, I'll do nothing. If I'm not told where to go, I'll go nowhere."

Sync slowly dropped his arms and curiously looked at Tacyturn, having never heard him say so many words at once. It was less like an emotional confession and more like it was a programmed response.

"What? What kind of a fucking person is that?"

"If I'm not told who I'm supposed to be, I'll be no one."

"Is it because of . . ." He pointed to his own head, indicating the wound on the side of the driver's head. "Or are you brainwashed?"

Tacyturn crossed his arms and turned his head away.

Sync wondered if he had to wait another week to hear that many words from him again.

"If you're into it, it's Sync, not Synclare. That's what I'm called if I'm in trouble. I guess I'm in trouble now, though, huh? Still, Sync is . . . better."

The driver nodded, plucking Sync's vidphone from the charging hub and handing it to him.

They didn't speak again until night came.

Sync exited the shower and put on his pajamas—fluro leggings and a T-shirt. He also gave in to socks because the cabin was so cold and he was tired of being pissed about it. He didn't yet give in to wearing his daytime sweater, not wanting the filth of the day on him at night.

He saw Tacyturn in his usual seat.

"Do you bathe when I'm asleep? I know you rinse off with the pump outside, but that's not very fucking effective, is it? This cabin already has a fucking weird smell, don't make it worse."

Tacyturn acknowledged his question with the shake of his head.

"Why not?"

The driver said nothing, but the young redhead had an idea.

"Poor fucking bastard having to watch over me at all times. Can't imagine being a mindless drone."

Tacyturn kept his same serious look, but looked him right in the eyes. Sync nervously averted his eyes.

The young heir rubbed the back of his neck as he thought for a moment. He adored his hot showers and couldn't imagine going without them. He had been certain the old cabin's water would be cold, but it luckily had at least a basic boiler.

"You've got to be fucking suffering. What can I do to get you in the shower? You just have to be able to see me, right? See that I'm safe? Make sure I'm nearby so I can cower behind you?" He pet the cat as he formulated an idea. "So, I'll just go in with you!" He awkwardly coughed, then he specified, "I mean, in the bathroom, at least. I'll just play on my vidphone and sit on the sink in the corner."

"Sync in the sink."

Sync wrinkled his freckled nose. "Ha, yeah? Is that you trying to be fucking funny? It's weak, but it means you're listening to me. But I'd like a real answer." He ignored the irony of his statement. "Will that work or what?"

The young man watched as Tacyturn looked around. He then stood up and went to the bathroom, looking out the door from the direction of the shower. The sink was tucked behind a tall cabinet, hiding it from the door. One slide of the cabinet could hide the corner entirely to anyone not familiar with the layout of the bathroom.

"Well?" Sync huffed impatiently.

Tacyturn nodded.

"Great. So, whenever you want to—" Sync nearly dropped his vidphone when he saw Tacyturn beginning to strip in front of him. "Whoa! Shit!" He quickly pressed his face into the crook of his arm. "Let me get into position, you sick fuck! Fuck me!"

As Tacyturn turned on the shower, Sync climbed up onto the counter and sat in the small sink. He tried to give the driver as much privacy as he could by turning towards the wall and leaning his head against an old hanging mirror. The shower was an open type and the only thing separating them was a single glass pane.

He hugged his legs and glued his eyes to his vidphone. The barn cat stared at them both from a nearby shelf.

Unable to focus on anything on his vidphone, Sync put all of his effort into not looking at Tacyturn. He could see him partially through the mirror, but not very well. He could see that he had dozens of marks on his body and he was curious to see them better.

Holding his breath, Sync stole a look of the driver in the shower. He was a lot more fit than he had originally thought. He knew his arms were strong, but he didn't know his body was practically all muscle. He seemed much lankier with his clothes on.

Sync was surprised he wasn't covered in tattoos—he looked like the type. He thought he saw one on his right inner wrist, but it was too small to focus on it.

What grabbed his attention the most was that Tacyturn was covered in scars, like his face. Some had been healed for a long time and some looked as recent as a few weeks.

Sync felt ashamed. He had always let his cigarette scars define him, reminding him of what a weakling he was. He flinched whenever he even smelled a cigarette. He couldn't imagine what kinds of pain Tacyturn went through. Just with a brief glance, he knew he had gone through a hell of a lot.

His scars were gnarly—Sync had a few dots.

The young man glanced at the driver a few more times until he realized that Tacyturn was staring back through his wet magenta hair. Sync tried to make himself smaller, pressing his forehead against the mirror and closing his eyes. He remained that way until he heard the water shut off.

He heard Tacyturn reach into the cupboard for a towel. He still didn't move until he felt a gentle touch on the back of his arm. It was where one of his scars was.

When he whirled around at Tacyturn for an explanation as to why he touched him, the driver reached up and brushed his thumb gently across the trio of scars on his right cheek.

Sync then saw the tattoo on his wrist better. He thought it was a bit inane looking for a hitman—it was a small black circle with a squiggly line through it. There was a dot inside the circle and one outside the circle. It looked like a child tried to draw a taijitu.

Instead of deciding to ask him about it, Sync voiced his annoyance with a yell and shoved his hand away.

The driver's eyes moved from one cigarette burn to another, then sought out another.

Sync thought it looked like he was counting them.

"I have twenty of them, if that's what you're wondering," Sync said as the driver spotted one on his collar bone, peeking out from the saggy neckline of his shirt that was caught off his shoulder.

The young man didn't know what to do about the awkward moment, so he decided to keep talking as he tugged on his shirt to stop it from exposing so much of his shoulder.

"What about you? Do you know how many you have?"

Tacyturn shook his head.

"I could count them for you if you ever wanted to know. Might take a while, but I'd do it. I've got nothing else to do."

The driver acknowledged his offer with a nod, then left the bathroom. Sync was relieved that Tacyturn didn't say anything back.

In retrospect, he thought it was a weird thing to say and felt like a creep. He had just reminded himself about how bad he was at interacting with people. He slapped himself in the forehead in a scolding manner.

Knowing that Tacyturn wanted to keep an eye on him, he went into the bedroom where Tacyturn was putting on a fresh outfit from a small suitcase the young man didn't know he had. It was another magenta shirt that matched his hair.

This gave Sync an idea and he dove into his own personal bag. He pulled out a small vial and turned the dial to the correct colour.

"I have the perfect fucking colour for you!"

While tying back his hair, Tacyturn curiously glanced over to Sync.

"I bet you've never painted your nails before. My father would never let you even if you wanted to. I find that it draws the attention away from weaknesses I don't want people to see. Your hands are all fucked up and this would make people less likely to notice. Instead of grimacing and feeling pity, they are preoccupied about their personal opinions on the fashion. Isn't that why your hair is that magenta colour? To distract from your head wound? I mean, a hat would be more effective or just, you know, maybe not shaving the sides of your head."

He paused just in case the driver would say something. He didn't.

Sync showed him the vial as the driver buckled his gun holster to his body.

"It's a little more fluro than your hair, but it's pretty fucking close. I mean, I can keep adjusting the dial a bit to try to get it even closer. If you've never done it before, I'll do it for you."

He wanted to mention that he used to paint Brayd's nails, but he decided he wanted to avoid being sad. He was sad anyway, remembering her favourite purple shade that was in the same vial he was holding.

There was such a long pause, Sync was starting to feel embarrassed.

He watched as Tacyturn finished tying his magenta tie and tucked it under his collar. He then inserted the metal lock on his black master access wristband into the mechanism implanted into his left wrist and securely looped the tight band back into place.

Then the driver offered him his hand.

Sync perked up and grabbed it, pulling the tall man into the other room. He pushed him into the couch, then sat on the arm of it.

They sat in silence as Sync painted the nails on his right hand. The young man wanted to talk, but he couldn't figure out what to talk about. He was just glad to have a reason to interact with someone without having to talk about guns or fighting or his family—or how pathetic he was.

At least he was good at painting nails—a nice useless task for a crime boss heir.

He often glanced up from what he was doing to try to read Tacyturn's expression, but it was impossible. The driver kept his eyes averted.

Just as he was finishing his thumb, Tacyturn lunged forward. Sync cowered back in fear and fell backwards off of the couch. His back hit the floor and he found himself briefly face-to-face with a dangerous snake.

He relaxed when he saw that the snake was in Tacyturn's grasp.

Very quickly, the driver threw the snake towards the door and unsheathed his gun. Before he could do anything further, the barn cat appeared and attacked the snake, killing it.

"Fucking cabins!" Sync yelled, pulling himself up. "Fucking snakes! Like our fucking lab snakes! They are deadly and always fucking pissed, but I don't blame them! They are used for some fucking cruel shit. I get pissed when I'm used, too."

The cat proudly went to Sync with her kill and he appreciatively pet her.

"Got yourself a meat forest noodle there."

He leaned away from the tattered snake and shook her playfully until she dropped it.

"It's extremely grody, though. You can do better, Bandit."

Tacyturn stared at the cat. He wanted to say something, but he just subtly tilted his head.

Sync saw his expression and assumed what it was about.

"What's that fucking face for? I decided to name her Bandit. You know, just staying with the theme of my family's business." He rubbed her head and she looked like she was in heaven. "I'm fucking spelling it right, though."

Sync thought it was strangely dramatic for his family to banish the letter "I" from names and replace every instance with the letter "Y". They had once been the Thornwrights, but it changed when his great great grandfather had his eyes cut out. In defiance, he claimed he didn't need "eyes" and removed them all from his family.

He decided the letter "Y" was much stronger, a letter that represented inner wisdom—one doesn't need "eyes" with inner wisdom, according to the inflated pride of his great great grandfather.

Sync thought it sounded like he was overcompensating.

"Well, what would *you* fucking name her?" Sync asked, feeling like the driver's silence was being extremely judgmental.

The driver watched the two of them for a moment before saying, "Chanceuse."

Sync groaned loudly. "Oh, don't start with the random nonsense again, okay? You've been around my father too much. Answer seriously."

"Lucky."

"Oh. Not much better, is it?" Sync wrinkled his nose. "Yeah, my name is way fucking better. Maybe I would have chosen that name ten years ago. It would be up there with Angel or Princess. What about Fluffy or Smokey? Are those good too? Maybe you are actually ten years old. Shit, you look old as fuck for ten." Then, he clapped. "I got it. Kitty. I bet your second choice was fucking Kitty."

Tacyturn then received a message on his vidphone from Ephraym Thornwryght.

THIS IS TAKING TOO FUCKING LONG, TACYTURN.

[41]

The driver clenched his fist.

"Are we doing your other fucking hand or not?" Sync asked, huffing impatiently because the driver had rudely pulled out his vidphone mid-conversation. "Unless you have someone better to talk to, which is likely. I'm sure all you servants send messages amongst yourselves and laugh at the rich hellions and their superficial shenanigans. Be sure to ask them their opinions on all the cat names. I bet at least one of them will suggest Cinderella. I'll be pissed if they suggest it with a 'Y', though. Cinder I could agree with. I mean, I'm already set on the name Bandit, but if a second cat appears, I might be tempted to go with Cinder. But not Cynder. You know what I mean."

Tacyturn stared suspiciously at the snake's corpse for a moment, then kicked it into the fireplace to burn.

Just as Sync was holding the barn cat's paws and considering painting the claws, Tacyturn sat back down next to Sync and offered him his left hand.

Tacyturn swore that the barn cat looked relieved.

VI.

"The killer is out to earn his reward outright."

WHEN SYNC WOKE UP, HE cried out in fear when he felt a knife at his throat—he was not unfamiliar with the gesture. He quickly realized that the person he was crying out to for help was the one who was threatening him.

Tacyturn was leaning over him, pressing the edge of the blade against his skin. Sync was too afraid to speak.

When he started to move his hands to maybe hide his face, he felt something in his grasp. When he tightened his grip, he realized it was Tacyturn's holstered gun. He knew then that his hand had been purposely placed there before being woken up.

"Why the fuck do you keep doing this?" Sync whimpered. "Are you hoping it'll trigger some sort of Thornwryght reflex and I'll hurt you while defending myself? Do you do this a lot? Is that why you always have fucking black eyes? What if I killed you? Is father making you do this?"

Tacyturn pressed the blade harder, but purposely turned it flat to keep it from cutting him. He hoped the pressure change was enough to make a point—without the point.

"Killing someone isn't the way to prove myself, is it? 'Cause I've already fucking done that. It didn't fucking work. It just kept me alive a little longer . . . but now look at me. Can't say I've spent my time alive very well. There must be something else I can do. I wish I could fucking . . . help someone, or something. That's not the Thornwryght way and I'm probably too fucking pathetic to do that, either, but . . ."

The pressure from the blade relaxed.

Tacyturn said, "You can save someone from a snake, but the killer gets the reward."

Sync tilted his head. There was something weirdly specific about what he said.

Once Tacyturn saw that the young man was reading into his words, he backed up and sat on the edge of the bed.

Tacyturn pulled his vidphone out of his pocket, reading the message from Ephraym again. Then he let his phone drop to the floor. It automatically reverted back to its cube shape from the impact.

Not wanting to loom over the young redhead anymore, he slid down to sit on the floor and leaned back against the bed, looking non-threatening.

Sync moved to the edge of the bed, laying on his stomach.

"What the fuck are you doing on the floor? Watching for more snakes?"

Tacyturn said nothing.

"Did you want me to thank you for stopping the snake? Fuck. I didn't fucking know I had to. I don't thank people. I didn't even thank you for killing a bunch of dudes for me and destroying perfectly good cars. What the fuck do I have to be thankful for? It's like getting a glass of expensive rose water while you're drowning. I didn't even thank the fucking cat. I mean, maybe I did? Sort of? I didn't thank her with . . . words. I—"

Sync was terrible at reading people, especially when they were impossible to read—like Tacyturn. He bit his lip and thought for a moment about what he was about to try.

He lifted his hand and gently touched the top of Tacyturn's head, like he had touched Bandit. He didn't flinch and that made Sync feel like he wasn't doing the wrong thing—but Tacyturn was also not the flinching type.

The young man began to affectionately touch the driver's head, running his fingers gently through his hair.

Tacyturn closed his eyes and relaxed. Sync felt this and was immediately proud of himself. It was the first time in a while he did something odd during human interaction and it was turning out fine.

Just twenty minutes later, both of them were asleep.

Tacyturn woke up a few hours after that to a perimeter alarm only he could hear. He wasn't sure how long it had been going off and cursed how slowly he was rising from a deep sleep.

Sync was sprawled on the bed with his arm limp around his shoulder. The cat was lying in the cradle that the young man's legs were making.

He was disappointed he had allowed himself to fall asleep and quickly sprung to his feet, hunting down his shoes to put them on. As he did so, he scanned the area around him and listened closely.

He heard a car. The car was coming in their direction—and it was already moving fast.

Tacyturn put his hand on Sync to gently wake him up.

"What the fuck is it this time?" the young man groaned, feeling for a knife at his throat.

"Get ready to go," he suggested firmly.

Sync was going to question it, but then he saw Bandit was suddenly spooked by something. She flailed and ran to hide. Sync scrambled to his feet and quickly put his shoes and sweater on without another word.

Tacyturn positioned himself near the front door. He peeked through the window and could see the vehicle driving towards the cabin at high speed. Its lights were off and its engine was completely silent—the 1983►► Joßerand Whisperunner Supercar was designed that way.

Tacyturn took out his gun and pointed it in a specific direction, standing in a specific spot.

Several seconds later, the vehicle came crashing through the front of the cabin. The driver's window landed in the path of his gun and he quickly shot the driver in the head, shattering the glass.

He reached in and unlocked the door, opened it, threw the body out and got in. He put the vehicle in reverse and moved it out of the cabin. As he did so, he saw a handful of armed men approaching the damaged cabin on foot.

Because the swap was so quick, none were aware of the fact that the driver of the vehicle had changed.

When he looked over to the barn, he saw armed men there, as well. They were dismantling something under the hood of the Aphotic. He also knew more cars were on the way.

Very quickly, he drove the vehicle into the men who were approaching the cabin. He parked the car, pointing the driver's side door at the gaping hole that was the front door. He made sure to take the key fob out of the glove box.

As he slid methodically out of the car, he crisply shot each injured man to make sure they weren't going to get up.

Tacyturn grabbed their personal bags and threw them through the broken window of the Whisperunner.

Sync was cowering in a corner until Tacyturn grabbed his arm and led him quickly towards the car. The young man grimaced at the sight of the dead body.

Then Sync stopped. "Where's Bandit?"

Not caring, Tacyturn continued to pull him. Sync yanked out of his grasp when he saw that the china cabinet by the front door was now face down.

"That was one of her favourite hiding spots!" he cried out, moving to the broken cabinet.

Panicking, he tried to look underneath, but could not see anything.

Tacyturn didn't want to waste any time, but he also knew that arguing would waste time. He lifted the edge of the broken cabinet and a small fluffy bundle darted out and hid under the couch.

Sync scrambled mindlessly over to her and reached under to try to grab her. As he did so, a bullet flew in and hit Tacyturn in the neck.

Just a second after that, bullets showered the inside of the cabin.

Tacyturn grasped his neck and pulled the couch out, shoving Sync behind it. Just as Sync was safely blocked, a bullet hit Tacyturn in the thigh. The driver then squatted down behind the couch.

The young redhead had just gotten a hold of Bandit and was holding her in his sweater. Her claws were digging into him, but he held her tight.

Once Sync saw that the driver was injured, he didn't know what to say. He could only produce a concerned and confused whimper as the driver remained calm and focused, not showing any signs of feeling pain.

Tacyturn fumbled whilst holding his bleeding wound and his gun, also trying to handle the key fob from the Whisperunner. The young man could see that the bleeding was heavy, but at least the bullet had only side-swiped him and not gone straight in.

Sync thought they were in a dire situation trapped behind the couch with his bodyguard injured.

"This is all my fucking fault," he whined.

Then he noticed that there were severed wires sticking out of the bloody wound in Tacyturn's neck. He stared curiously, wondering what they were.

Tacyturn then grabbed Sync's wrist and pressed his palm up against his neck to hold his wound for him. Sync did his best to apply pressure, allowing the driver to do what he was trying to do.

With the key fob, Tacyturn activated the remote control of the midnight blue Whisperunner. He guided it around the cabin, hitting a few men in the process. He stopped it just beside a window nearby.

In one quick movement, Tacyturn shot the window, scooped Sync up with an arm around his lower back and pressed their stomachs together, sandwiching the cat safely between them.

The young redhead continued to apply pressure to his neck, also clinging protectively onto the cat with his other arm. He did not want to mess up his two main tasks. He added a third as he pressed his leg up against his bleeding thigh.

Tacyturn rammed his back into the weakened window, crashing directly into the driver's seat. He immediately saw that a bullet had destroyed the rearview mirror and the car had swiped against the cabin, crunching the side mirror into a useless state. The dashboard screen was also destroyed.

Not wanting to waste time now that the enemies were certain of his position, Tacyturn quickly put the car in reverse. Sync was confused and felt a bit awkward because he was still straddling Tacyturn in the car seat, the way they had stumbled in.

Tacyturn didn't acknowledge it and reached around Sync to steer the vehicle as if he wasn't there. Sync tried to make himself as small as possible, peeking over his shoulder to see what was going on behind them.

As Tacyturn drove into the woods, he heard cars behind him. He instinctively tried checking his mirrors, but they were useless. He tried to turn his head but felt his wound stretch in a way it shouldn't.

Sync, being so close to him, felt hyper aware of what was going on in his head. He thought he heard electricity crackling sometimes, wondering what part of the car was doing it.

"There are two of them," Sync told him. "One is a car's length behind us and the other one is trying to come up on your side."

Calculating with what had just been told to him, Tacyturn braked the car hard and swerved in reverse, weaving his way between the two cars and ending up beside the one furthest back.

With his gun, he shot the driver and the vehicle went wildly into a tree. The vehicle that was now ahead started shooting and Tacyturn protectively pushed down on Sync's head.

Just before he lost sight of the view out the back window, Sync saw another car.

"There's another one! It's that one Jeep," he said in awe, recognizing it

[47]

from their garage. "The one with the huge fucking wheels with weird gnarly armour on the top of the—fwuh!"

Without any warning, Tacyturn turned into the dense forest. The Whisperunner was not entirely cut out for off-roading, but the other small enemy vehicle wouldn't be able to follow him at all.

"You know you're going exactly where the Jeep wants you to go, right?" Sync was puzzled with his decision. "They usually bring it out when they plan to run someone off of the road. You should know that and you've probably done it yourself."

They drove for a while as Tacyturn expertly dodged all of the trees. Sync was shocked that they were not hitting any. He could see so many trees flying by and even feel them as they went by the broken window. Some leaves showered them.

Sync could hear the Jeep and it was terrifying because of how powerful it sounded. It was gaining quickly.

The young man held on tight to the wriggling cat and also Tacyturn's neck. He kept an eye out for the vehicle.

"It's fucking here!" he exclaimed the moment he saw it.

Finally spotting what he wanted, Tacyturn slid the vehicle to sit alongside an overhang. He then performed a very quick and efficient action that reversed them down the hill alongside the edge, dropped the Whisperunner down a less dangerous part of the overhang, then drove back up and tucked the vehicle below where he had started.

He then opened the sunroof and dirt and leaves showered them.

"Fucking really?" Sync whined, protecting Bandit with his sweater.

Tacyturn responded by quietly turning off the car and its lights.

As they waited, the Jeep was getting louder and louder. Sync's insides twisted up more and more the closer it got until it was right on top of them. He was usually impressed with the sound of its engine, but now it was like the sound of a monster in the woods.

Sync closed his eyes, terrified as the Jeep drove directly over the top of them, dirt and debris flying into the car. The front wheels hopped over them and the back wheels crunched just the edge of their car.

As that happened, Tacyturn aimed upwards and shot out all four of the armoured wheels where their only weakness was. The Jeep continued to roll down the hill as Tacyturn maneuvered their car back onto the main dirt road.

"Fuck yeah!" Sync exclaimed when he felt things were calm again.

Just as Sync was trying to slide into the passenger seat without letting go of the driver's neck, he spotted a car.

"Ah, shit, that car we lost track of is back."

The enemy car remained very far away from the Whisperunner, quietly following. It only ever gained on them when a passing lane showed up, but still never got too close.

The driver figured that they were trying to see where exactly Sync was in the car. He knew it would be best if he remained where he was, confusing any sensors they might have. He hoped they would become disinterested, thinking he was no longer in the vehicle.

Occasionally Tacyturn would speed up in an attempt to lose them, but they'd eventually find their way back into view.

At one point, the car passed them and Tacyturn pushed Sync's head down. Before going down, he saw that one of the Thornwryght medics, Yenvieve, was in the car—she looked terrified. The person next to her offered no comfort.

Tired of the tense chase, Tacyturn aimed to shoot them the next time they went by.

"I think Tobyas is in there," Sync pointed out, mumbling against his chest. "I think he has a camera and, of course, one of our medics. Fucker's always afraid to do anything dangerous without one."

Tacyturn quickly drew the gun back into the car. Sync wondered if he wasn't allowed to kill any of The Nineteen—especially with Tobyas as the oldest one.

"What's wrong?"

"The killer is out to earn his reward outright."

Before Sync could respond, Tacyturn sped up and sideswiped the other car. After that moment, the enemy car became more aggressive.

With Sync telling him everything the vehicle was doing behind them, Tacyturn managed to escape the long car chase with a few scrapes, leaving the enemy car sliding to a stop upside down.

Sync thought he should have been more afraid of being in such an unsafe position during a precarious chase, but he always knew when Tacyturn was about to do anything dramatic and could brace himself—the driver would wrap his arm protectively around Sync like a seatbelt.

Just as the enemy car was downed, they were now in the city again.

"Coffee?" Tacyturn asked as if nothing exciting had just happened.

Sync was about to object to getting himself a treat when he was the cause of all the chaos, but saw that they were already at a drive-thru coffee shop.

A barista emerged with an ube macchiato. She hesitated when she realized something was off.

Cautiously approaching, she stared and slowly processed what she was seeing—the driver with a noosed young man on his lap holding his bleeding neck, both coated in broken glass, dirt and leaves.

Just before she spoke, Bandit peeked her head out from between them and loudly meowed. The barista jumped and Tacyturn caught the drink as she dropped it.

"Nursewryght," Tacyturn tersely said as he held onto Sync's coffee with an arm dangling from the window.

Recognizing the word, the barista quickly nodded and disappeared. Tacyturn pulled the car up to the back of the small building and an older woman emerged with a medical bag.

The driver opened the car door, letting debris fall out onto the street. The woman sighed seeing his bleeding leg and neck. She wanted to speak, but knew better.

Once Sync was freed from holding his neck, he slid into the passenger seat and Tacyturn handed him his coffee drink without looking at him. Bandit stretched and jumped into the back seat, needing some space.

The woman quickly patched Tacyturn up like she had done it many times before. She handed Tacyturn the bullet from his leg, then she went right back to work in the coffee shop, leaving a wet cloth hanging on the car door before she left.

"Are you okay?" Sync asked him when they were alone again.

The driver nodded whilst handing the cloth to Sync and tossing the bullet into his cup holder.

The young man cleaned the blood off of his hand and attempted to soak blood out of his leggings, but decided he would just toss them later. He handed the cloth back and Tacyturn then cleaned his own hands and the steering wheel. He then tossed the cloth into the nearby dumpster and drove off.

Sync quietly stewed in his anxiety as he went through everything that had just happened.

The driver looked calm as always.Suddenly he shoved the drink towards Tacyturn. "I don't deserve this! It's my fault you were fucking shot! Twice! That's two more scars for you! Throw this fucking thing out the window!"

Tacyturn gently pushed the drink back to the young man.

"I failed to be prepared."

"What? How? You're always super fuckin' prepared and knowing exactly what to do and shit."

"I fell asleep," he confessed.

Sync was confused. "So? It's almost like that fucking happens every night, or something. Are you not supposed to sleep?"

Tacyturn said nothing, leaving Sync to wonder about several things.

He had never seen Tacyturn eat or drink. He was implying he wasn't supposed to sleep. He also had wires in his neck. He didn't seem to be in pain, but he also didn't show emotions for anything else. He had zero fear. He didn't talk unless he had to. His control over cars was mechanical and precise, as was his shooting. He needed commands to act on.

The conclusion he was coming to sounded silly, so he kept his mouth shut about it. 1983►► was advanced, but not that advanced. If his family had a contract that big, he would have known about it. Brayd kept Sync in the loop of everything, especially if it was something cool—and androids were really fucking cool.

Tacyturn bled, so he assumed he had to be human. He also had a heartbeat that Sync could feel the entire time he was with him in the driver's seat.

It was unnerving how calm it stayed, though—but it kept Sync calm, too.

"We can't keep going on like this," Sync mewled. "Even if I wanted to prove myself to my father, how can I do it if we keep getting fucking hunted down? How will we get them to stop looking for me? When do you stop looking for someone?"

"When there's nothing to look for."

VII.

"Movies aren't real."

BY THE EARLY EVENING, SYNC had chewed two coffee straws into mangled clusters—and was working on a third. The young man wanted desperately to talk about what they were going to do, but he mostly wanted to avoid talking much at all. He was worried about what the plan was going to be, especially after Tacyturn's last unpropitious comment—because he wasn't wrong.

Sync had also made several excuses throughout the day to distract from the bigger picture, whining about petty things.

He had first mentioned that Bandit looked like she needed food. Tacyturn took him to a convenience store to grab some. Sync had angrily yelled at people when they were gawking at the blood on their clothes and how dirty they were. He showed several people his middle finger as they returned to the car—even people who were minding their own business.

Once he turned his back, an offended thug had stomped towards him, looking for a confrontation. Tacyturn had quietly stepped on the bottom of the man's baggy pants, causing the man to trip and fall hard to the ground. He yanked off the man's trousers in one quick and efficient tug and deftly tossed them in the bed of a truck as it went by.

Not wanting to lose his wallet—and also embarrassed by just being in his underwear—the man had run off just as Sync turned around to see.

"Some weird fucking people in this world," Sync said as Tacyturn opened the car door for him.

Next, Sync had complained that the car was too dirty. After waiting for a direct command and not getting it, Tacyturn finally gave in and drove the vehicle to a remote location and swept out dirty leaves and rocks with his hands.

After the back seat was cleaner, Sync took out a squashed black fedora with an orange trim-ribbon from his bag, flipped it over and used it as a makeshift cat food bowl. Bandit happily crunched on her meal. He then rinsed out his empty coffee cup in a drinking fountain and filled it with water for her.

Seeing the cat eat made him hungry and he casually complained about how loud his stomach was growling. Tacyturn, again, waited for a direct command or a suggestion—and got none. Feeding Sync was part of taking care of him for Ephraym, so he eventually stopped at a sandwich shop in the early afternoon and then drove to an auto glass shop.

Whilst Sync ate, Tacyturn mended the broken window in the Whisperunner, concerned with how cold Sync was getting during their car rides. The young man admired how the driver was able to do it himself, but complained that it took an hour.

Weaved in among all of their activities, Sync complained about being physically dirty with the blood on his clothes. Tacyturn seemed to ignore him about it, but the main destination for the day was going to take care of those issues. He didn't want to stop to be vulnerably disrobed and showering anywhere even remotely close to where they had last been spotted, so they drove for several hours.

Just before dark, Tacyturn and Sync arrived at a public indoor pool that was temporarily closed for renovations. The driver took the car around back and broke in, pushing the large doors open wide enough for him to back the Whisperunner expertly into the main pool area. It was an insanely tight squeeze, but he did it with ease.

As Sync stepped out when his car door was opened, he saw that the pool area was a mess, covered with debris. Sync let the barn cat run around and play.

Thankful that the showers worked, they bathed themselves and took advantage of the washer and dryer they had on site. Anything that they had been wearing that had too much blood on it ended up in the trash.

Tacyturn's magenta shirts seemed to hide blood well. Sync wondered if that was why he chose the colour in the first place.

Once clean, Sync wasn't sure what he was dressing for—it was either going to continue to be a car ride or they were going to sleep. He decided to meet in the middle with a fresh T-shirt under his green sweater and with his fluro pinstripe pants. The noose around his neck was non-negotiable as usual and he threw it on, as well.Sync peered down into the main pool to see that it was mostly empty of water. He sat at the edge of the pool with one leg dangling in and the other tucked against his chest. His chin rested on his knee.

He finally tugged the final mangled straw out of his mouth—he had been chewing the hell out of it for hours.

"You're not going to drown me, are you?" Sync asked, knowing that Tacyturn was right behind him. "See if I fight back and unleash my suppressed Thornwryght potential or whatever?"

Tacyturn stared down at the water. "It's too shallow for a Sync to sink."

The young man was expecting silence, so when he heard him talk, he made a face.

"Wait, that's another one of your weird fucking comments. Is that humour?" He looked up at his dull expression. "I can't fucking tell! I hope you don't have any more."

"Synchronized swimming."

Sync put his head in his hand and groaned.

"Jesus fucking Christ. You have been my father's bodyguard for way too fucking long." He offered the end of his neck rope to the tall man. "Here's this, because I'm going in to end it," he said. "It looks deep enough for *that*."

Sync didn't expect Tacyturn to react—and he didn't.

The young man resumed analyzing the room. What he saw told a clear story to a crime syndicate youth. He picked up a bullet casing.

"This place isn't closed for renovations, is it? It's closed for repairs." He gestured to the walls, which were covered in bullet holes. "A gunfight went down in here. A pretty serious one, from the looks of the damage. I'm not a stranger to old blood spatter." He looked up at Tacyturn who wasn't bothering to look around, himself. "You were here when it all happened, weren't you?"

The driver remained silent.

"That's how you knew this place was here and empty for us to use. Was it a deal gone wrong? A set up? Were you the ones who set it up or did you get tricked?" Sync didn't know why he asked so many questions when he knew he wasn't going to get many answers. "How many people did you kill?"

"All of them."

Sync grasped his chest as he felt it go hot with fear—but also hot with admiration.

To hide his fear, the young heir angrily huffed and stood up, throwing the bullet shell across the pool. He yanked his vidphone out of his pocket and shoved it into Tacyturn's hands.

When the driver looked at it, he saw it was recording video—currently Sync's shoes.

Sync dramatically got down onto his knees and grabbed the driver's wrist, pointing the camera at him.

"Whoever kills me and gets video proof gets to claim the company, right? Who fucking better than my father's right-hand man? At least you'll keep that company badass and murderous like it's supposed to be. I am not a good fit because I am neither of those," he whined. "I should be put out of my pathetic pointless and miserable life. My purpose is to die, no matter what I do. I'm weak and I'm a coward, so do it quickly."

Tacyturn knew that Sync was just being dramatic like he always was. He hid fear that way—but also showed it tenfold.

Sync trembled for a moment, allowing his mind to go blank long enough for the possibility of his histrionics coming true. Anger then pushed him back onto his feet and he snatched his phone back.

"Fine, I'll just do it myself! Maybe I can do it in a way that makes it look like you did it. Give me your fucking gun so that physical evidence will definitely point to you."

When Sync turned around to look at Tacyturn, he was holding his gun out towards the young man, gripping it by the barrel and offering the handle.

The young heir sighed heavily, realizing he had given something that resembled a command, but he wasn't serious. He felt bad seeing how easy it was for him to disarm the loyal driver—or the man was just humouring him.

"Fucking don't," he said as he shoved it back towards Tacyturn. "I don't know what's going to happen, but I'm only pretending I have any control over it. You made it very clear that the only way I'm going to stop being hunted is if I die. The only other way is if I became magically fucking bulletproof so that they fucking *can't* kill me. So, that must be the next plan. I have to fucking die."

"A suicide would be perfect."

Sync froze with his back towards him. "What?"

[55]

"With proof," he added as he tucked his gun away.

The young man stared beyond the shadows on the walls. "*What?*"

Tacyturn said nothing else and Sync whirled around to look at him.

"Are you fucking serious? This is your plan?"

"Like a movie," he added.

Sync angrily approached the tall man with no intentions of grabbing him, but made it look like he was holding back from doing so. "THIS ISN'T A FUCKING MOVIE! THIS IS MY REAL FUCKING LIFE! MOVIES AREN'T—" He paused as a light turned on in his head. "Movies . . . aren't real . . ." He made a clicking sound whilst fidgeting with his fingers. "Movies aren't real."

He cast his eyes down to see the barn cat rubbing against his legs. Her presence helped calm him quickly.

"I need to fake my death, don't I?"

Tacyturn nodded when Sync looked at him.

"That's . . . actually a really fucking good idea." He kneeled down to pet Bandit as his mind raced. "If I did that, no one would be able to take over the company by killing me. Father would have to figure something else out and The Nineteen would just have to fucking be patient. They'd stop looking for me and start kissing his ass, if they knew what was good for them." He looked up at the driver, hitting a dead end. "But after that?"

"Come back from the dead to claim your empire."

Sync quickly stood up and shook his head. "I couldn't possibly! Are you fucking crazy? I'd take one step back on that peninsula and have nineteen fucking bullets in me! I know I've mentioned before that I'm not fucking bulletproof! But I'll mention it again, anyway." He grasped his own shirt. "*I'm not fucking bulletproof.*"

"You'll learn to fight."

"I'm not interested in hurting people," Sync mewled, putting his head in his hands and teetering backwards. "I have no desire to kill anyone."

"You already have."

"AND THAT'S HOW I FUCKING KNOW I DON'T WANT TO DO IT AGAIN!" he sobbed.

Upon taking another step back, Sync felt the floor disappear. Just as he went over the edge of the pool, Tacyturn grabbed the rope around his neck and held it tight, keeping Sync from falling in. The redhead grabbed the knot itself to keep it from tightening in the process.

The driver effortlessly wound the rope around his wrist and reeled the young man in. "Learning to fight doesn't mean you're learning to hurt people."

Sync scoffed. "Pretty fucking sure that's exactly what learning to fight means."

"You're learning to protect yourself and it gives you confidence."

"Is that why you learned?"

His response this time was just a usual headshake. Sync's expression begged for further explanation.

The driver said, "I had to learn to prove that I was more useful alive than dead."

"Shit. My family's great, huh?"

Tacyturn tugged Sync away from the edge, then unwound his hand.

"So, I send my family a video of me killing myself so that they leave me alone long enough for me to train, then return home and prove that I'm worthy?"

Tacyturn nodded.

"Fuck." Sync rubbed his wet eyes as he took a moment to process everything. Then, he sighed. "So, where do we start?"

"Hollywood."

"Hollywood? Fuck, that's so fucking far," he groaned. "But that makes sense. They've got their movie magic that makes shit look real. When do we go?"

"Up to you."

"We're driving, right? Of course we're driving, look who the fuck I'm talking to. Well, we've been driving all fucking day and I'm—" He paused and watched Bandit happily knocking around the bullet casing he had thrown. "I mean, Bandit is tired of being in a car. Look how fucking happy she is."

He checked the time on his vidphone—10:23PM.

"It's fucking early for me, but I'll close my eyes for bit. For her."

Sync went to the car and took out her hat bowl of food and coffee shop cup of water, setting them down on a nearby bench. He then saw that there was an old blanket folded neatly in the back seat.

"Where did you find that? It looks like it smells like shit."

When Sync grabbed it to confirm, several packets of tea fell out of the folds. The pleasant scent of spiced biscuits enveloped him.

Sync looked up at Tacyturn who had already sat himself in the driver's seat. Sync wondered how he did it—the car was parked right at the edge of the pool on that side and he had heard virtually no sound of the man maneuvering himself.

Sync crawled into the backseat of the car and wrapped himself in his nice-smelling blanket whilst the driver kept watch, having positioned the car in the optimum way to do so.

Then Tacyturn felt a gentle and brief touch on his head.

After Sync settled down again to sleep, Tacyturn closed his eyes and sighed.

VIII.

"When he's dead, you'll be free."

THE TRIP TO HOLLYWOOD HAD been long—but not as long as
it could have been if Sync had a less efficient driver. Tacyturn's speed cut
the time nearly in half, and his ability to lose the police who often tried to
pull him over for speeding or for having only one intact mirror and several
suspicious bullet holes. He somehow could tell when a plain-looking vehicle
was an undercover police car.

Sync was always in awe and felt extremely lucky to witness such talent.
He loved the moments where the driver would lose them by drifting into a
hiding spot and turning off his engine. It gave him an adrenaline rush that
he felt like he could get addicted to.

Bandit was indifferent to it all, which was a compliment from a cat. She
slept peacefully the entire time, trusting Sync to keep her from flying into
the windshield.

The young redhead also decided to start sitting in the front passenger
seat—the first time in his life, aside from after their escape from the cabin.
That had given him a taste and he liked it. He liked being right next to
Tacyturn and watching him in action.

They had arrived in Hollywood in the late afternoon, but Sync had
hoped it would have been at night. He was anxious to see the enhanced and
remodeled neon city he had only ever heard of or seen in films.

When they stopped at their destination, Sync remained quiet and
followed Tacyturn. He looked up at the building they were at—a company
called Electric Reel.

Instead of going inside, Tacyturn walked around the back to a large
open lot with several cars lined up and drivers ready for their cues.

Nearby was a man controlling a UAV camera drone that buzzed about
in the air. The moment he saw Tacyturn, he put up his hand towards the
expensive cars to indicate he needed five minutes. He jumped and caught
the drone, then walked up to the driver and the syndicate heir.

"Holy shit, Tacy! You're . . . back?"

The way he offered his hand seemed like he was nervously testing the waters.

The man relaxed when Tacyturn shook it. The man smiled, then.

Sync eyed the man. He was a Pacific Islander with a neat side part hairstyle that was partially dyed pale lavender. He was not as tall as Tacyturn—but much taller than Sync. He looked older than Tacyturn and nowhere near as fit, but rather average. He was covered in tattoos, revealing them with his tank top and shorts—even though it was cold and was just starting to rain.

The young redhead averted his eyes when the stranger looked at him.

"Who is this? What's with the noose? Is that a new style I'm unaware of?"

When Sync didn't hear Tacyturn respond, he realized he was meant to.

Sync ignored the comments about the rope around his neck. "I'm . . . Sync."

"Sync? That's a name that'll make you fit right in here. Sounds futuristic like the world we're suddenly in. I mean, I'm assuming you're not named after the kitchen sink. Either way, much better than the name Tacyturn," he teased.

"Right?" Sync said, jumping on an agreement to make the situation less awkward. "What kind of fucking name is that?"

"Probably the same fucking kind of name as K-1-M-0 Rilang."

Sync wrinkled his nose. "Is that you, then?"

"That's me, then," he responded with a grin as he offered Sync his hand. "But honestly, I only add the numbers when I write my name down. You just have to say it with a regular 'I' and 'O' on your mind."

Sync weakly shook his hand and groaned. "Believe me, I will."

Kimo pointed to Sync's hand. "Better work on that handshake if you want to have anything go your way around here, though." He leaned in and examined his face. "But you are very cute and that will definitely help. Look at all of those freckles! Some of them look a little . . . afflicted, but makeup can fix that. Are you wearing eyeliner or is that natural? Those are some gorgeous emerald eyes. They look far too big for your face. You're a little Irish doll, aren't you? The accent indicates you're an Irish from Boston. You'll be a hit here talking like that. How old are you?"

". . . Twenty," he responded with an uncomfortable scowl.

"Damn, look at that baby face. You'd be perfect playing a high schooler. Or we could pretend you were underage and please—"

Tacyturn interjected, "We need your services."

"Who is *we*? Who *is* this kid to you?"

"I'm not a fucking kid!" Sync barked. "I'm *his* boss!" he pointed out, looking to impress.

Kimo looked skeptical. He stared at Tacyturn who ignored the pointless chatter.

"We need a video of Sync killing himself."

"Whoa, whoa, *whooooa-no!*" Kimo wagged his hands furiously as he looked over his shoulder. "I don't do snuff films!" he added through gritted teeth.

Sync's eyes widened. "Hey, fuck you! I'm not actually going to kill myself! It's gonna be fake, idiot!"

Kimo heaved a sigh of relief and put his hand on Tacyturn's shoulder, using it to support himself from the overwhelming relief he was feeling.

"Oh, thank God! I was about to be all up your ass for that," he responded, as if Tacyturn was the one that had clarified. "Absolutely I can make you one of those. Wouldn't be my first. Duration?"

"Quick, one clip," the driver said. "Not even a minute long."

Taking out his vidphone, Kimo flipped through his calendar.

"I'm busy the rest of today, but I can make room for you tomorrow. I'm usually way too busy on Saturday nights, but I've got a clear evening just for you, Tacy."

"And me," Sync grumbled, feeling invisible.

"How would you like to die?" he asked Sync without acknowledging that he had said anything first. "Is that where the noose comes in?"

Sync's jaw dropped slightly, but then he quickly answered, "I'd shoot myself in the head at the top of a building during a very rainy night. I'll use the noose around my neck that's attached to a neon sign, so when I fall off, I'll hang myself if I fucked up somehow with the gun, which I'm likely to do. If that fails and the neon shatters, I'll fall to my death while being showered with glass, so the building has to be too tall to survive. Maybe I'll land on my back and drown in the rain while paralyzed from a broken spine if that doesn't do it."

Kimo stared at Sync and Tacyturn stared at the ground.

". . . Oddly specific, but that saves me from dicking around too much in my own dark imagination. Saturday night works out well, then, for everyone." Kimo modified his schedule. "Probably just go with the first portion of your little emocore drama, though, if you want it to be quick and realistic."

Tacyturn took out his wallet.

"We'll figure that out later," Kimo said as he pushed the wallet down. He moved closer to Tacyturn and slid his hand across his lower back. "I want you to know that I still take other forms of payment, by the by."

Sync saw this move and gaped.

"I'm working," Tacyturn said, flatly.

"When do you get off?" Kimo asked coyly.

"I don't."

Kimo stared Tacyturn in the face, trying to read his expression. "Does that answer both my questions?"

"But that was only one question," Sync chimed in with an attitude.

Kimo looked down at Sync, then back at Tacyturn. "What do you do now?"

"Bodyguard."

The man clicked his tongue. "Ah, an *escort*. That's around-the-clock work."

He pointed at Sync with an inquisitive look and the driver nodded.

Kimo clapped once. "When he's dead, you'll be free."

Sync narrowed his eyes at Kimo.

"Also, Tacy, what's with the outfits? So goddamn formal. You're welcome to rifle through the wardrobe storeroom and see if anything takes your fancy. Ellenoir will be *very* pleased to see you, too." He saw Sync's nosy expression. "My wife."

"Why the fuck do I care tha—!"

Suddenly Sync jumped when a driver in the lot impatiently revved his engine and honked.

Kimo was amused and waved behind him without looking, clearly consumed with unknown, but pleasing thoughts.

"I've got to get back to work while there's still daylight and before it starts pouring," he said, seeing the droplets of rain on his vidphone. "These videos are usually very personal, so you should have a script ready. Even if you just jot down a few lines, I'll make it work. I don't know what your intentions are, so I can't do it for you. I will see you both tomorrow when we kill little Sync together!"

Kimo cheerfully smiled and waved before turning back to his drivers, relaunching the drone with an enthusiastic skip.

Tacyturn went back to the Whisperunner and Sync followed close behind. The young heir remained quiet as the driver opened the door for him and he sat in the car.

Just as Tacyturn sat down and closed his own door, Sync said, "I don't like him."

Tacyturn said nothing and started the car.

"Do you like him?"

"I like that he's going to help you."

Sync hummed in thought and crossed his arms, slouching in his seat. Bandit crawled from the back seat into his lap, yelling in his face for attention. He tried to relax as he petted the cat, but stewed in his thoughts. He scratched under Bandit's chin and she lifted her head up and tightly closed her eyes.

Seeing her bare neck, Sync thought it might be nice if she had a collar of some sort, imagining a tiny rope like his own—but safer, with a breakaway buckle.

Then he started thinking about his own daytime outfit—the same thing he had worn all his life. He had built his look up from the requirements for being on the Thornwryght peninsula as an heir, but it still felt like he was limited to his full fashion potential.

Most of what he wore he found—like his pins from various places. Also his black diamond earrings he found in his mother's belongings as they were being removed from the mansion to sell.

Or what he wore was what he needed—like his cardigan sweater he wore underneath his jacket to make his arms look thicker. Also, he was always cold, even in summer—but only when he was thinking about it.

Sync thought it might be nice to find something new to wear.

"Are we going to the wardrobe storeroom?"

Tacyturn shook his head.

"Is it because you don't want to see that Ellenoir chick?"

"Coffee?"

"Shutting me up with a coffee?"

Not even giving him much time to respond, Sync heaved an annoyed sigh, knowing that Tacyturn wasn't likely to answer his question even if he did.

"Fuck, fine. I'd love to chew the fuck out of a straw right about now."

IX.

"Are you an android?"

I DON'T UNDERSTAND HOW EVERYONE knows to get one of these fucking things prepared before we even get there," Sync wondered out loud, holding the ube macchiato in his hands. "Hollywood isn't close to our peninsula."

"An order is automatically placed when we are within range."

"Must be a system that father sold to the industry and had a perk added on the side."

Sync sipped his drink, impressed with the efficiency—until he realized how flawed it was. "What if you're just driving by and have no plans to pick it up?"

"Up to them."

"Figures my father doesn't care what gets thrown away along the way," Sync mumbled, leaning dramatically against the window. "Or who."

When he looked out, he saw that they were out of the city and in the rural outskirts.

Deciding not to ask where they were going, he waited, figuring that they were going to come upon another unenhanced old cabin or something abandoned.

They just continued to drive.

Just as the rain started to pour, Tacyturn parked the car in the middle of nowhere and stepped outside. Sync wondered if he was going to stop to drain water, so he quietly minded his own business. He huddled in his blanket further, glad to not be in the rain—he wasn't in the mood.

Then the door on his side opened and the wind and water flooded in.

"What the fuck are you doing?" Sync hissed. "I'm not getting out!"

Tacyturn patiently waited.

"It's getting dark and, I don't know if you noticed but . . . IT'S FUCKING RAINING! And not even a little bit. See, I like a little bit of rain. Maybe even a fair amount of rain. Perhaps even a dramatic amount of

[65]

rain. But this? This is a FUCKING STORM!"

The driver continued to be patient.

"Are we abandoning the car?" Sync whined. "Why didn't we abandon it near a hotel?"

Continuing to grumble, Sync stepped out of the car. Once out, he realized the rain wasn't as bad as he thought, but he was still annoyed as if it were. He left his blanket behind, knowing it would just become a wet and heavy mess.

Bandit crawled out from the backseat and meowed from the center console.

"What about Bandit? We have to take her with us. She won't like this rain." He grabbed his bag and unzipped it. He tried to coax her into it, but she refused. "Don't we have an umbrella?"

"In the Aphotic."

"Fucking great." He pulled his jacket up partially over his head. "The hitmen didn't pack anything useful?"

Tacyturn popped open the trunk. Inside was an entire arsenal of weapons.

Sync peeked in. "None of those are particularly useful to stop rain, are they?" Then he spotted something he liked. He reached in and grabbed a fedora. "Fucking nice! This one isn't flat and doesn't smell like cat food! Probably left over from some poor bastard who had to spend some time locked up back there. Wonder if it was a one-way trip or they just needed to think about what they've done."

The syndicate heir put the hat on and leaned to look in the one intact side mirror. He hardly had a chance to see how it fit before he grimaced with pain. Bandit climbed onto his shoulders, using her claws. She curled around his neck, staying decently dry under the rim of the hat.

Tacyturn shut the car door and began walking.

"Wait, what about our bags?"

"Later."

"But we're abandoning it, aren't we?"

"It'll look like something happened."

Sync thought a moment, then said, "One of The Nineteen might find it and see that we left all our shit behind? Then they'll be suspicious one of the others had something to do with it and got to us first? Then they'll start investigating them instead of where we might have gone on our own? Fucking nice!" He looked up to see Tacyturn was already several steps away. "Walking is still NOT FUCKING NICE!" he called out after him.

Bandit nipped at his freckled cheek with her sharp teeth, something he was noticing that she did whenever he sounded too angry too suddenly. She'd either be close enough to bite—or move closer to him and bite him. It had made him angrier at first, but now it calmed him like a hysterical person getting slapped in the face.

Sync tucked Bandit closer to him to make sure she wasn't getting too wet, grabbed his coffee drink out of the car, then caught up with the driver.

After they had walked longer than Sync had ever seen Tacyturn shower, he spoke up.

"Is it okay that you're in the rain this long? It's not gonna fuck you up in any way, is it?"

Tacyturn curiously looked at Sync.

The young man suddenly felt embarrassed. He found himself concerned with Tacyturn and had forgotten that his suspicions were silly. But with the way the driver had looked at him, he thought he might as well just find out for sure—or at least see Tacyturn's reaction, as minimal as it might be.

Sync stopped walking and Tacyturn took several steps before Sync got out the question he wanted to ask.

"Are you an android?"

Tacyturn stopped and turned back to Sync.

Deciding not to let the awkward silence linger too long, Sync decided to throw out all of his reasons why he suspected it. He wanted to quickly prove that his question was not as stupid as he was thinking Tacyturn thought it was.

"You must be one of my father's experiments, or a personal perk for selling the technology to the highest bidder. I looked up your name in cyberspace and it corrected my spelling. It showed me the real word. I didn't even fucking know that was a word! You were programmed to be quiet and obedient? Then he marked you as one of his by giving you one of these fucking 'Y' names. Servants don't usually get names like that."

Tacyturn continued to stare. Sync nervously continued.

"You had fucking wires in your neck! I saw them! They were severed, weren't they? Is that fucking you up somehow? Also, you don't really sleep, do you? You don't seem to have any mortal fear or human emotions. You also didn't seem to care that our dicks were practically pressed together for an entire car chase! Your heartbeat never changed that entire time. And the way you control a car is so precise. It's the same the way you move and handle a gun. You also have to do whatever a Thornwryght wants, right? You can't function without commands to give you some sort of direction? That must be programmed right into you.

"You also don't eat or drink! I've never seen it. I mean, whenever we get one of our many coffees, you don't ever get one. I thought it was because you were supposed to stay in your place as a servant, but I've never seen you drink *anything* and—"

Sync abruptly stopped when he saw that Tacyturn was slowly approaching him. He ended up so close, they were almost touching. Sync averted his eyes and leaned back, uncomfortable being so close to another human body—or possible android body.

Then Tacyturn leaned down and quietly took a sip of Sync's drink.

Sync turned back to object to it, but was too curious by the gesture. As he looked back at Tacyturn, he detected the mechanical whirring and glint that he always thought he saw when the driver looked at him.

When he focused on Tacyturn directly in the eyes for the first time up close, he saw that his right eye was magenta and his left eye was denim blue. It was extremely obvious now that he was really looking—further reminding Sync at how bad he was at making eye contact. He felt silly for never noticing his heterochromatic eyes before that moment.

"There are no androids," Tacyturn said matter-of-factly.

He could see that Sync was still feeling embarrassed by what he probably thought was a childish assumption. The driver pointed to the terrible scar on the side of his head.

"But I was implanted with a fragment of experimental programming while being repaired."

Sync's green eyes lit up with interest. "Like . . . you're testing it out? Is that why your eyes look bruised all the time?" He peered closer and could see strategic surgical scars amongst the discolouration. "The tech inside is doing that?"

Tacyturn nodded.

Sync sighed, feeling bad. "Sounds about right that my father made you a fucking guinea pig." He fumbled with his coffee cup, then asked, "What can it do?"

"Detect motion within a certain radius."

"So no one can sneak up on you?"

Tacyturn nodded.

"What else?"

"Intervene with other technology to a certain degree and scan and show information only I can see."

Sync was eager to hear more. "What's the coolest thing it can do?"

"When my eyes are closed, I can still see."

"Whoa! How do you know when your eyes are closed, then?"

"It's darkness, but with lambent wisps showing contours of objects, like an electric tapestry."

"So, you're like a cyborg hitman with neon radar?" Sync almost threw his drink with enthusiasm. He ignored the claws of Bandit who did her best to hold on as he excitedly flailed. "That's really wicked cool!"

Tacyturn's expression softened at his reaction.

"What are you detecting right now?" Sync eagerly asked.

"The night lights of Hollywood are turning on."

The young heir leaned over to look around the driver and could see the city within view. The sun was setting and the neon lights were starting to show their ghostly dominance over the rising darkness.

Sync was still excited and grabbed Tacyturn's hand, yanking on it.

"Let's fucking go!"

It wasn't long before they arrived back in the city. Sync wanted to be in the heart of it as it became the darkest it would become for the rest of the night.

Tacyturn stopped him just before he ran into the wet neon streets.

"What?" Sync huffed in the rain.

"Your shoes would fit right in."

The young heir looked blankly down at his shoes.

When he realized what he meant, he exclaimed, "Oh, fuck yeah they would!"

Sync quickly squatted and turned on his neon checkered shoes.

Before moving any further, he asked, "Can your . . . technology help you read minds?"

Tacyturn shook his head.

"Are you sure?"

Tacyturn nodded.

Sync hummed in thought, then dismissed it when he remembered what they were doing.

They both wandered side-by-side into the new neon Hollywood. Sync was in awe and loved every moment of it. Tacyturn kept an eye on him and the world around him. Whenever anyone looked at Sync wrong, his fingertips touched the gun under his jacket.

Sync thought it was interesting that every location's entrance and exit had a grand display for complimentary umbrellas. Anyone could take any umbrella they wanted and use it until their next indoor or covered destination. Then they would just leave it there for the next person. He wondered why his own city didn't do such a thing—it rained just as often.

The redhead didn't like to use umbrellas, so he was stoked when he found a kiosk that would attach a plastic hood to any outfit. Handing the woman his jacket, she hesitantly placed the expensive piece of clothing into her machine to attach tich buttons all along his under collar. Out of all of the plastic hoods, he chose one that was slightly green with a subtle checkered texture and attached it.

He enjoyed the sound of the rain hitting the plastic, though he was often giving it up to cover Bandit when she would retreat to his shoulder, hiding from people trying to take her. At one point, she even used it as a hammock—testing the strength of the buttons.

To keep people from assuming she was a stray, Sync stole a glowing purple braided mood bracelet from a tourist stand and put it around Bandit's neck. He insisted that she should have something that was stolen to coincide with her name. He also thought of his sister—the barn cat's secret full name was Bandit Brayden, so the collar was fitting.

Tacyturn let Sync wander around until midnight. He usually just looked around outside, only once showing interest in leaving the rainy neon night to go into a virtual gaming café. He played a few old game machines that were not being used.

The driver tried one that had a physical gun to hold and beat the highest score. When Sync insisted that Tacyturn play something he wanted to play, he mounted a virtual motorbike. Sync couldn't tell if he chose it just because it was the closest one to him or if he actually revealed something he enjoyed to do.

He destroyed the record in that game, as well—but that was probably just Tacyturn's natural proficiency that made him excel at everything he did.

Sync had wanted to see more, but Tacyturn was suddenly intent on moving along, going outside through the back door, climbing out of the convoluted sunken alley. Sync was confused, but thought it was fun—he momentarily felt like he was on a secret mission with a cool hitman.

For a brief moment when Tacyturn was pulling him up over a high ledge, he thought he saw that Tacyturn's right eye had turned yellow—but blamed the wild variety of lighting that was around them.

Bandit quite liked the climbing, too, jumping off of Sync's shoulders to do it herself.

To apologize for dragging him out of the game bar, Tacyturn bought Sync a halo-halo from a dessert street vendor. Sync asked for every topping available and it was served in a coconut shell. Bandit returned to his shoulders at that point and licked his spoon whenever she got the chance.

As he ate his dessert, Sync hopped up onto a bench and was peering closely at Tacyturn's right eye, confirming it was magenta.

When the driver looked at him, Sync quickly looked into his dessert, seeking out his next bite.

Once he finished, they moved on.

Every move they made was purposeful and planned, even though Sync thought they were just wandering. The driver had made sure to direct the young heir to end up at a specific building right as midnight struck.

They entered the old building through a back door with a digital key from the driver's black wristband. He had to knock on the door a certain way for it to work.

After weaving through a few small dilapidated hallways, Tacyturn opened up a door labeled 7Y3.

Inside was a very modest, cheap apartment.

Bandit immediately jumped off of Sync's shoulders and shook herself off.

Sync looked around. "Is this where we're staying?"

By the way the place was decorated, he knew it was one of his father's many properties—the syndicate logo was everywhere. There was one thing that was off, though.

"This couldn't be a Thornwryght hideout. It's on the ground floor and looks like total shit!"

He checked the kitchen for a fancy coffee maker and confirmed his suspicions—there was none.

"Besides, won't my family think to check here before we get the video done? Father made all his property available for any Thornwryght to use. He can't use DEL\Lync on any of them, so I'm sure one of my ex-siblings is already going through the list. Luckily, we're pretty fucking far from the peninsula, so this would probably be one of the last apartments that would be checked out. I mean, unless they decided to fly to the other side of the country and then start checking places one by one on the way back home by car. Then this would probably be one of the first ones they'd check."

Tacyturn handed Sync a vidkey—it was for a film called *Blade Runner* that he had never heard of. The label looked like a faded amateur printout.

Sync automatically went to a display screen and reached out to plug it in.

"Here."

Tacyturn was pointing to a cracked wall tile. Part of the crack did match to the shape of the tip of the vidkey, but Sync would have never thought to put it there.

Approaching the crack, Sync inserted the Y shaped prongs. Just as he did so, Tacyturn grabbed him by his jacket lapel and tugged him towards him.

Sync thought it was rude and resisted—until he looked down to see that the wooden floorboards were seemingly dissipating. He hopped quickly into Tacyturn who kept him from falling in.

In a hole in the ground, there was a ladder. Bandit had curiously wandered over, peeking down the new opening.

"What the fuck?" Sync mumbled, surprised.

He leaned in and could not see the bottom. He was uncomfortable with how Bandit looked like she was going to jump down and protectively scooped her up.

"No fucking way! Tacyturn will go first."

Tacyturn snatched the vidkey from the wall, grabbed Sync around the waist and slid expertly down the ladder as if it were nothing. The hole sealed above them.

Once they hit the bottom, Sync pretended he hadn't hidden his face in Tacyturn's chest.

Down inside, Sync could see that it was just a storage room.

"Oh. Wicked cool," he unenthusiastically said, setting Bandit in a box.

She liked it, indicated by her purring.

"*No*, Bandit, I was being sarcastic. This is awful. This is worse than the shitty apartment above. I miss the shitty apartment above. No, I take that back, this room makes me miss the fucking *cabin*."

Sync huffed and saw Tacyturn messing with a vent. Tacyturn used the vidkey to pull out a screw, then put the screw in backwards—the other end looked just the same.

The young redhead hid behind Tacyturn when it felt like the wall he had been leaning on heaved a sigh. The wall then slowly peeled away square by square folding upon itself.

Once it finished, the frame of the wall lit up in a neon purple colour and familiar words turned on in their own glow, as well—**Y/OUR FUTURE IS Y/OURS**. The second 'Y' frequently—and strategically—flickered off.

With how bright the light was, Sync couldn't see very deep into the darkness of the next room and was fearful of what might be in there.

Tacyturn entered the room and scanned his wrist across a panel in the wall. He then pulled Sync into the room by gently grasping his upper arm.

Sync watched as an entire hidden apartment lit up bit by bit, different colours of neon shapes turning on. The young man gasped in awe as a luxury fluro bunker revealed itself before his eyes.

On each wall, there was a slightly sunken-in digital window that looked real. When each one turned on, it showed a different angle of a neon cityscape. It felt like they were miles high instead of underground in a basement.

Sync was speechless until the apartment finally settled in a brilliant stillness.

"Now *this* is a fucking apartment!" he yelled as he ran from room to room. He found the expensive coffee maker in the kitchen. "Now I see why the place above is on the ground floor. I bet my father is the only one who knows this room is here, right? Well, and obviously *you*."

He went up to one of the windows and clicked through some of the scenes—an empty field, underwater, a snowy mountain, out in space, on Mars, a busy street market, a rainy beach and a sunny forest.

When the forest popped up, Bandit jumped on the windowsill, pleased. She bathed in the imitation sunrays, clicking at birds she could see go by. Sync decided to leave it on that one, making a note to check out the rest later. He tried to make the window bigger for her, but couldn't manage it.

"Ah, shit, this apartment must be somewhat old. It has the old screen windows that don't expand, back when them just looking like an actual window blew people's minds so they didn't think to make them do cool shit real windows can't do. Have you seen those fucking things? They can take up an entire fucking room!" He patted Bandit, who didn't look disappointed and was, in fact, quite happy. "Sorry, Bandit. I was going to make the whole room look like we were outside."

The young man turned to Tacyturn, who was just watching him.

"So, why do *you* know about this place?" Sync asked. "I mean, not that I don't think you should, but . . . why would father keep it so hidden, then reveal it to someone who he has only had working for him for five years? Or maybe you've known him longer, what the fuck do I know? Definitely not as long as his first children, you're not *that* old." He paused. "Are you that old?"

"I lived in Hollywood for two years preparing to work for your father."

"Oh, so you stayed here?"

"I stayed in the one above."

"Then why do you know about this one?"

"I was expected to keep this one dusted."

"I bet he was testing you to see if you'd give in and try to secretly use this place instead of the shit place upstairs," Sync pointed out, then noticed a small Zen garden landscaped in the signature Thornwryght symbol. "You probably had to come down here just to keep that stupid and pointless fucking thing all nice, huh? And keep the coffee maker clean? What a long fucking test to take . . . Two fucking years! Fuck that! But you obviously passed. You . . . proved you were more useful alive, huh?"

Tacyturn nodded.

Feeling embarrassed and responsible for his own family's actions, Sync changed the subject—and his emotions.

"Well, I'm really fucking tired, but I don't seem to have any of my shit," he pointed out, angrily. "I wonder whose fucking fault that is? I hope you're not planning on having us walk all the way back to the fucking car, because I'm not going to do that. And you can't leave me alone. And Bandit, look at her! She's starving and where's her food?"

Bandit rolled over happily on her back, oblivious of the conversation.

"Oh yeah, in the fucking car. Great fucking job. And she doesn't even have anywhere to piss."

He grabbed the Zen garden and tossed it onto the floor in the corner of the laundry room.

"Wait, there we go. Took me two fucking seconds to solve. You had two years to prepare for shit like this and you parked the car like nine hundred miles away from where we're fucking staying!"

The driver took the Whisperunner's key fob out of his pocket and started the remote-control program.

Sync blinked at the fob, then shuffled away to the nearest charging hub, plugging his vidphone cube into the slot. He was trying to hide how stupid he felt.

"Well, you should know by now that I'm worth fucking ignoring, so if I ever say anything you don't like, *fuck you!*"

X.

"My blood can reconstruct him."

ONCE A SCAN OF SYNC confirmed that he was asleep, Tacyturn finally called Ephraym back—there had been over twenty calls he had purposely ignored.

He leaned against the furthest corner of the apartment from where the young man was asleep.

"Where the fuck have you been?"

The call was audio only, but Tacyturn could tell how angry he was. He was holding back, possibly having to keep quiet with someone else nearby. It was unsettling not being able to monitor Ephraym's safety until he checked in with him—that was still an unshakeable part of his job.

"Why is your tracking not working? What the fuck is going on?"

"I was shot in the neck."

"Hm. I believe you, even though you're hiding from me on this call. The nursewryght who healed you reported to me when she saw I wasn't in the car. Of course, that meant I had to do something about her because she can't keep her fucking mouth shut. Did it cause any other damage?"

"Visual glitches and electric shock."

"You deserve that for a while, don't you think?" He paused to let Tacyturn think about it before continuing. "This should have been over by now. What have you been doing? Has he been using you or have you just been acting on my orders?"

"He has not told me anything he wants."

"Have you been training him? Is he as hopeless as he seems?"

Tacyturn glanced over to Sync, scanning his body again. He was still sleeping peacefully with Bandit beside him. His technology glitched enough to sting him and he closed his eyes, the right one now redder.

"We are going to make a video that looks like he's committing suicide."

"WHAT?"

"It will stop The Nineteen's blood hunt and give him more time."

"Interesting idea. You must be in the Hollywood apartment, I take it? The timing seems about right for that. How's my Zen garden?"

Tacyturn wanted to deny being there, but knew he would just ask for video proof. He watched as Bandit went over to the Zen garden and started digging in the sand. It was as though she knew the timing would be perfectly disrespectful.

Ephraym didn't bother to wait for a real answer. "This is a waste of time. Movie tricks aren't going to fix your inadequacies. Whatever you're doing, it's not working. I want you to try something else, something more dramatic. If he won't tell you what he wants, you'll have to show him how you act how you . . . wanton. My blood *will* kick in, but you're just not inspiring it hard enough."

The boss' tone darkened. "I want you to get fucking killed if you have to. He'll be safe where he is. Only I know about it, like only I knew you were at the cabin."

The silence that followed that statement was telling.

"I can pick him up later and help him hide your body. It's a good father and son bonding experience he shouldn't miss out on again. If I don't get this fucking ridiculous suicide video from you, I'll assume you succeeded. So, I fucking hope I don't get it. What a waste of time. You're just delaying the inevitable. The ending is even closer now that you're damaged and starting to fail me. You can't avoid it forever. You're destined to die for a Thornwryght."

Even though Tacyturn was silent as usual, Ephraym knew something was off and knew just how to set him straight.

"If you don't let Synclare kill you, you might as well kill *him*. Then The Nineteen can prove themselves by killing *you*. That would be more impressive than killing that little shit, and also possibly impossible. Then whoever killed you would really deserve to take the company, don't you agree?" He had to laugh. "So, I want you to tell me what I should be expecting from you."

"If you get the video, it means I'm training him to fight like a Thornwryght and if you don't, it means I'm dead and he's still exactly the same."

Tacyturn felt the annoyance seething through his phone.

"I still hope I don't get the video, Tacyturn," he growled. "You should have already changed him by now. That's on you. His future is on you. If you don't know what to do to him, try looking into your own fucked up past. Do to him things that have been done to you, things that made you want to kill in retaliation. You must break him. My blood can reconstruct him."

Ephraym was about to hang up, then the driver said, "He may figure out my tell."

"Hmph. Think that'll give away your intentions? Got him paying closer attention to your eyes, have you? How can he even see your eyes close enough to tell? What colour did you show him?"

"Yellow."

"You were being cautious, were you? Well, I suppose I can give you permission to stop it from happening, but it won't stop it entirely." Tacyturn could hear his boss typing. "Your eye will still change if you're not paying attention. Lucky for you, you're an expert at paying attention."

After a moment, Tacyturn could feel a string of programming enter his tech remotely, merging flawlessly with it.

"That should help you at least revert it back to the default colour. Don't get too comfortable because I'm taking that code back as soon as you're back with me. Unless you're dead, of course, then enjoy your authorization as a little farewell gift from me to you, Tacyturn. Goodbye."

Then the call suddenly ended and Tacyturn let his vidphone drop to the floor. He looked up at the rainy digital window and stared into it. He flipped through the dial until he stopped at the video of the Jeu de Balle Flea Market in Brussels. His right eye went blue.

Then he felt a motion alert and took out his gun, the eye quickly changing to yellow. He glanced over to where Sync was still asleep.

He then looked into his chair that he had positioned to keep an eye on the apartment. Bandit was sitting in it and staring at him. It was like she was staring directly at his right eye, knowing exactly what was going on with it.

Tacyturn stared at her for a long while. He glanced up to check on Sync and saw he was still comfortable and asleep—even though he looked like he was in the most uncomfortable sleeping position possible.

When Tacyturn's eye became magenta again, Bandit stretched and curled into a ball. He approached the chair and watched her until she scanned as fast asleep.

The driver pulled the chair back a foot, then grabbed a stool from nearby and set it down in front of it. He sat down, loosely holding onto his gun.

Using the tip of the barrel, he slid a piece of paper from the coffee table closer to himself and picked it up. It was the script for the suicide video.

He read it over again, starting with Sync's terrible handwriting and then where he had made Tacyturn write the rest, learning about his perfect cursive—Sync had insisted again that he was an android because it was too perfect.

Looking beyond the handwriting, he looked at the words. He was not looking forward to hearing Sync say any of it.

Then he closed his eyes—one blue and the other now grey—and kept watch through the electric tapestry.

XI.

"Everyone knows the Thornwryghts."

THE TIME FOR THE MEETING arrived far too soon—Sync hardly felt ready to "die" by then.

He was hardly living after twenty years.

Sync was having a panic attack on the drive over to Electric Reel as his "life" flashed before his eyes.

"It's never gonna work. No one's gonna believe it. Can someone really die if they've never really lived?"

"You've lived."

Sync scoffed. "Have I?"

"You're not an android, either."

The redhead sighed. "I dunno. I get what you mean, but I think I'd be living one hell of a fuckin' life if I was an android. I'd be bulletproof, wouldn't I?"

"To some degree."

"Hm." He rubbed the most recent burns on his hands. "I'd take any degree at this point."

"The third?"

Sync relaxed just a bit. Tacyturn sounded serious, but he was pretty sure he was teasing him with word play again.

He also appreciated that Tacyturn specified he was talking about the third degree, not third-degree—which he already had twenty tiny round bits of.

But what he appreciated most of all was that Tacyturn actually listened to him. He listened to his mumbling, his loudness, singing to himself—even his bitching.

He tried to calculate a smart response. "You're talented at . . . first-degree, aren't you?"

"Most serious, but somehow also least harmful."

"You know which one I mean." Sync was amused. "There are a lot of degrees out there, huh?"

"Temperature, music, mathematics, grammar, law, medical, genealogy, education."

"This is a really fucking stupid conversation that could go on for a while," Sync groaned. After a moment, he softly touched the back of Tacyturn's head and then acted as if he hadn't.

His anxiety was suppressed for the rest of the ride as they bantered about all the degrees of degrees.

The word now sounded like utter nonsense.

Tacyturn made sure they showed up promptly. By the time the two of them approached the set and Kimo's eyes were on them, it was exactly 7:30pm.

Sync tried his best to walk beside him, even though he always wanted to follow behind.

As they walked, Sync suddenly noticed he was now one step ahead. He figured Tacyturn must have hesitated, but it hadn't been noticeable at all. Sync was concerned—he had never seen Tacyturn hesitate.

He still hadn't, but he knew he must have.

When he looked up to where Kimo was, he saw a woman beside him. She was smiling and whispering to Kimo, not taking her eyes off of Tacyturn.

She was a few inches taller than Sync and wore all blacks, whites, and greys—except for a choker that was magenta. Her hair was something Sync was having a hard time figuring out—the top layers of her hair were black and crimped short and ragged whilst the underneath of her hair was white and long. Her bangs were black and white and defied gravity. Her makeup looked like it was inspired by the Egyptians.

She took out a cigarette—it was Sync's turn to hesitate.

Luckily, she seemed to be having an issue with it. It was a digital prop cigarette and kept turning off just as she was trying to trigger it with a lighter. Sync could see that Tacyturn was focusing on it until she gave up and discarded both items onto a messy table.

"Tacy! I didn't believe it when Kimo said you were back! Look at how much you've grown!" she exclaimed, putting her arms around the driver. "You just couldn't stay away, could you? You're back for more!"

"You must be Ellenoir," Sync flatly said, unable to stop his nose from wrinkling at her.

"Of course I am," Ellenoir haughtily responded, without even looking his way. "You're the Irish doll I heard about." Her tone indicated she didn't care to know anything more than that. "Look, I wore a little something to celebrate!" She pointed to her magenta choker that matched Tacyturn's style.

Sync could tell Tacyturn was uncomfortable, but he hid it well.

Suddenly the roof opened up and rain began pouring down on the set. It startled Sync, but gained the attention of both him and the driver.

The set looked like the very top of a tall, old, dilapidated building. There was an inflated mattress on the floor beside it.

Kimo saw that all eyes were on him and he called out, "Sorry! Just getting the set wet. We'll close it as we practice, then open it again when we film. We better hurry up because I don't think this perfect rain is going to last. With just the four of us, I don't think we can make convincing rain ourselves. The less people involved in a fake suicide video, the better." He approached Tacyturn with his hand out. "Got me a script?"

Out of his jacket pocket, Tacyturn pulled out the folded paper and handed it to him. Kimo quickly scanned it with his vidphone, then handed the paper back.

Tacyturn, Sync and Ellenoir waited patiently for him to finish reading.

When he did, he whistled. "I don't know what's going on, and I don't want to know, but I see why you're doing this," he said to Sync. "I know who the Thornwryghts are."

"You don't know fucking shit," Sync growled. "And you're not special. Everyone knows the Thornwryghts."

"Back to minding my own fucking business, huh?" He chuckled dryly and looked at Tacyturn, revealing in his expression that he thought Sync must be a handful. "Let me quickly lay out a plan here. Ellenoir will help him with his acting and you can come with me to choose the camera."

"I can't let him out of my sight," Tacyturn warned.

"Don't worry, Tiger. They're just right over here."

Tacyturn handed a reticent Sync the paper script, then followed Kimo.

"I gathered all of my handheld vidcams that would work best. Wanted them to be a manageable size. You'll be the one filming, so you have to pick what you're comfortable with."

Kimo gestured to a table covered with all sizes of video recording devices. Tacyturn picked up the oldest one and handed it to him.

"This one from the fifties? Well, all right." He picked it up and checked to make sure it had a cassette inside. "It's easy enough to transfer it to a more modern format."

"We'll take it on the cassette." Tacyturn kept his eyes on Ellenoir and Sync.

"On the 8mm? You're fucking crazy, no one has the shit to watch those anymore." He saw Tacyturn's serious expression. "Okay, fine. That's actually trickier for me, but I see why you want it that way. It'll look like it couldn't have possibly been edited." He slapped the cassette slot shut and handed the camera to Tacyturn. "Have a minute for me to teach you to use it?"

After the small bit of training was over, the four of them reconnected. They closed the roof to stop the rain. Then Kimo and his wife left to work on the official script.

Sync wandered up to the rooftop set and examined it, admiring how real it looked. He stomped in a few of the puddles.

Pretending Tacyturn asked him how it went, he said, "She told me to go to a dark place, but I told her I was already there." He handed Tacyturn the paper script back. "We should probably burn this. I'd be wicked cool if I took out a lighter and did it myself, but I don't like lighters. You do all the wicked cool shit, so I'll leave it to you."

Tacyturn took out his gun and adjusted a small dial to its enhanced electroshock setting. He twisted off the cartridge and exposed two electrodes. As he pulled the trigger, an electric arc formed and Tacyturn used it to set the paper on fire as he held it in his teeth, then let it flutter to the ground as ashes.

Sync stared in awe, suddenly very aware of his heart beating.

As usual, he began rambling more than necessary, feeling awkward afterwards. "See? All the wicked cool shit. Whatever degree of cool means the coolest. You're too wicked cool. What the fuck?"

When it seemed like no time went by at all, Kimo and Ellenoir returned and copied their script to Tacyturn and Sync's vidphones. It gave all of the visual descriptions of what the final piece was going to look like, as well as what the camera was going to be doing and when it would cut out. There had even been a small note about which neon light should be flickering—a small distant sign that said "Digital Head" in red. The first letter and last three letters would be the only working ones.

After a few practice runs, Kimo opened up the roof and let the water pour in. Tacyturn and Sync climbed up to the rooftop and got into position. Every light was turned off in the warehouse and the neon lights of the old fake building lit up.

Tacyturn was directed to turn the camera on whilst holding it casually, catching a crooked shot of a city below that was going to be added in later. He then held it up and pointed it at Sync who was just finishing his anxious pacing.

He was supposed to start off by sounding like he was answering a question that Tacyturn had asked, but not captured on camera.

"—this because I need to show them. I need to address my family without getting pumped full of fucking holes. I'm not fucking bulletproof." Then he turned towards the camera that Tacyturn was now holding steady and straight. "Are you fucking ready already? Okay."

Sync took in a deep breath, then let it out slowly.

"You don't know me, but my name is Synclare Tymotheos Thornwryght. Okay, you do know who I am, but you *don't* fucking know me. I'm making this to show you who I am because . . . well, I don't know why, because none of you fucking care."

At this point, he was supposed to sound like he was going off script. Sync added in looking at the burn scars on his hands.

"All of you just want me to fucking prove myself." He began pacing again. "I have to prove that I am worthy of being next in line so that you don't want to kill me to take it for yourselves." He laughed, making sure he sounded like he was snapping. "Funny how all you fucking non-bloods have to just kill me and that somehow proves you're worthy. Kill *me*, the weakest fucking link!" This was the moment that he knew for sure what he was going to do. "I'm the link that just breaks on its own in time . . ."

At this point, Sync pulled out a prop gun that looked real. Tacyturn nudged the camera like he was shocked and ready to stop Sync from whatever he was doing, but Sync put up his hand and then firmly pointed to indicate that he should back off.

Then, he laughed. "According to the rules, I'm going to finally prove that I'm worthy. I'm checking all the boxes needed to be the next Thornwryght boss. So, in the end . . . I proved you all wrong. For a fleeting moment, the empire is mine. Good fucking luck figuring out the next one."

There was a long pause before Sync said to Tacyturn, "Please mail this home for me. Leave my corpse where it falls."

Then before Tacyturn could do anything, Sync turned the gun on himself and shot himself in the temple. The electric gun kicked just like a real gun would. It also sounded like one—the sound was deafening to Sync.

Even up to the point of filming, Sync was terrified of using the fake gun. Even though it was on the weakest setting that kept it from firing a hot bullet made of light, it was unnerving.

With the barrel pointed at him, all confidence drained from his body. Even though Ellenoir told him to try his best to hide it, it could still be seen for a brief moment, making the video a little more tragic than what was intended to be more of a laugh in his family's face.

Ellenoir had also tried to teach him how to react to being shot with a gun, but Sync made it clear that he was no stranger to seeing people get shot and knew how it was supposed to look. His fingers froze around the grip of the gun and took it with him as he fell limp over the edge.

He landed on the mattress, then Ellenoir and Kimo quickly moved it out from under him while Tacyturn hesitated, processing the situation. Sync re-positioned himself on the ground the way that he was supposed to while Tacyturn ran to the edge, purposely letting the camera dangle like he no longer cared about it, like this was something he needed to see with his own eyes and not through the lens.

Just as he got to the edge, the camera was positioned in just the right way to be able to peek over and capture an accidental glimpse of Sync's body, which would be scaled down to look much further away later.

At this point, Tacyturn was supposed to utter one word, but he wasn't supposed to say it as if he was shocked or heartbroken or even disappointed— it was a failed job and that was it. In one single word, he revealed that he knew he screwed up big time and could not possibly go back to the peninsula to face it, excusing his own absence now that he lost his charge.

"*Fuck.*"

Then the camera was turned off with a clear sense of urgency, making sure to capture Tacyturn's distinct clothing to confirm that it was him filming. The last frame was the Thornwryght logo on Tacyturn's tie.

Once the recording stopped, Kimo and Ellenoir applauded.

Tacyturn and Sync stared distantly at each other as the realness of the scene drained away.

The ceiling then closed, the rain stopped, and all the bright indoor lights turned on, clicking them out of their film noir numbness.

"Fantastic!" Ellenoir exclaimed. "And only one take!"

"Don't get ahead of yourself, we've got to check the camera work," Kimo said. "It could be shit."

Sync barked as he picked himself up off of the wet ground, "Are you implying that Tacyturn did something imperfect? Fuck that! It's perfect and I don't even have to check."

Ellenoir chuckled slyly, "Think Tacy's perfect, do you?"

"I think . . . that you can fuck right off with that tone."

"Oh, little Irish doll, your cheeks are red," she responded condescendingly.

"They get that way when there's a huge bitch nearby that won't shut the fuck up," the young redhead growled, turning away. He wanted to storm out, but he had to stay near Tacyturn.

The Rilangs looked at Tacyturn as he climbed down from the building. Without acknowledging any conversation, he offered the old vidcam to Kimo.

Kimo snatched the camera and they all gathered around to watch it on its small screen.

Sync was shocked at how genuine he sounded—it was disconcerting to watch. He was glad that it looked fake and felt no desire to see the finished version.

"I'll let you know when I'm done," Kimo said, cradling the camera like it was precious. "It shouldn't take too long at all."

"Yes, so you should be free in no time," Ellenoir purred and coquettishly leaned up against Tacyturn. "We're ready to tell you all the things that we want in return."

"He's not a toy!" Sync barked at her.

Ellenoir chuckled. "You see this?" She rubbed her hand seductively across the scar on the side of his head. "You know what this is, right?"

Sync was getting hot with what he thought couldn't possibly be jealousy—it had to be anger.

She continued, "He has brain damage that makes him do whatever you want him to do. I understand he can't right now because he's got a job

[86]

protecting you, so *you're* his master, but after that he'll be free. Then there's so much fun stuff to do with him!"

"Did you know that he knows how to do several accents?" Kimo asked. "It's because we told him to. Just for fun! And even though he hardly talks and he'd have no use for such a talent, he fucking did it!"

Ellenoir giggled. "His French accent is the best one, in my opinion. We'd make him show you, but he's not ours at the moment." She saw Sync's hard stare. "Haven't you been making him do whatever you want as your escort?" She seemed genuinely confused.

Sync looked to Tacyturn who continued to react to things how he normally did—not at all.

"No, because that's fucked up," Sync hissed. "He's a person, not a pet." Feeling weird talking about him like he wasn't there, he said firmly to Tacyturn, "You're a person, not a pet."

"But he does so many neat tricks like a pet does!" Ellenoir giggled. "Did you know that one of his eyes changes colour depending on his mood?"

Sync furrowed his brow, thinking about the time he thought he saw his eye turn yellow.

"What?" he asked as he looked up at Tacyturn.

"Look! It's pink right now, right?" She stood on her toes and leaned closer to Tacyturn's face. "That means he's either happy, feeling love or, my personal favourite, he's embarrassed!"

Sync scoffed. "It's like that all the time! Around me, anyway. I think."

"Is it?" Kimo pretended to hide a knowing look. "Maybe it means you're really embarrassing to be around."

The young redhead forced a fake laugh, humouring the couple who were obviously getting a kick out of what they were saying.

Ellenoir leaned in closer to Tacyturn, pushing her body up against his. Sync felt his insides getting hot again. He wanted to shove her away but remained frozen in shock.

"My other favourite is making it turn red or purple," she said.

"Don't forget white," Kimo said to his wife.

"Ooh, yes, white. That one is tricky."

Ellenoir eventually backed up and tilted her head when she saw that his eye never changed. "It doesn't seem to be working anymore!"

"He is working for someone else, dear. We have to wait until he's dead."

"Maybe if I hurt him, it'll trigger red," she mumbled as she looked for something sharp.

"What the fuck kind of people are you?" Sync asked, feeling stupid just listening to them.

"We're in the business of getting what we want because we have what people want," Kimo said, wagging the camera to make his point. "You should know all about that being a *crime syndicate heir.*"

"He's *your* servant, isn't he? I bet he got hired by your family and taken away from us five years ago. Probably heard about him and snatched him up to become a bodyguard. He's meant to be ordered around." She laughed. "Can't let a monster like that make his own decisions."

Sync was about to go into a full rage, but Tacyturn put his hand on his shoulder. The young man knew at that moment that the footage was in danger, so he quieted. He said nothing to the Rilangs again, letting Tacyturn wrap up the evening with as few words as possible before they left. He even let Ellenoir stab him with one of Sync's lapel pins just to prove that his eye would remain the same.

Sync thought that it was unnecessarily brutal that she insisted on stabbing it entirely through his hand—and Tacyturn had let her. He also showed no pain, which was a relief and a worry at the same time.

The last things that the Rilangs had said to them was confusing to Sync—but pissed him off anyway.

"You should never have run away from us with your tail between your legs. You still have work to do, Tacy. We're so ready for you to listen to us again."

"The tiger counts on the city and the city counts on the tiger."

Sync was certain that Tacyturn would have some clever word play to say in return, but he remained silent—compliantly or calculatedly, he was not sure.

Once they were back in the Whisperunner away from the awkward situation, Sync finally spoke up again.

"What have they done to you?" he asked as Tacyturn pulled the pin out of his hand and handed it back to the young man.

There was such a long pause, Sync wasn't sure if Tacyturn was going to respond at all.

Then he said, "At sixteen, I was dropped off here and I had to do whatever I was told for two years."

Sync could tell he wanted to say more, but it felt like he was caught. He knew it was hard for Tacyturn to say more than one sentence at a time—maybe two. He wondered if it really was how he was trained, or if it had something to do with his head injury.

The young redhead decided to help him move along by making it a conversation, not a story.

"Shit. What the fuck happened with that?" he asked, trying to sound casual as he wiped the blood off of the 'OUT RAGE OUS' pin and put it back on his jacket.

"Some people caught on when they thought it was brain damage and took advantage of it."

Sync remembered something that his sister had explained to him before. "It's cause of your eyes. I mean, your pupils. You ever look in a fucking mirror? You don't seem like the type. They're different. It has a name. Annie something. I mean, it's obviously not some bitch's real name, unless it was named after some bitch. I don't know what—"

"Anisocoria."

"Yeah, her! Or . . . that!" Sync felt stupid and decided to pretend his interjection didn't happen. He was ruining the tone of the serious conversation. "That explains that Ellenoir bitch. She wasn't even fucking subtle about it. Did you really do *everything* you were told?"

Tacyturn nodded. "Following that path, I became a stuntman and learned to drive and fight that way."

"I didn't realize learning to do stunts helped someone kick so much *real* ass! Have I seen you in anything? Probably! I've seen a lot of fucking movies."

"When I made it through, I became your father's driver and bodyguard and no longer had to do what anyone else wanted."

Sync was saddened by what he heard, but tried not to show it. He couldn't imagine what Tacyturn had gotten into by always having to do what people wanted—especially in a corrupted city like Hollywood. Someone could have told him to cut off his own tongue, or limb—or kill himself.

Tacyturn was lucky—but so very unlucky as Sync thought of what he may have done. He thought of what he may have had to do to other people. He wondered how many of his scars were self-inflicted. He wondered how many of his wounds were done by other people making him let them—he now was going to have two new pin-sized ones.

But then he perked up when he realized, "So . . . you *don't* have to do what they want!"

"I do until that cassette is ours."

"We didn't have to do it this way. I'm sure they're not the only ones who could have done it for us! They're clearly fucking toxic." He put his hand on Tacyturn's injured hand as he was about to switch gears to get the car moving. "Why the fuck would you do this to yourself?"

"They have dark secrets, so they'll keep ours."

"Dark secrets that you know?"

Tacyturn nodded.

"Dark secrets that you're a part of?"

Tacyturn let the rain that started to pour answer for him—he had nothing to say. The driver just stared at Sync's hand resting on his own. Thinking that the driver was annoyed with the lingering gesture, Sync quickly retracted his hand.

Realizing how young he was when he arrived, Sync wasn't sure he wanted to know any of Tacyturn's dark secrets. But he wasn't blind to young corruption—everyone in his family had to kill someone before they reached puberty. It was an important Thornwryght sacrament—if you didn't complete it, you were executed. When he was little, a few of his siblings had disappeared so suddenly that Sync thought they were his imaginary friends that just stopped coming back.

He still had hope that they were just mind-wiped, renamed and relocated somehow.

Sync then wanted to talk about why Ellenoir wanted to stab his hand in the first place.

"Is it true about your eye? Does it really change colour depending on your emotions? Is that something your tech does?"

When Tacyturn looked at him, his eye was magenta like he always thought it was.

"What the fuck use does that have when you never show emotion anyway, right? You're always so . . . stoic. If I had it, it would always be red or blue. That's anger and sadness, right? What's the colour of fear?"

"Purple, white or yellow."

Sync quickly dismissed the time he thought he saw Tacyturn's eye be yellow—there was no way that the driver was afraid of anything. He then thought about Brayd's favourite colour being purple.

"I feel like colours are emotionally different for different people. Purple makes me think of . . . bravery."

"Purple can also be that."

"Oh." Sync scratched his head. "Then what the fuck is the point of having a colour indicate your emotion when it can be interpreted so many different conflicting ways? I mean, unless you are aiming to confuse people, like maybe the Rilangs." Sync chuckled dryly. "I do see why you never mentioned it before, though. Is magenta your default? Must be, because it matches your style perfectly."

Sync also thought about the fact that Tacyturn likely had a lot more emotion when he was sixteen. Deciding that the Rilangs weren't lying, his colour-changing tech was probably more active until he became a desensitized adult. But then Sync realized that meant that they were abusing him when he was just a child.

"So, you were here when you were sixteen?" He counted on his fingers. "Two years here, five with my father . . . So, you're . . . twenty-three?"

The driver nodded.

"You're only three years older than me? I thought you were way fucking older!" He coughed, fumbling over what he thought may have been an insult. "Not that you look old. You just look . . . I don't know, like you've been through a fucking lot. And you have been. With that in mind, I don't look like I've been through anything . . ."

Sync crossed his arms and slouched, hiding his baby face under his hat.

"And you know what? Maybe I really haven't. Maybe that's why I'm the weak link. I'm a blank fucking slate." He tightened the noose around his neck, then loosened it several times in a row. "I've been alive for twenty years and I've got nothing to show for it."

After a moment of pouting, Sync wanted to direct the conversation away from himself.

"If you hadn't let the Rilangs have the last words, what would you have replied with?"

Tacyturn said nothing as he started to drive back to their flat.

"Come on! I know you had some wicked cool shit in your head but you are so well behaved, you kept it to yourself, right?"

"There were two on my mind, an insult and a threat."

Sync sat up eagerly, no longer messing with his neck rope. "I knew it! What were they?"

"A tiger doesn't lose sleep over the opinion of sheep."

The redhead clapped and laughed. "That's the insult for sure! And the other?"

"A tiger doesn't lay low because of fear, but to aim."

Sync felt hot admiration again, pressing his flushed cheek against the ice cold rainy window.

XII.

"You have me."

WHEN TACYTURN DIDN'T OBJECT TO Sync picking up the *Blade Runner* vidkey that they used to get into the apartment, he curiously plugged it into a small hub on a pedestal. The pedestal then disappeared into the floor and Sync looked around, wondering where the screen was.

A moment later, lights cut through him and he stumbled backwards into the couch. The screen was a projection that came up from the floor in the center of the entertainment corner. It was a little opaque, which is why the wall behind it was so empty and painted white. He used a nearby controller to make it as big as he could.

Impressed, he watched the video that played. The quality was not very good—it was like a memory of a movie. Watching the film was like a dream floating in a fog at the back of his mind. The audio sounded exactly how voices sounded when thinking about them. He recognized Harrison Ford, but knew he wasn't in any movie called *Blade Runner*.

What was even stranger was that the film took place in 2019, but looked a lot like present time 1983►►. The most obvious thing that was missing were the spinners—the flying cars.

"Where the fuck *are* the flying cars?" Sync asked out loud to himself and to Tacyturn, wherever he was.

They had just finished their showers, but he knew he was close—he always was.

Near the middle of the film, there was a figure that lit a cigarette. It didn't seem to fit—there was still an unrelated scene going on. When he saw the smoke hitting the ceiling above the screen, he tilted his head at it.

He also heard scratching and it spooked him a bit. He soon realized it was the muffled sounds of Bandit meowing under a locked door.

Then Tacyturn materialized out of the smoky science fiction film, holding a cigarette up to his lips. Sync flinched and jumped up onto the couch, a half-assed attempt to get further away.

"I didn't know y-you fucking smoked!" he whined with a dry swallow, embarrassed by his reaction.

Tacyturn said nothing and approached the young man. Sync was extremely uncomfortable with the lit cigarette getting closer to him, so he moved to get off of the couch. Tacyturn grabbed him by his arm and shoved him back into the seat, holding him down.

"What the fuck are you doing this time?" Sync asked, fearfully annoyed, watching him unbutton his sweater nimbly with one hand.

Tacyturn took another long drag of the cigarette and then exhaled smoke slowly up Sync's entire body, starting with his thighs. When he moved across his stomach, he lifted his shirt to allow the smoke to touch him directly. Then he moved to blowing the smoke on his neck.

The young man tried to get away, but his attempts were feeble, as the smoke acted like his kryptonite. Tacyturn put his leg up on the couch to help support his strength over the much smaller man and applied pressure to his exposed freckled stomach.

"Th-this isn't going to fucking work! It's j-just gonna make me mad enough to run away and make your bodyguarding job a lot more inconvenient!"

The driver's smoky breath ended at Sync's lips where it dwindled in light smoky wisps.

Bringing the cigarette to his lips, he breathed it in again. Then he slightly opened Sync's mouth with a thumb on his chin and kissed him.

Sync's jaw would have already dropped on its own with shock if Tacyturn hadn't made him do it first. The kiss was mellow, but eager—like a farewell kiss from a lover about to be long lost.

It was clear that the young man wasn't sure how to react. The cigarette was putting his senses on hold, shutting him off like prey pretending to be dead, hoping that the predator would lose interest and just go away.

When their lips parted, both of their mouths seeped the smoke. Tacyturn put his hand holding the cigarette on his freckled cheek and Sync flinched. Sync felt as the driver's hand ran down his body. He ended up on his thigh, pushing his legs apart so that he could get closer to him.

Sync watched as one of his hands was grasped by Tacyturn and raised to the driver's own throat. He hesitated a moment to see if Sync would choke him, but he didn't. He then pushed Sync's hand down his fit body in a similarly seductive manner and then left it to grip on the handle of his holstered gun at his side.

"You have to keep doing this d-don't you? It's something my father *wants*."

Sync coughed, trying to make his voice sound strong—but failing. His lungs felt weak, like the smoke in his mouth had done something to them.

"It's not going to fucking work! You're just going to have to fail this time! You're allowed to fucking f-fail sometimes, you know! I won't t-tell him!"

Tacyturn leaned forward and put most of his weight on Sync, taking another drag of the cigarette, blowing the smoke into the small space still left between them. He grasped Sync's jaw with one hand and slowly put the cigarette closer to his throat.

Sync's eyes widened and he tried to wrench himself away, but couldn't. Tacyturn's weight and strength kept him from getting away.

Then Tacyturn pressed the cigarette hard into his neck. Sync cried out and flinched hard enough to make his body ache with the fear that surged through him. He closed his eyes and saw his entire family holding him down and burning him with cigarettes, one by one.

But there was no pain.

When Tacyturn removed the cigarette, Sync could see that it was a digital one—the same one that Ellenoir had discarded. The tip lit up, but there was no actual heat. He gasped, unable to reduce his heavy breathing—the fear of it had been real.

Tacyturn saw that the young man had instinctually pulled the gun from the driver's holster and was pointing it under his ribs. His finger was caressing the trigger.

Once Sync looked down to see what he was doing, he choked on his shock and immediately pried the gun from between them and threw it.

He was dismayed—he had almost done it. He had almost killed again.

Before he could find any words to express himself, Sync heard a faint electronic crack. He saw a fragmented glint in Tacyturn's magenta eye, then watched as the cigarette short-circuited.

The driver tossed the broken cigarette through the floating film, then stood up and pulled Sync up with him.

Holding onto his arm, he led the young man into the bedroom. He scooped up his gun along the way. Sync tried desperately to run away and hide—but he used no energy to fight back.

Tacyturn forcefully removed his sweater and then threw him down onto the bed, tossing the gun down beside him. Sync could see that there was also a candlestick and a kitchen knife on a side table and a spanner and his neck noose on the headboard—all within reach.

The driver then produced his own iridescent knife and expertly unfolded it as he climbed on top of the young man and straddled him. He quickly slipped the blade under Sync's shirt and, as the young man cried out fearing being gutted, Tacyturn sliced his neon graphic T-shirt open.

Sync looked down at his exposed torso, now very privy to how heavily he was breathing.

"Tell me that you want me to stop," Tacyturn said as he pushed himself against the young man.

"I—I—!"

"It's that easy."

Sync could not manage to say anything further.

"Tell me you want me to turn this knife on myself," Tacyturn said as he removed his own shirt by cutting through it with the blade.

The young man continued to say nothing.

Tacyturn rubbed his hand all over Sync's body, sliding it down the front of his leggings.

Still, there was silence from Sync as he held his breath.

The driver leaned in to kiss his neck, holding his arms down.

"Even if you just want me to stop, I'll surprise you with how I do it."

Tacyturn underestimated Sync's consternation. He put his hands on his own trouser zipper as Sync looked about to overflow from bottling up.

"Tell me what you want and I'll stop," Tacyturn desperately said, changing his tone a little for the first time in Sync's presence.

"BUT I DON'T WANT YOU TO FUCKING STOP!"

Tacyturn paused. Sync covered his mouth as his freckled cheeks went red.

Once the driver reverted his white eye to magenta, he pulled back from his neck to look at his face. Sync saw his eyes and turned away, wanting to bury his face into the bed.

Tacyturn hadn't expected the direction this was taking, but he felt like he was closer to getting Sync to finally tell him what he wanted. He had told him what he didn't want before—it was not always accurate when turned around. He needed to hear the right words.

"So," the driver said softly, "tell me what you want and I'll obey."

"I don't want you to . . . *obey* me," he huffed.

"What do you *want*, Sync?"

Sync hid his face with his hands and crisply said, "*You!*"

"You have me," Tacyturn said. He grasped his wrists tightly and pulled them away from his face, making him look at him. "What do you want me to do?"

"W-Want me back?"

"What do you *want me to do*?" he asked again, raising his voice.

He averted his eyes by turning his head. "I-I want you to—"

Tacyturn turned his face back to look at him. Sync thought he could see in his eyes exactly what Tacyturn knew he was going to say—and maybe *wanted* him to say. His magenta eye seemed redder.

"I WANT YOU TO FUCK ME!" Sync exclaimed, tightly closing his eyes.

Hearing his first real command, Tacyturn wasted no time. He had to prove to him that being assertive and commanding would get him what he wanted. He had already calculated that what Sync wanted was within the foundation of Ephraym's commands—albeit unlikely what Ephraym had in mind.

Sync braced himself as the driver sat him up, no longer wanting him to be in a vulnerably submissive position. He tore the remnants of their sliced clothing off and tossed the fabric aside.

Then Tacyturn leaned in and kissed him—the kiss was much gentler than the one before. There was something affectionate about it—something he wasn't aware that a man like Tacyturn could do.

The driver went slowly, waiting for Sync to react before giving it more passion. Sync's hands floated with uncertainty at first, but then he grabbed onto him tightly.

Tacyturn kept the kiss going so he could feel his reaction when he began giving his body attention all over with his hands. When he finally did remove his mouth so that he could use it other places, he unsealed a strew of swearing from the young man—it sounded more and more like Sync was himself again.

During it all, Tacyturn began gently preparing Sync—one finger at a time.

"I told you to fuck me, so why the fuck are you going so—ah—s-slow?"

"Everything I do is to keep you from getting hurt," Tacyturn responded.

"Is it just a part of your ongoing objective to not want to hurt me? Is that the only reason? Would you hurt me otherwise?"

"I would rather you hurt me before I would ever hurt you," he said softly, kissing one of the scars on Sync's stomach.

Sync thought about it and realized he was right. Tacyturn had never caused him any pain. He had applied plenty of pressure to show him direction or try to get a rise out of him, but he never hurt him. The cigarette that he had touched him with had been fake. The knife at his throat had enough pressure just to feel it was there. He had shoved him several times, but with just the right amount of force so that Sync was able to catch himself, or it was into something soft.

He was in awe of Tacyturn's self-mastery. He was strong, but prudent.

"What if you're ordered to hurt me?"

"I'd have to pinch you." Even though the act mentioned was childish, he sounded serious.

"What if you're ordered to hurt me *a lot?*" he asked through a pleasurable gasp.

"I'd have to pinch you a lot." He sounded less serious, but only by accident.

Sync laughed. It was the first time Tacyturn had ever seen the young man genuinely and purely happy because of him. He was surprised—but also confused with the line of questioning.

"What are you trying to tell me?" Tacyturn asked.

"Nothing, nothing. I just thought you should prioritize what I want over what anyone else wants, maybe?"

Tacyturn nodded. "You've relaxed."

"Have—ah!—I?"

"I've almost got my whole hand in," he said against his lips.

Sync's face went red again and he laughed in disbelief. "Ah, fuck me!"

"As you want, Synclare Tymotheos."

Sync got a thrill out of hearing his full first name and his rarely spoken middle one.

"Ooh, I'm in trouble," Sync excitedly breathed.

XIII.

"My family stole the future."

I'M STILL FUCKING PISSED ABOUT the cigarette, but I think you've made up for it. Maybe not for cutting my shirt, though. I fucking liked that shirt."

Sync was sitting in Tacyturn's lap and leaning up against him as the driver leaned up against the headboard. Tacyturn's arms were around him and Sync was looking at his scars.

"I want to ask you why you would do that to me . . . but I know why. You work for a Thornwryght."

Sync felt the arms tighten around him. There was something quietly apologetic about it.

Before asking anything else, Sync jumped up suddenly when he heard Bandit yelling.

"Fuck! We forgot to let her out!" He slipped on his briefs. He thought he saw Tacyturn look disappointed and he scoffed, "Hey, I don't want her to see my dick, that's fucking weird!"

After opening the bathroom door and apologizing on Tacyturn's behalf, he jumped back on the bed and dove into Tacyturn, whose quick reflexes caught him into an embrace.

Bandit yowled the entire way until she hopped up onto the end of the bed. The driver thought he saw her give him a silent, dirty look.

"If you hadn't told me that you weren't an android, I'd definitely think you were one by now. Like you're some perfectly programmed pleasure model." He blushed, then added, "You're very experienced in a lot of things, aren't you? Like, not only experienced, but fucking mastered." Sync decided to be bold about his curiosity. "When was the last time you were with someone?"

"A month ago."

Sync was surprised it was so recent, since they had been together for a good part of the last month. "Who?"

[100]

"I was with a woman while your father talked to her husband."

"Oh. What about . . . the last time you were with . . . someone like me?"

Tacyturn's silence made it clear that he wasn't certain what Sync meant. Sync could tell. "Oh, someone with a dick is what I meant, I guess?"

"Earlier that same day."

Sync was shocked. "Whoa, what?"

"I was with the husband while your father talked to the woman."

The young redhead wasn't sure what to think about it. It was impressive in a seductively suave kind of way, but it also made him feel bad.

"My father forced you to do that, huh? Were you a distraction?" He paused, then asked a question sounding like he didn't want to know the answer to it. "How many people have you been . . . forced to be with?"

Tacyturn shook his head, indicating that he wasn't sure.

"What about just . . . been with?"

He shook his head again in the same manner.

"My father really reprogrammed you to do whatever he wanted, didn't he?" He groaned. "That pleasure model comment was supposed to be a compliment, but the reason you're so experienced is because of everything you were forced to—!" Sync hit himself in the face, mewling. "And I just fucking took advantage of that, didn't I?"

"You told me not to stop," Tacyturn said, grasping his wrist to keep him from hitting himself again.

The young man huffed. "Yeah, and?"

"I believe that's called consent."

Sync sighed heavily. "Fuck, I'm not good at this shit. Human interaction is not my strong point. I don't . . . know how to do this. *All* of my experiences before now with romance, or whatever you call it, were not what I wanted, but I went with them anyway." He sat up and fumbled with his hands. "I mean, I liked it for sure . . . but they were . . . oh, never mind."

"I drove them," Tacyturn said.

Sync turned away from the driver and bit his lip. He realized that Tacyturn knew about the prostitutes that his father had bought for him when he was still a virgin at eighteen.

"My father has paid for every fucking intimate human interaction I've ever had. There was even a girl that he had paid to pretend to fall in love with me, but I couldn't have been with her. Not because she was paid, but I just . . . couldn't have loved her back . . ."

He turned to see Tacyturn's subtle curious expression.

"Yenvieve. The medic with the French accent? I . . . killed her brother. She doesn't know I'm the one who did it. How could I be with someone with a secret like that?" Sync whimpered, feeling the heartache all over again.

Sync decided to coat it with anger as he continued, "And you know what? Maybe her brother was paid by my father, too, to sacrifice himself for my sacrament. I mean, *he* wasn't paid. He wouldn't have been able to use the money, but maybe his father? Their father was a Thornwryght mechanic. He disappeared after it happened, probably because he bought his freedom and fucking left!"

Sync's anger softened and he was sad again. "I just don't know what experiences in my life are real anymore. I don't think I've done *anything* on my own. Like, even right now." He leaned into Tacyturn, an excuse to get affection and not allow the driver to see his facial expressions. "I don't know where I'd be without you. But it's all been my father's plan all along, hasn't it? He put you in my life to save me from myself. It's the same pattern. Every important turn is planted by a person pointing in the direction I have to take."

"You're always going to cross paths with someone else, but the path you're on is no one else's and the direction it chooses to go rests on you," Tacyturn said, interlinking their scarred hands.

Sync hummed in thought, enjoying Tacyturn's calm heartbeat. "That's a lot of words coming from you." Then, he smiled fondly. "And yet still just one fucking sentence. I've heard you do two." He tapped his lip. "I think."

"Too many words?"

"No, just the right amount." Then, he laughed. "I do prefer you quieter, though." He lifted his head up to show Tacyturn that he was teasing him and not being serious. "Only because I know you're actually fucking listening to me. I can feel it. There have been too many people in my life talking at me and no one fucking listening. It's why I have to yell and swear. I don't want to yell and swear. I want to stop talking but—"

Sync's words were cut off when Tacyturn kissed him on his lips.

The young man smiled and blushed. "I like you, Tac—"

He was cut off again by another kiss.

"Well, now I'm going to keep talking so that you keep—Mm."

He embraced the third kiss planted on his lips.

Knowing that he had interrupted Sync from watching the film, they decided to return to the entertainment corner and start the film where Sync had left off. Sync stole a magenta shirt from Tacyturn's bag, considering it a favour in return for cutting his own T-shirt up.

Tacyturn was left to just put his navy-blue trousers back on, as his extra magenta shirts were in the wash. He considered his jacket, but Sync objected to it.

"Where did this movie come from?" Sync asked near the end of the film, watching the visuals flicker like a damaged reel.

"Memories."

The young man turned to Tacyturn, shocked and excited by advances in technology.

"What do you mean? Was this REW\Lync of a movie they had already seen? Or FFWD\Lync of a movie they hadn't seen yet? Has it been developed enough to actually be visual now? Maybe now we can see what the future would have been like through the future's eyes, not our eyes!"

The expression on Tacyturn's face made it clear that he didn't know what Sync was talking about.

"Do you . . . know what the Thornwryghts are responsible for, Tac? Do you know what it means that we live in an enhanced world?"

"When I think about it, it's fragmented."

Sync realized then that his father must use DEL\Lync on Tacyturn after any occasion where their secrets were revealed in his presence—and he felt terrible about it. But, in the long run, it was what kept Tacyturn safer. He knew he could help, then, because it only worked on those who didn't know it existed.

Sync paused the film.

"I might not have everything right, but it's what I was told. If you start to get bored, be sure to stop me from talking in that way I like."

He bit his green painted nail, wondering where to start. He had never had to explain their crime syndicate to anyone before—it was forbidden.

"During World War II, my great great grandfather invented a truth serum with a weird fucking name, Hones+Linc 3413. The 'T' is a plus sign. It's named after—"

"Abraham Lincoln and a Bible verse."

"That's fucking right! Was that a guess or did you know?"

"Both, to a degree."

Sync chuckled, then continued, "The Thornwright Syndicate sold Hones+Linc to whoever was willing to pay. No one had the sole rights to it, like he advertised at a fucking insane price. He just gave it to anyone who asked, to any side that asked. He offered men from the syndicate to kidnap, torture and administer the serum for them, to keep their hands clean and to keep people from taking it to a lab to try to duplicate it. People caught on to the double-crossing and he ended up getting his eyes cut out of his head and Franklin Thornwright became Franklyn Thornwryght." He laughed, knowing it sounded the same when spoken out loud. "You know what I mean."

Tacyturn nodded, confirming he was listening intently.

"Well, eventually our family figured out that this serum wasn't a truth serum. It was actually a serum that revealed what has already happened, forcing the person to think about it. So, they called it a new name, this time with a 'Y' instead and also written really fucking weird. They added a slash to make the code name look more like cyber code."

Sync used his finger to write how it was written out on his vidphone and showed it to the driver—REW\Lync, pronounced like 'Rewind Link.'

"Thinking that they could potentially reverse it, they began tweaking REW\Lync to try to be able to tap into a mind's *entire* lifeline and learn the future. And you know what? They fucking figured it out!" It was clear that Sync was impressed. "They were not able to visually grab anything, but they were able to tap into it mentally. Like, tap into the words in thoughts."

He showed Tacyturn the new word on his vidphone—FFWD\Lync, pronounced 'Fast-Forward Link.'

"When *this* is given to someone, they go into a weird fucking stupor where all of their senses go out, except for their ability to write and think their future thoughts. So, they write it all down. And once it's written down and someone else reads it? Their future changes. When the right person was given the serum, future technology invented or produced by that person gets revealed to a world thirty or forty years before it was supposed to happen."

Sync rubbed his head. "Ugh, this is where it gets confusing, but it's why anyone privy to it marks two arrows at the end of whatever has been greatly enhanced, but typically just doing it to the year covers everything.

They started doing this to keep things organized on paper. Paperwork is important, even for a crime syndicate."

"I did know about that and did it myself."

"Technology from the seventies and eighties was invented prematurely in the late forties. Then technology that would have been from the nineties was in the fifties and sixties. So, there was once a 1983, but that's not the one we're in. We've been enhanced and now we're in 1983▶▶ with the silent fast-forward arrows, which is pretty wicked cool, right?" he asked as he drew the symbol out to show the driver. "Now that I'm thinking about it, this movie is probably from the unenhanced timeline somehow." He pointed to the flickering still of *Blade Runner*. "A new serum must have grabbed this from someone's mind before the future changed where it never happened. Or it was a fluke of the current serum? Who knows."

Tacyturn nodded again, feeling the fragmented pieces joining together. He realized he knew more than he thought.

"So, now we're at my father. He realized that the younger the person given FFWD\Lync, the further into the future we can get, but obviously they would still need the ability to hold a pencil. He began sending his children, like yours truly, out as bait to lure in young minds to try to find those with a future set to invent great things. A lot of the times they had nothing to offer, but sometimes they had something amazing. He wanted to keep having very young children to help him, so he continued to make more and more children with more and more women.

"Eventually my father became sterile, so the youngest he has, or *thought* he had, are the twins that are just a year younger than me. That's when he started urging The Twenty-One to start having more and more children for him to use. Great reason to have children, right? Anyway, the Thornwryghts are basically responsible for stealing people's futures and selling it to whoever has the most money. All the amazing technology that exists in our world was not invented by those who claim to have invented it. It's all stolen. My family stole the future."

He rubbed the headache that was brewing in his mind from all the explaining.

But he also felt relieved to finally tell someone—relieved and delightfully disobedient.

"They stole it and brought it to the past. It's definitely fucked up, but

I'm glad I get to enjoy all this wicked awesome technology at twenty, not at sixty. It's also pretty fucking impressive compared to any other crime syndicate and whatever the fuck *they've* ever stolen. I mean, not the part where we steal *children* and their bright futures, but definitely much cooler than a bank heist or drug smuggling or emptying a defenseless pharaoh's tomb."

"I see why the technology was sold and not kept in the family."

"Right. Us Thornwryghts would look super suspicious if we invented everything. We don't want the attention, we just want the money and, most of all, getting away with it. My family will kidnap children to drug and tap into and also murder anyone who might fuck all this up for us. That's probably your main job, you know? Killing people who learn too much. It needs to stay in the family where we're all too spoiled to ruin it for ourselves, right?"

"And now there's The Nineteen who know."

"Shit, right. My father's going to have to do what he can to keep from pissing them off. Then he'll have to kill them. DEL\Lync can only be used on those who don't know about it."

"Like me."

"Yeah," Sync responded softly. "But father deleted everything from you that would have secured your execution by Thornwryght rules. He erased shit to keep you alive. That's surprisingly nice of him. He must like you."

"He put a lot of work and time into me."

The young man huffed and leaned into Tacyturn, but then said, "Yeah, that's probably it."

Sync then triggered the film to continue.

Not long later, Tacyturn received a message on his vidphone. He ignored it until the movie was over, keeping his arms around Sync

By the time the film finished, Sync had fallen asleep against Tacyturn's chest. The driver picked him up and carried him to the bed, readjusted the messed-up bed sheets and tucked him in.

As he picked up his gun off of the floor, he checked his vidphone to see that he had a message from Kimo.

"Get me a coffee, I'm not fucking sleepy," came a mumble from the bed.

Tacyturn looked behind him to see Sync groggily sitting himself up.

"What time is it?" Sync asked.

"Three."

"Fuck, that's nothing."

"Your cassette will be ready sometime today."

"Today? Already? It's only been, like . . . eight hours! Did you just get a message?" He saw Tacyturn nod through rubbing his eyes. "What the fuck are they doing up so late? It's fucking three in the morning!"

Tacyturn was amused. "That's nothing."

"They must be eager to get you out of your commitment to me . . ."

He had to agree, but the driver didn't show it. But he did pick up on Sync's body language suddenly looking shy.

"Before we pick up the cassette, could you teach me to be more like you?"

"That would take seven years of Hell I'd never let you see."

"Damn, you and your wicked cool one liners," Sync teased—but really was genuinely charmed by it. "You know what I mean, though. Just pretend. I know we're going to get into training me to actually be able to maybe be a fraction of how fucking cool you are, but I pretended to kill myself, didn't I? Maybe I could pretend to be a force to be reckoned with? I just want to be able to look like I should be taken seriously."

Sync grasped Tacyturn's hand.

"I want you to teach me to act like the boss worthy of having someone as wicked cool as you by my side."

XIV.

"Time to die."

THE CASSETTE WAS FINISHED ALMOST exactly twenty-four hours after it was recorded.

Kimo and Ellenoir invited Tacyturn and Sync to meet them in their wardrobe storeroom.

There were endless rows of costumes, like an overflowing department store that couldn't decide on a theme.

At the back was the area where Ellenoir worked creating each one herself. There were mannequins, sewing machines, and an entire wall of fabrics, appliqués, patches, buttons—there was everything she could ever need to create whatever was needed on film, on stage, or on the red carpet.

Sync and Tacyturn approached the two of them through the only narrow pathway between clothing racks. For once, Sync was taking the lead.

Kimo had been watching the cassette using the old vidcam that it was filmed with. He liked to obsessively look at his completed work just to make sure it was perfect. He popped the cassette out and stood up to wave cheerfully at the two of them.

After catching sight of himself in a nearby mirror, Kimo plucked a checkered knit cap off of a mannequin and put it on to hide his disheveled lack-of-sleep look.

Ellenoir looked up from her work with her digital prop cigarette in her mouth.

Once Sync stopped, he made sure his back was straight and his shoulders were relaxed. His hands were behind his back to channel any fidgeting or flinching he might do. He wore his fedora with his plastic hood over it to partially obscure his young face. Tacyturn stayed beside him, a single step back.

All Sync had to do was hold his position and trust Tacyturn to keep him safe.

"Got your video here, Tacy!" Kimo wagged the cassette.

"Don't fucking talk to him," Sync firmly said.

The man was stunned and annoyed. "Excuse me?"

"You fucking heard me."

Ellenoir put her work aside and stepped beside her husband, staring at Sync. She put a hand on her hip, showing a bit of attitude.

"What is this? The little Irish doll is playing pretend, is he?" she asked.

"You underestimate me," Sync said. "That's good. The weak handshake was a nice touch, wasn't it?"

"My wife and I couldn't care less about you. We just want to spend some time with Tacy to make up for lost time. Once we do that, you'll get your cassette."

Sync chuckled. "That's not how this fucking works. Tacyturn is mine and not allowed out of my sight until my family sees that cassette."

Kimo flipped the tape around in his hands. "How do we know we'll get any time with Tacy when he's done babysitting you?"

"Oh! I can tell you absolutely that you won't," the young heir said matter-of-factly, adding a slight dry chuckle. "Tacyturn doesn't want to play with you."

The Rilangs laughed.

"There's no way he told you what he wants," Ellenoir said.

Sync smiled. "Tacyturn, I want you to show me on those two mannequins exactly what you want to do to the Rilangs."

Expertly, Tacyturn pulled out his gun and fired two shots. One hit the male mannequin in the left wrist—the same hand that was holding the cassette. The other shot hit the female mannequin in the right wrist—the same hand that was holding the electric cigarette. Two hands shattered on the floor.

Sync did his best not to flinch to either of the shots. Tacyturn had suggested that Sync squeeze his hands together to help channel his emotions. His admiration kept him looking pleased—but he felt like he was about to break the bones in his hands.

Sync said with a subtle snort, "He's the fucking coolest, hands down."

Kimo and Ellenoir were in shock, now feeling afraid. They huddled together.

"How dare you threaten us!" Ellenoir hissed. "Don't you know who—!"

"Tacyturn, please show me exactly what you want to do if the very next thing that Kimo does *isn't* giving us the cassette and if the very next thing Ellenoir does *isn't* discard her offensive cigarette."

Two more precise shots were fired—both right in the forehead of each mannequin.

"He just blew your minds, didn't he?" Sync teased—he now understood why his father liked wordplay, no matter how dumb. When you're confident enough, everything you're bold enough to say—despite everything—is satisfying.

Ellenoir dropped her cigarette and it shattered. Kimo threw the cassette at Sync as if it were suddenly red hot.

Sync remained motionless as the tape came at him, trusting Tacyturn to intercept. He did.

Tacyturn then calmly handed Sync the cassette. The young man looked it over, nodding approvingly. Then he tapped it on his lip in thought.

"How do I know this is the right one? How do I know it doesn't have anything else added into it?" He spotted the camera and pointed. "Tacyturn, I want you to get me that vidcam." He crossed his hands behind his back to prepare for whatever happened next. "We'll be taking it with us."

Before the driver could move, Kimo grabbed a gun from the workbench and pointed it at Sync. The young man's insides twisted up and he nearly broke his fingers behind his back, but he remained outwardly calm. He knew it had to be fake—if it were real, Tacyturn would have already put a bullet in the filmmaker.

Tacyturn could see that the red light on the prop gun wasn't on—the light that indicated if real bullets were loaded into it.

"Oh, thank you for reminding me. I'd also like to take that prop gun with me. Tacyturn, if you would be so kind?"

Tacyturn quickly disarmed Kimo and tucked the gun into the back of his pants. He grabbed the vidcam and looped it around his shoulders by its strap.

"Don't you want to play with us, Tacy?" Ellenoir quietly asked, reaching desperately out to him.

"We've all had so much fun together, haven't we?" Kimo added.

"I *said* don't fucking talk to him!" Sync called out.

Kimo mumbled, "Who the fuck does this little shit think he is?"

As Tacyturn returned to his side, Sync responded, "This little shit is a Thornwryght who has no problem with his hearing, by the way." He examined the vidcam as he added, "If I find anything wrong with this tape, I know where to find you."

"And I know where to find your family!" Kimo defiantly stomped forward. "I'll just contact them and tell them everything I know about this."

Sync laughed. "Oh my fucking God, please do. The shit you know about a Thornwryght will get you killed and the shit I know about *you* . . . will get you killed. You can't make threats without clean hands, fuckface."

After that, Sync turned to leave, not needing the satisfaction of seeing their facial expressions.

Tacyturn followed.

"Your bodyguard's hands are the most unclean of us all, Thornwryght, and yet you threaten us with him. You have no idea what kind of a monster he is, do you? How can you even trust him?"

Sync paused as Ellenoir spoke. Tacyturn stopped when he did and gave no reaction.

"He'll turn on you once someone more worthy of commanding him steps up," Kimo added.

"There is no such person," Sync said.

Kimo and Ellenoir both laughed.

"You're no one, doll face."

Sync smiled, knowing exactly what to say in his role as a confident master—he had seen enough movies with badasses to help him, on top of what Tacyturn had taught him.

"I'm the one with the monster. There's only one thing worse than not having a monster on your side, you know." He turned around to show his smile off to the Rilangs. "Pissing off the person who does." Sync pointed to his face. "If my smile fades, you're in a lot of fucking trouble."

As the young redhead turned back towards the exit, Ellenoir and Kimo lapsed into a palpable silence.

After a few quiet moments to make certain his advice stuck, Sync started to walk out of the warehouse again and Tacyturn followed.

Without turning around, Sync called back to them, "Putting your pointless chit-chat aside, I appreciate the work you did for us and I will not leave you empty-handed for it. Before you arrived, we took the liberty of leaving a tidy sum in a pocket of one of your outfits here."

The driver opened the large warehouse doors for Sync. The redhead wished he could see the looks on their faces as they scanned the thousands of outfits—with more than twice as many pockets.

They stepped outside and the large doors slowly closed on their own. As they did, Sync thought he heard Ellenoir and Kimo mumbling to each other, but couldn't hear what they were saying. He looked at the driver and could tell that he was able to hear them.

Tacyturn pulled out his vidphone and sent his brain tech feed to it, having it translate into the written word.

WE'LL SEND SOME OF OUR PEOPLE AFTER THEM,
SO DON'T DO ANYTHING RIGHT NOW.
TACY WILL BE OURS AGAIN, DEAR.
WE'LL MAKE TACY PUT AN END TO HIMSELF
LIVE
IN FRONT OF MILLIONS OF PEOPLE.
OH, GOOD IDEA. EVERYONE WOULD LIKE
TO SEE THAT HAPPEN TO THAT MONSTER.
EVERYONE WILL ADORE US FOR MAKING IT HAPPEN.

Just as the large door was about to click shut, Sync threw his hand inside and stopped it with an echoing thud. Tacyturn opened the doors for him again.

When the doors revealed his face to the Rilangs, his smile was gone. He found himself pleased with the fear in their eyes—he thought maybe his Thornwryght blood was starting to boil, or he could at least act like it was.

Reading Sync's body language, Tacyturn started to move towards them, but Sync put his hand up.

"Don't kill them. I want you to just make it hurt and permanent." He returned his hand to his pocket. "Also, I want a couple trophies to remember them by."

The young heir held his breath as he watched as Tacyturn swiftly came down upon them before they could do anything. He grabbed a pair of pliers nearby and seized Kimo first.

As he held him down, he yanked out one of his molars. His howl of pain would have been heartbreaking if Sync didn't hate him.

Whilst that happened, Ellenoir was screeching and trying to hide amongst her costumes. Just as she decided to try to attack Sync with scissors, Tacyturn was on top of her.

The young redhead realized that Tacyturn had somehow never told them about the extent of his brain tech, otherwise they'd have known better about whispering or trying to hide—they should have kept quiet or run away.

The driver allowed her to see that his magenta eye was now a bloodthirsty red. Then he yanked out one of her molars, too.

Her cry of pain pleased Sync more than Kimo's—it was making him concerned with himself because it made him smile. While he would have been disturbed if anyone else was being cruel, he was gratified that Tacyturn was doing it—and he was doing it for him. He wondered if he was doing it for himself, too.

Tacyturn then handed both of the molars to Sync. Inwardly, the young redhead was grossed out. Outwardly, he thought he looked pretty cool casually taking a pair of bloody teeth into his bare hand.

Kimo was cowering in a corner and Ellenoir was huddled on the ground nearby, crying.

Deciding that nothing else needed to be said, they left the warehouse.

Keeping his act up, Sync and Tacyturn walked across the street and around the corner to the Whisperunner.

Once out of sight of the Electric Reel warehouse, Sync collapsed with relief, his entire body aching from being so stiff. Tacyturn caught him.

"Holy fucking shit, that was fucking hard!" He tugged the plastic hood down off of his head, even though it was still drizzling. "I can't believe I pulled that off."

"You were perfect."

"*You* were fucking badass, as usual. I got the feeling you've been wanting to pull out their teeth for a long time." Remembering he had them in his hand, he gagged and dropped them. "You know, when I said I wanted some trophies, I was thinking maybe something less grody?" He went to a nearby drinking fountain and washed his hands. "Like maybe something interesting from their pockets or Kimo's wicked cool checkered hat right off his stupid fucking—!"

Before he could finish his thought, Tacyturn produced the checkered knit cap from the pocket inside of his jacket.

Sync was super excited. It was mostly black and had a neon-lined checkered star on the front, divided by different triangles of colour.

"Wicked!"

As Tacyturn scooped up the teeth off of the ground, Sync grabbed his tie to keep him from standing up straight again. When the driver curiously looked up at him, Sync put the knit cap on his head, then took a step back to admire it.

"Shit, you look better in checkers than I do! Ah, not your fault, though. You look good in everything, I bet." He nervously chuckled as he fumbled with the cassette. "Not to mention you also look fucking good in nothing at all. You also look wicked cool with blood on your hands, but I insist you clean up in that bubbler."

Sync held the cassette up and looked at the moon through its holes as Tacyturn washed his own hands.

"Guess it's time to review this ancient fucking thing and then mail it home. Ugh, I didn't want to see it done."

Getting comfortable in the Whisperunner, Tacyturn tossed the teeth into the driver's side cup holder, which still had the bullet from his leg. He then set up the camera and they watched the video on the tiny screen.

The result was terrifying and real—and they *knew* it was fake.

"Damn, he *is* good," Sync uttered under his breath once the video went to static. "I see why you wanted to use him."

They fast-forwarded through the rest of the tape on both sides to make sure nothing else was on the cassette. It was entirely empty except for Sync's suicide.

Without delay, they went to a self-serve kiosk in the lobby of the post office that was closed due to it being a Sunday. While messing around with the machinery that cut and built boxes in the exact size desired, Sync accidentally cut himself. Tacyturn automatically grasped his hand to take care of it.

Getting an idea, Sync suggested that he handle the box once without wiping his hand off—having Sync's blood with Tacyturn's prints was a perfect touch.

Then the only thing they put as the return address was the number zero—The One was now dead and there were no Thornwryght children left.

Just before dropping the package into the outbox, Sync shrugged and quoted one of the clearest lines of dialogue from *Blade Runner*, "Time to die."

Returning to the car, Sync kept replaying the video in his head, wondering what everyone was going to think about it. Seeing himself get shot in the head was disturbing—especially because he couldn't fight off the feeling that he deserved it.

Sync sat down in the passenger seat and, just as Tacyturn was closing the door, he stopped it with his hand.

"I just died and I want a kiss."

The driver obediently leaned in and gently kissed Sync on his lips.

When he pulled back and tried closing the door again, Sync shoved it back open.

"Fuck me, what the fuck was that? I just *died* and I want a real fucking kiss!"

Without hesitation, the driver climbed on top of Sync. In one quick motion, he reclined the seat as far back as it would go and passionately kissed the young man.

In no time at all, the situation escalated and they both had forgotten about the depressing video.

While making love, Tacyturn's scanner sensed someone watching them. He looked up in their direction and put his hand on his gun until they got the hint and left.

"What's—ah!—wrong?"

"Someone was filming us with pare tech."

Sync was aware of the illegal lens that peeled back layers of the world, letting the viewer see through anything they wanted and at any angle.

"Is it bad I kind of like that?" Sync thought for a moment, then asked, "You've got pare tech, too, don't you? That's how you looked right at them." He saw Tacyturn nod. "Why didn't you tell me?"

"I thought it would make you uncomfortable."

"No, I—ah!—I like it."

He grasped the driver's magenta tie to pull him closer to him.

"You're too wicked cool, Tac. I don't care how much of a monster you might be. I don't even deserve to be fucked by you."

He slipped the knit cap off of his head and pulled the band out of the driver's magenta hair, letting it fall free. He ran his fingers through it.

Sync then urgently added, "Don't you dare stop, though."

"Ever?"

The young man laughed once he realized that Tacyturn was implying that it could be something to panic about if his demand was just about the current session never ending.

Now he was curious. "If someone wanted you to do it forever, could you?"

"Someone or you?"

"Mm, me."

"Then no."

Sync cocked his head, thinking he should be offended. "Why not?"

"You are heavenly and I am only human."

Sync's cheeks went red, but then he snorted to try to hide his embarrassment.

"I don't know if a crime boss should be described as—ah!—heavenly, though!" he pointed out, but knew he shouldn't be running his mouth and ruining Tacyturn's stimulating words. "The Thornwryghts should all be hellish, right? Not fitting in is what caused all this shit in the first place, so I should be trying to f-fit in. Aren't you going to be teaching me to be hellish like my family? Or is just having the blood enough?"

"Hell is beneath everyone."

"Well . . . yeah . . . That's a good point, but—"

Tacyturn firmly gripped him and softly spoke against his lips. "Nothing surpasses Heaven."

Synclare Thornwryght felt himself filling with confidence—and Tacyturn.

X V.

"If he can't have you, no one can."

FOR THE NEXT SEVERAL DAYS, Tacyturn tried to teach Sync how to handle a gun and how to defend himself. Sync tried his best to remember everything he was told and mimic everything he was shown, but he was having a hard time—even just using the prop gun.

"I'm much better at doing this shit in video games, Tac," he would say in defense of his difficulty learning. "There's nothing to lose in those except one of many, many lives. There are also fun cheats that you can do in God mode. It makes you invulnerable! But I'm *not* fucking bulletproof in real life!"

The young man was so tired of being forced to learn to fight, he would even stop playing violent video games and solely focus on a piano simulator he was working on. He found it relaxing, but hid that he was doing it, worried he might look like a dork.

Sync's best tactic to get out of training entirely was distracting Tacyturn by giving him small commands for affection. He never liked to demand sex, but he was always pleased when it happened. He liked it to be a surprise—he discovered that he liked Tacyturn to *take* him.

He wanted to be submissive around the driver—and learning to fight went against that image he wanted to convey to the much more dominant man.

Sync didn't want to tell Tacyturn that, though.

Tacyturn thought that Sync was being too playful and not taking the training seriously. He tried not to worry about it. It had only been a few days and Sync's supposed predisposition for violence couldn't unlock that fast, he thought.

To help Sync relax, he had taken him back to the virtual reality gaming café for most of one of the days. He observed how Sync handled violence in the fake world. He was very good, but it was because he had no fear—his life was not actually in danger. Tacyturn could bring him back to life with the money in his wallet. Sync could also kill enemies whilst laying snuggled safely and comfortably up against Tacyturn in a chair they shared while the driver held his drink for him that Sync could sip hands-free.

On the evening of the sixth night, Sync fell asleep in the bed beside Tacyturn and the driver slipped out to go to his usual seat in the apartment. He set his motion alerts for anything larger than a fluffy cat and closed his eyes, holding his gun on his lap and wearing his black penny loafers, ready to go.

An hour later, Tacyturn detected motion and saw the electric silhouette of Sync approaching.

Once Tacyturn opened his eyes, Sync could see the faint mechanical glow of his irises.

"Wouldn't you be better off getting more sleep if you want to protect me?" Sync asked, hoping he would decide to come back to bed.

"This is the best place in the flat for me to be," Tacyturn responded.

Sync suddenly looked hurt and pouted. "If you think harder about that, that's not fucking true."

Tacyturn said nothing, but waited for an explanation.

The young man crossed his arms and turned away. "A long time ago, men and women slept near those they wanted to protect with no special tech and just a sword by their side. I'm not saying your way isn't good, but it's not the only fucking way."

He turned back and leaned close to the driver.

"I think you could protect me just fine from a comfortable bed. You don't need to drain yourself, Tac." He gently touched Tacyturn's scarred cheek. "Get some real sleep for once. Just closing your eyes doesn't fucking count. I know you'll still be able to protect me even if you're in a deep sleep."

Tacyturn stared into his concerned green eyes. Sync grabbed his hand and Tacyturn willingly let him pull him over to the bed.

"I'm still using my gun," Tacyturn said as he stepped out of his shoes.

"I should fucking hope so!" Sync huffed as he crawled under the covers. "This isn't the fucking Dark Ages, you know."

Tacyturn's expression softened with amusement.

Once he got himself into bed next to Sync, it wasn't long before the young man had nestled into him.

After just a half an hour, Sync had to remove his sweater because

Tacyturn emitted so much heat and he felt like he was being cooked alive. Sync thought that made them a perfect match—Sync was always cold and Tacyturn was always very warm. He wondered if that was why he wore a short-sleeved shirt under his required jacket.

That night, they both slept better than they ever had before. Tacyturn could still see electric shapes with his eyes closed, but he ignored them as best as he could.

At one point, Sync had affectionately began petting him—like he had at the cabin.

Tacyturn was actually having a hard time not wanting to focus on the neon lines of Sync's face looking at him so sweetly. He had seen his hesitation in doing it, but he must have assumed that the driver was asleep to make him feel bold enough to do it again.

The driver couldn't help but open his eyes and it made Sync's cheeks feel hot.

He pulled his hand away. "Am I bothering you?"

Tacyturn shook his head.

"Are you sure?" Sync bit his lip.

The driver lifted his hand up and rubbed Sync on his head the same way that the young redhead was doing to him to show him how it felt.

Sync pleasantly shuddered. "Oh, shit, that does feel fucking amazing, doesn't it?" Then, he couldn't stop a small sad chuckle, "Or maybe it's because we're both just not used to shit like that? Even the simplest thing is rare and amazing. Just having my fucking hand held makes me feel the same way, honestly. That's not pathetic, is it?"

The driver quietly slipped his hand into Sync's and the young redhead couldn't help a charmed smile. They both fell asleep while their hands were interlinked.

Tacyturn woke up later to a message on his vidphone from Ephraym. He was shocked when he saw that it was noon. Sync was sprawled on top of him and he tried his best to reach his vidphone and check it without disturbing him.

I DIDN'T WANT THIS VIDEO, TACYTURN, BUT I DO WANT YOU TO TRAIN HIM.
I'M ACTUALLY A BIT DISAPPOINTED I KNEW

THIS VIDEO WAS FAKE BEFOREHAND.
WHO WOULD HAVE THOUGHT THAT SUICIDE WAS
THE BRAVEST THING HE'S EVER DONE?
I'M ABOUT TO PRESENT IT TO THE NINETEEN.
THIS ALL BETTER TURN OUT PERFECT.
REMEMBER WHAT THAT MEANS? YOU'RE
SUPPOSED TO DIE.
THAT'S THE ONLY REASON YOU'RE STILL ALIVE.
SYNCLARE IS SUPPOSED TO KILL YOU. YOU
CAN'T AVOID IT FOREVER.

Just as he finished reading it, Tacyturn deleted the message and dropped his vidphone to the floor. He wrapped his arms protectively around Sync and closed his eyes, waiting patiently for Sync to wake up on his own. He did his best to stay in the moment and not let his mind wander too much.

Once his active scan of Sync let him know the young man was awake, the driver spoke gently. He knew that The Nineteen had seen Sync's video by then.

"Your video reached the peninsula."

"That's good news," Sync said as he stretched. "But what about a good fucking morning first?"

"Good fucking afternoon," Tacyturn said.

The young man checked his vidphone. "Whoa! See? Slept fucking great, didn't you? I know I did. Woke up dead, though," he chuckled and stared at his phone a little longer than he needed to. "Guess I'm officially dead, huh? You're the only one who knows I'm alive."

"And your father."

Sync turned to Tacyturn, shocked. "WHAT? You *told* him?" He groaned. "I guess your fucking loyalty *is* to him first and me second. Why the fuck did you tell him? Is it because I specifically didn't say that I wanted you to not tell him?"

"We don't want to force him to choose someone else."

Sync sighed, now feeling stupid about his anger. He also made a quicker attempt to look outwardly calm as he saw Bandit coming closer to him with a determined look on her face, likely ready to bite him because he was acting pissed.

"Okay, yeah. You're right. I mean, you usually are. I also wouldn't want him to send people after you because you'll look like a deserter when you don't return to him. You're his property. You've got his expensive tech in your head. If he can't have you, no one can."

The young redhead gently caressed the scar on the side of his head.

"I also don't want to find out if you have anything implanted in there that'll go off when he has no use for you anymore."

Tacyturn closed his eyes and leaned against the young heir. The gesture surprised the freckled young man. Sync realized that he must have verbalized a fear of his that he had never expressed before—and probably would still never.

Sync wrapped his arms around him. "You must be tired of my shit, Tac."

The driver pulled back to look at him in the eyes, seeking what he was getting at.

"Now that you don't have to protect me from The Nineteen and their hitmen, you can probably go off on your own. I mean, you don't have to stay away because you're still training me, but if you want to go and take a breather . . . I think you should."

Tacyturn looked apprehensive—in the most minimal way that Sync could only detect now that he had been around him so much.

"No, actually . . . I fucking *insist* that you do. I . . . want you to."

Sync could see it in his eyes now that he knew he had to. Sync squeezed him tighter, every-so-slightly flinching when he gripped his wounded hand a bit too hard.

Tacyturn picked up Sync's hand that had been cut by the post office kiosk and kissed the healing wound.

Sync melted inside as he desperately added, "Just fucking promise me that you'll come back, okay?" The young man then quickly shook his head. "No, wait . . . That leaves doubt."

The young man tightly squeezed Tacyturn's hands, ignoring the pain.

"I *want you* to come back to me," Sync tenderly ordered. "I want you to *always* come back."

X V I .

"You're proof that there is no God."

Tacyturn WASN'T SURE IF HE would have been able to go off on his own without Sync wanting him to, but he did—he was told to by a Thornwryght.

He waited a few days to make sure that Sync was certain about being left alone.

He was.

Tacyturn then waited until Tuesday evening where the darkness was on his side and few people were out and about on a work night. He also wore the checkered knit cap to hide his hair.

He had spent two terrible years in Hollywood and he didn't want to bump into anyone from his past. He scaled back the range of what his scanners would pick up on so that he wasn't bothered too often by anything he didn't care about. He didn't want to be pinged about all of the places he has done terrible things and all of the people he did terrible things to—pinging also still caused him to be hit with electric shock due to his damaged wiring.

He would only know if something was too close already—but not too close to handle.

As he was walking nowhere in particular, the tech in his eyesight did ping him, but it was not something he wanted to ignore. He had marked the individual who had been filming them making love in the car, but also the camera that had been used. His radar had picked up on the camera's location.

He knew now what he wanted to do with his time alone. Interacting with the pare tech recording of Synclare would reveal where the young man was and the timestamp would reveal that he was not actually dead—the recording needed to be destroyed before it entered cyberspace. It had already been ten days since it had been recorded and the driver hoped he wasn't too late.

Tacyturn went to the location that was flagged—it was the worst place for the footage to be. It was a virtual reality cyberspace bar called Journeymind Escape. He was uncomfortably familiar with it and had only ever been there twice.

To get him started in Hollywood, Ephraym had demanded that he go and connect with every simulation that had to do with satisfying a fantasy of killing yourself. He insisted that his body be injected with simulated pain, as well. He had to complete each one and send him the results.

The second time was the last task he had before he left Hollywood. He had to use a custom simulation that had a realistic virtual copy of himself scanned into it. He had to do to himself everything he had ever done to anyone in the two years he had been there. It was surreal—and was the final cherry on top of being totally desensitized to anything.

He had never been back between both of those times—luckily no one had ever asked him to.

The driver walked in through the neon drapes and went down the tunnel that led to dozens of small hallways, like a circuit board. The closer he got to the center, the more dead the building felt.

The first dozen rooms attached to the first hallway were lit up and fancy, like a popular club might be. Some pods had people actively using the services. Ads for different simulations surrounded him, trying to entice him.

A few waiting eyes were on him—some looked eager, some looked embarrassed and others looked desperate.

Tacyturn ignored everything and walked far beyond where any customer was meant to be. Walking straight through the dimly lit and disorganized maze, he narrowed in on his target.

From behind a series of computers, a petite dark-skinned woman slid her stool out into Tacyturn's line of view. She was in circuit board themed aerobic gear in pastel colours of green, yellow and purple. She was fit like a gymnast and had her blonde hair in finger waves. She wore contacts that made her eyes purple with star-shaped irises. Her leg warmers were small tool belts, as were her elbow-length fingerless gloves.

Tacyturn recognized her as the owner. He had never crossed paths with her before because Ephraym had purposely distracted her from Journeymind Escape on the two days that Tacyturn had gone into the cyber bar. It was far more difficult to infiltrate a company when the owner was on site.

After staring at him for only a moment, she grinned.

She had a Liverpudlian accent. "Oi, Whisperunner fucker! Here to experience something again? Or something new?"

Tacyturn approached her with his hand under his jacket.

She wrinkled her nose at him. "Oh, come on. You can't be mad that you were being filmed. You weren't being subtle, you know. You were out in public." She hopped gracefully to her feet and approached him. "I'm a bit jealous of the ginger. I'm developing new software that will make one person look like another. That way, I *could* make myself look like the ginger, and—"

The driver took his gun out.

"Shit, you're a serious one, aren't you? Let me finish my story before you get your panties in a twist. What you're thinking is not why I'm inventing it. Well, that's how it will be abused, but that's not where I got the idea."

She danced over to her monitors, checking up on her clients as she talked.

"I thought it might be nice for same sex couples that want children. I can take a couple like, for example, my wife and I or a couple like you and your lil' ginger and swap one of the partners with an actor of the opposite sex, either a sperm donor or a surrogate, so that they can feel like they're producing children with the one they love. Each actor will be connected to the other partner so that they have to do exactly what they do. It will be beautiful . . . if done right."

Tacyturn relaxed the hand that was holding his gun.

She noticed and grinned again. "See? I thought you might like that. Maybe you'll use it one day with your lil' freckled ginger?"

Tacyturn was annoyed that her video was detailed enough for Sync's freckles to show up.

"What is the film for?"

"Don't even want to know my name first?" She saw no reaction from him. "Visard Lum is who I am, anyway. Middle name Rebel. Sometimes called Visa, if you're looking for a pet name. And you?"

Tacyturn said nothing.

Visard innocently shrugged. "Thought I'd try, anyway. To answer your question, it was for inspiration."

She picked up a digital sketchbook and showed her plans for a simulation of a situation exactly like what had happened in the Whisperunner.

"We usually have to pare down many more levels before we get something like *this*." She giggled and shrugged like it was no big deal. "My underling was just on my way to mail an in-home virtual order and there you guys were. It's usually in the back seat, but we liked your way. Cute how your leg was still hanging out of the wide-open car door like you just didn't give a fuck about anything *but* a fuck."

"Delete it," Tacyturn demanded in a threatening tone.

"Is that why you're here? I can delete it, luv, of course, but it's already in here forever. Hope you can live with that." She pointed to her head. "Are you sure you didn't just come here to get a copy? All you have to do is ask." She picked up a helmet covered in wires. "I could plug you in and you could experience it like you were my underling at that time, or move into a free seat nearby or, if you're into seeing how good you are or how you look from different angles, you can be the ging—"

Tacyturn shoved the helmet aside. It hit the floor hard.

Visard threw up her hands defensively. "Fine, fine, I'll delete it." After a few clicks at her computer, she said, "Done."

Tacyturn was able to interact with her computer screen without having to see it and confirmed that was exactly what she did. He saw the recording device nearby and it was still plugged in. She had deleted it from the device itself through her main computer.

As he was turning around to leave, he looked at the helmet on the floor. It looked like complicated encephalon technology.

"You're good with technology interlinked with the brain."

Visard smirked. "I'm brilliant. I don't own this company because I'm gorgeous."

"I have damaged wiring."

"You want me to fix it?" She excitedly approached him. "You've been kind of an arsehole, but I can never resist getting my hands on brain tech. Where are these wires?"

Tacyturn pointed to the old wound on the side of his neck.

"Even better, we're going to have to dig in!"

She ran to her desk and dug around in a sphere-shaped drawer that rotated open in the wall. She pulled out two small devices. She wirelessly connected them as she walked back over to him. She gawked up at him towering over her, then she slid a chair over with a dramatic swoop of her leg.

Tacyturn sat down.

"I have these blockers designed for customers who want to get out of their situation quickly. They apply them anywhere safe on their body and it'll work."

She showed him the jointed device that was covered in small fish hook-like pins.

"It makes it so that it can be anything in the simulation and gets into their skin to block the tech. It's set to cancel all tech for one hour. After one hour, their body has relaxed and returned to reality so that it's safe for them to get disconnected and then my equipment automatically terminates. It also gives me time to handle it, be it one person or a large group."

The driver stared at the blocker, then glanced at the other device she had.

"This is just a timer for when I'm using it outside of a simulation and want to know how much time I have before it automatically shuts off. Like right now!" She handed him the timer. "So, is it okay if I apply the blocker? Like, it's not gonna kill you, right? Haven't got any important tech keeping you alive, do you?"

Tacyturn thought for a long moment, then nodded his approval for the blocker.

"Terrif!"

Visard wasted no time and stabbed it on the back of his neck. She was impressed that he didn't flinch. The extra pins that didn't make contact with flesh retracted and the device tightened to the surface of his skin.

Just moments after, Tacyturn's tech flickered out. His mind was suddenly very, very quiet. The constant mechanical humming was no longer there. It felt as though he had suddenly floated into space. He felt like he could relax—if he was anywhere else. But he also felt blind.

At first, he thought it was him when the world seemed to go a lot darker than normal—he thought for a moment that he had just forgotten how dark the world was without his tech, but it was too dark. He blinked hard as he looked around. He could only see anything if something was glowing or backlit.

Visard noticed his behaviour and shrugged it off like it was no big deal.

"Yeah, I forgot to mention it sort of dims your sight, as well. That's part of the easy transition. I suppose it's sort of like throwing a blanket over a bird's cage."

She peered into his eyes to see what the blocker had done on the outside first.

"Though, your sight has dimmed differently because your tech is mainly ocular, yeah? Your right eye has gone and lost its colour entirely, while your left one is just dimmer. Tech is mostly on the right side of your head, is it? Your eye was pink in the video I took, then it was matching your other eye when you came in here. Gives you the ability to just customize the colour of one eye? That's . . . half rad, I suppose? Ginger find the rose-coloured eye to be more romantic?"

The woman went to put a needle in his neck, but Tacyturn pushed it away.

"Fine. Like pain, do you?" she asked as she put on a headset and clicked the light on.

Tacyturn didn't show any emotion as Visard re-opened his wound to reveal his severed wires.

"Now that's some shoddy work. Who the devil did you have do this? They just twisted the wires back together like bloody pipe cleaners!" After examining them further, she said, "You must get some serious electric shock every time you try using any of your abilities having to do with NAVSTAR or trying to get it to work while you're moving very fast."

Tacyturn already understood why he couldn't successfully use his tech while driving, but it did confirm that he was in the hands of someone who knew what she was doing.

"The wires are pretty frayed. Best thing for me to do is to cut them down and strip them, then connect them with a fresh piece and a bit of soldering. I've got exactly the right wiring here in my shop, very special wire just for brain tech. You've hunted down the right bitch for the job."

In between her work, Visard examined his face. She didn't want to be rude, so she didn't stare at the scar on the side of his head peeking out from his hat or the bruises across his eyes—but when she finally caught a long look, the driver could see that she was close to realizing something.

"Do you mind removing your cap? It's a little bit in my way here," she mumbled, trying to sound as casual as possible.

Without hesitation, he pulled it from his head. Tacyturn knew what she was about to say because she suddenly looked very pale seeing his unique magenta hairstyle.

"You're the Magenta Tiger," she stated.

Tacyturn showed no reaction—he wasn't surprised with her statement.

When his scarred and magenta likeness was requested anonymously by Ephraym, he went into the simulation with an infiltrated temp worker that kept him a prisoner in the digital world until Ephraym deemed him done abusing himself. If he killed himself, another likeness would be dropped in—the body of the previous one would remain. Tacyturn had nearly overheated from the duration of the simulation. Tacyturn figured she must have learned all about it, even though they left hardly any trace of it.

She further explained as she worked, taking great care not to sound worried as she spoke.

"I remember getting a scan of you from Electric Reel about five years back because you were requested. You must remember that, it's hard to get scanned for virtual reality without knowing about it. You need to give your permission. You looked a lot younger, but it's definitely you. Hat hides a lot, though, so I didn't see it sooner. That's probably the idea, innit?

"I didn't know you or your name, so I just labeled your scan as Magenta Tiger. Since you were scanned nude at first, I could see that you had so many scars then. You looked like a tiger. You must have so many more now. I also considered the raccoon angle with your battered eyes, but I didn't know that was permanent until right at this very moment with it still there five years later. Unless you just happened to get in a similar fight again just before visiting. Or is that some sort of weird makeup? Hope it'll catch on?"

Tacyturn said nothing and let her continue talking. It was information that he didn't know—he had been unaware of the origin of the name Magenta Tiger. He had never seen the specs before being thrown into the simulation himself. The name had caught on just as he had left to work for Ephraym.

She was clearly tense, though, and he made sure that she didn't use any tools that looked like they would meddle or link with him—or hurt him.

"Did you know that you're an object that can be used in any simulation? It's just that I don't know if you've ever been here and I can usually tell. I've seen simulations where there have been more than one of your scans interacting together, but not you as a customer. Many people come in to use and abuse you in all sorts of situations. They seem shocked you're an option. Most of them seem very personal. Most of them choose to kill you, calling you a monster. I have overheard some very interesting things . . ." Visard hummed in thought, wondering why she didn't make the connection sooner. "I can't imagine how much they would pay to do all those things to the *real*—"

Visard stopped suddenly when Tacyturn's hand was around her throat.

"H-Hey! That's not my thing! I'm just *saying*, luv!"

The driver squeezed until he saw real fear of possible death—he saw the moment just before her life would start flashing before her eyes, lit up by her torchlight visor. He then let go and Visard coughed and grasped her neck.

"I see why you're popular with people who look like they've been fucked somehow. That's just your style, innit? You're really fucking terrifying, mate. Why would God put someone like you in a body that's almost two meters tall? Jesus."

Fearful of what he'd do if she stopped working on him completely, she continued. She swallowed gingerly several times, still feeling the pain in her throat.

Checking the timer, Tacyturn saw that he still had fifty-four minutes left. He stared at the digital glowing letters until forty-nine minutes were left and Visard was sewing him up.

"Forty-nine minutes left until your reboot is done. Sorry, I'm just a fast worker. I suggest you stay here until it's over with. I don't think you want to try to get out of my maze until you get your tech back, right?" She pointed at his head. "I have a feeling the only reason you found me was because of it. This place is so complicated, I was thinking of turning the empty space into a virtual maze you have to escape from. What do you think?"

Not expecting a response, Visard hopped off of the stool she was squatting on and tossed her tools into a drawer.

"Are you thirsty? Or anything? I can get you something from the automat"

Without waiting for an answer, she disappeared around the corner. Tacyturn remained in his seat trying not to feel nervous being in an unfamiliar place and in almost complete darkness. He wanted to partake in a virtual cigarette, but the blocker would make it impossible.

A few moments later, he received a message on his vidphone he could barely read. It was an advertising notification from Journeymind Escape for a special event on August 30th, 1983—the current date. Visard was sending out a forced message to all of the users who had ever experienced time with the Magenta Tiger simulation.

She was letting them all know that the original copy was at Journeymind Escape—and indisposed for a short amount of time. She added in a timer that was counting down—it matched the forty-five minutes left on the device in his hand.

Visard had likely not been counting on Tacyturn being on that mailing list.

Wasting no time, Tacyturn stumbled around the room and tried to remember exactly how he came in. He was torn between just leaving or showing Visard how he felt about what she had just done.

Grabbing a large metal tube nearby, he began blindly smashing anything that was glowing. Visard came out of her hiding place to try to figure out a way to get Tacyturn to stop. It was just enough as he saw her move past one of the shattered monitors that was still emitting light.

He grabbed a wire that was on a large spool he remembered being nearby and wrapped it around her neck, pulling it tight into a complicated knot. He then threw her down hard onto the floor, tightening the wire. She gasped as she stared up at him.

He then let go of the wire and Visard gulped in air. The driver started to backtrack to try to leave the complicated building.

"You're proof that there is no God," she sputtered. "I've seen the Magenta Tiger simulations. What kind of a person would I be if I let a monster like you go back out into my city?"

Tacyturn didn't hesitate as he returned to her and her eyes widened, trying to scramble to her feet. He quickly turned the large spool, winding up the wire that was around her neck. The wire tightened and pulled her up onto her feet by her throat.

Just as she was barely standing on her toes, he grabbed her by the back of her neck.

"You're going to regret it if I need to come back here in forty-four minutes," Tacyturn said.

The driver then let go of the spool and slammed her face into a nearby shelf, breaking it and knocking her unconscious. She collapsed onto the floor. He then tied her hands behind her back and sabotaged the spool so that it would not unwind anymore.

He searched her body for something that might help him get out of the building more quickly, but he found nothing. He also lost track of the checkered hat.

Tacyturn tried to cancel the message that had been sent out but, without his tech, he wasn't able to. When he yanked on the blocker on the back of his neck, it tightened and he started to feel his flesh tearing.

The driver knew he had to get out just by remembering how he came in—and with a lot of luck, too. He started walking in the direction where he felt himself going uphill, knowing that the walk into the building had a slight incline. Whenever he felt the ground levelling out or dipping, he felt around until he was moving upwards again.

Once he was closer to the outer walls, he could hear rain and the noises of the active portion of the cyberspace bar and tried to follow the sounds.

With surprising accuracy, Tacyturn found his way back outside into the rain. He checked his glowing timer and saw that he still had about forty minutes left. He needed somewhere to hide for that long. His eyesight was worse now that he was out where there was less electric illumination and more pollution.

Knowing he had to get away from Journeymind Escape, he continued to backtrack.

It wasn't long before he realized that there were people nearby—he didn't need his eyes or technology to know that. One person had grabbed him and he deftly spun them away. He bumped into another person and was forced to step backwards.

He could sense that there wasn't just one person—there were twelve and he was surrounded.

Tacyturn still had thirty-nine minutes left before he could see properly again.

He didn't want to pull out his gun too soon—it was an invitation for people to start attacking. He also didn't want to waste time shooting the wrong person. The driver also was wary of pulling out the torchlight on his vidphone as someone may think he was getting his gun.

He slowly started to identify people as they started to taunt him. Voices overlapped, trying to get his attention.

"Do you remember what you did to me, Magenta Tiger?"

"I'm going to fucking cut you the same way you cut me!"

"Why did you kill my dogs? What did they ever do to you?"

"I don't understand why you did that to my sister, Magenta Tiger."

"My husband killed himself after what you did."

"I'll never be able to model again!"

"I was trapped in that basement for days before anyone found me!"

"You didn't burn my dirty money, did you? There was nothing wrong with it!"

"We never found the antidote. There wasn't one, was there?"

"Whatever you gave me made me fucking eat my friend's face!"

"I told you to stop! My back will never be the same again."

"Why did you dig up my family?"

The overlapping comments were overwhelming, but he remained outwardly calm—which pissed them all off further. Inside, all of his terrible memories were drowning him. He was still feeling like he was floating out into space, but now he felt that his oxygen was running out.

For once, Tacyturn didn't know what to do. It was just a matter of time before someone cast the first stone.

Then suddenly there was a bright purple light moving towards him.

The crowd grew quiet until one person said, "Fucking alley cats have no sense of danger, do they?"

The driver could see that it was a familiar fluffy dilute calico cat wearing her braided collar. One person shot at her, but missed. She flailed and hid behind Tacyturn.

"Don't fucking do that, you idiot! It's just a fucking cat and you might hit someone else."

"If you hit *him*, it should be fine, though."

"She's hiding behind the wrong fucking person," another person said.

Unable to focus on anything but Bandit's collar—which seemed to be glowing much brighter than usual—he watched her as she ran between a pair of people and jumped up on an old car. From there, she made her way up a broken ladder and to some pipes that wrapped around the building to the side street.

Tacyturn now knew exactly what he needed to do.

In one movement, the driver moved towards the two people that Bandit had gone in between and pulled out his gun, shooting both of them in the thigh. They dropped and he jumped nimbly up onto the car, up the ladder and onto the pipes, just like Bandit had. Shots followed him, but he was able to avoid them by continuing to move. He fired back a few shots, trying to aim for where he heard the shots originate.

Once around the corner, Tacyturn continued to run along the building, his fingertips always touching whatever was to his right. He could see partially with the glowing signs, but a lot of the time it was dark or the lights were red. Bandit let him know when he needed to jump by doing it herself.

The driver knew he wasn't dealing with anyone who was a serious hunter or hitman like himself, so he was able to escape.

He heard a few tires screech, indicating that some more people had been on their way to get him, but had likely spotted him on the rooftops and stopped suddenly to avoid losing sight of him. He thought he heard the Rilangs.

It wasn't long before Bandit led him into an open attic of an abandoned building. He quickly felt around and latched the window shut. He did his best to familiarize himself with his hideout by touch. He stopped when he heard footsteps coming up the stairs. He readied his gun.

Once the driver saw Sync's glowing checkered shoes, Tacyturn dropped his gun and collapsed into a seated position on the dusty floor. Even though he was tired and blind, he managed to not look dismayed.

The instant Sync saw Bandit sitting beside Tacyturn in the corner of the attic, he ran to him and hugged him.

"I'm sorry I followed you. It's not that I didn't trust you, I just . . . couldn't stand being away from you. I tried to stay out of your range so you wouldn't know . . . but you had to have known, right? You were letting me follow you, weren't you?"

When Sync pulled back and looked into Tacyturn's eyes, they were dim. His right eye had been drained of all colour.

"What's wrong?" Sync looked at the timer that Tacyturn placed in his hands. "What the fuck is in thirty-three minutes?"

"I'll be able to see again."

Sync gasped and held his hand. For the first time, the tone of the driver's voice was slightly different, but not weaker—it was more flowery, he thought, but couldn't understand why he thought that. Tacyturn was more breathless.

"I thought something was off. You would have been able to kick all of their asses!"

He had heard Tacyturn's attackers, but he did not want to know any more. He knew it was a small glimpse into the two years of Hell he endured—and caused—in Hollywood.

The young man looked at the timer again.

"How is this making you blind? Can we smash it?"

He raised it above his head. Tacyturn grasped his wrist and put his hand on the back of his neck to show him the blocker stuck to his skin.

"Shit! I suppose if smashing had been the answer, you would have already done it. So, we just have to wait?"

Tacyturn nodded.

"What if this timer runs out and you don't get your sight back to the way it was?"

Tacyturn remained silent.

"Can't fucking depend on me, that's what," Sync whined. "I'm a fucking waste."

"You did just save my life."

"No, I didn't!" he sobbed. "I didn't want to bring Bandit, but she snuck out! I tried to stop her from going to you when you were trapped by all those people. I did fucking nothing! I tried to stop her and if I had stopped her you might have been—"

Finding his lips using the soft glow of his shoes, Tacyturn kissed him.

Sync calmed a bit, but he wasn't going to stop talking.

"And before that, you saved her from the cabin. And before that, you saved me! So, you've basically saved yourself!" He fumbled with his hands. "I know I wasn't taking learning to fight seriously before, but I will now." He clenched his hands into fists. "I need to learn to fight so that I can help you. I don't ever want to be helplessly nearby ever again. I don't want to care about the danger."

"You need to learn to fight to feel safe," Tacyturn reminded him.

"But I do feel safe . . . when you're around."

"What if I'm not around?"

"Can't you just always be around?" Sync asked with a hopeful tone.

The bodyguard was worried that Sync was depending on him too much—or their relationship was blossoming into something else.

Tacyturn wondered if Sync was falling in love with him.

He couldn't imagine such a thing being true—he was to be used, not loved. He was a companion, but not to be someone's other half.

Sync leaned against his shoulder as they waited in silence for the timer to reach its end, quietly praying. He supportively held his hand and Bandit curled up in his lap.

He knew the driver was worried that he would become useless if he couldn't see and Sync wanted him to know that wasn't true. Sync knew he'd be the useless one to be able to support him the way he deserved. He knew he had to learn. He was ready to tell Tacyturn that everything was going to be all right—but he was trying to convince himself first.

The young man wondered if his tech helped with his brain injury at all, or if it had just been put in as an extra enhancement.

"You're not fucking up in the head, are you? Without your tech? Are you in any pain?"

The driver shook his head. "It's so quiet."

"Because I was shutting the fuck up for once?" Sync asked, trying to be funny.

"In my head."

The young redhead thought that might be something that would bring him relief—but it was probably just disconcerting. Tacyturn always knew what was going on around them and now he didn't.

Sync looked around the room, wondering if he wanted to know what was in the attic. He thought maybe part of the quiet was not being able to scan his surroundings.

"Nothing really interesting in here. Old vanity mirror. Some costumes and props, I think. Kind of feels like an old dance studio, actually. Downstairs, the room is basically one big mirror. Scared the shit out of me. Thought there was some other little punk in the building. Did you know the windows were locked with unenhanced locks? So fucking lame. Did you know you can unlock those with just fire? Not even a lot of fire. Just a little bit of fire. Father had an unenhanced lock on the wine cellar. I burned it right off. Though this whole place looks like it could easily go down in fire. I'm surprised it hasn't already."

Then he realized what they were sitting next to. It was an old enhanced piano. Getting an idea, he pulled the blanket off of it and sat on the attached bench.

"I've only ever played in a virtual reality game I have, but . . ."

After just a moment of mentally preparing himself—and hoping he doesn't sound terrible—Sync began playing a hauntingly beautiful tune. It was both chaos and tranquility hand-in-hand and the fact that the piano was not entirely in tune complimented this.

The title for his song was "Command"—it sounded like the sort of title he should be confident enough to make and follow as a theme song. It was a song for a Thornwryght.

The real name of the song was the save file for the progress in the virtual game. There was a hidden message that was a desperate plea of how he really felt.

"COMMAND.SAVEME"

Tacyturn closed his eyes and leaned against the piano. The anxious emptiness melted away and he felt honoured to be able to hear Sync play for him and not hide in his virtual game. Just by feeling the sound, he could tell exactly how big the room was and he could tell exactly where Sync was.

When the song messed up with a choppy glissando mixed with Sync swearing, he could tell exactly where Bandit was, too.

After opening his eyes again when he felt Bandit crawl across his lap, he realized he could see Sync's hands and face glowing in what he thought must be an old mirror leaning up against the wall. He was lighting up depending on the combination of keys on the old enhanced piano. His shoes were still glowing, as well.

When the timer beeped, Sync stopped playing and they braced themselves.

Just when they thought nothing was going to happen, the blocker on the back of Tacyturn's neck loosened and fell limp, spent.

Sync smashed it with his shoe, then stared into Tacyturn's eyes. There was a mechanical flicker, then a throbber filling up his right eye for a long moment. He watched as the driver's eyes brightened up again, pixel by pixel.

First his right eye was denim blue, like his other eye. Then it became more of a purple hue.

The driver closed his eyes as the mechanical humming returned to his head. It suddenly seemed so loud now that it had been gone for the first time in seven years. He felt like he was getting brain freeze as the contours of neon painted the tapestry behind his eyelids again.

When he opened his eyes, the room was much brighter and his tech analyzed it all in an instant. He knew what people were outside looking for him, but near a building further away. The dance studio was a hole in the wall that had been overlooked. He saw the boarded-up window that Sync's petite form had been able to climb through.

When he scanned further back where he had come from, he noted that he had killed one person and injured three. More people had shown up. He also did not experience any painful shock as he scanned the locations of people he tagged—Visard had actually fixed him proper.

When he looked at Sync's face, he could clearly see him again and Sync could tell by the way his eyes focused. His eye pixelated back to a magenta colour and his denim blue left eye was more electric again.

The young heir smiled and heaved a huge sigh of relief and kissed him. He was glad that Tacyturn wasn't going to need to depend on him because he wasn't ready.

"Who makes you feel safe, Tac?" Sync asked in a serious tone.

Tacyturn said nothing as he stared into Sync's earnest green eyes.

"*I* want to be the one who makes *you* feel safe," the young heir said. "I want to be able to save you if you need to be saved and I'll do whatever I need to fucking do to make that happen."

Very suddenly, Bandit fled the attic and went downstairs, escaping through the same window that Sync had entered. At the same time, Tacyturn looked back and straight down through the walls towards the street. He quickly pulled Sync's face closer to his chest, keeping it hidden while he focused on the person seeking them out with an electronic device.

"What is it?" Sync asked.

"Keep your face hidden."

"Pare tech?"

The driver nodded and pulled Sync's plastic hood up over his red hair, shrouding his distinct green eyes. Sync reached around Tacyturn to give the pare tech two middle fingers to look at.

Tacyturn could see that all of the people who were looking for him were now swarming around the narrow old building. People were approaching the front door and climbing up to the attic window. They were blocking all the possible ways out with weapons unsheathed and vidphones ready and recording.

After interfering with the pare tech, he grabbed Sync's wrist, yanking him downstairs into the main dance studio. He started examining everything around them.

"What's going on?" Sync desperately asked.

"We're surrounded."

Sync wasn't sure that Tacyturn knew what to do. This made him panic.

"I fucking distracted you by running my mouth off about myself, didn't I? About fucking feelings and fucking self worth . . . I'm not worth *anything*." He started to pull on his hair. "When will I ever stop fucking up? I'm not worth any of this!"

The driver began peeling away the walls around them with his tech to see where everyone and everything was. Sync continued to rant and hate himself a little bit more.

"How long do we have?"

Finally hearing a direct question, Tacyturn responded, "Until they get impatient and come in."

"That'd suck for them, though, right? You'd take them all out easily. Unless you think I'd get in the way of that . . . and you wouldn't be able to with my dumb fucking ass around."

Finding something he could use, Tacyturn put both of his hands on a nearby wall and focused hard. Sync remained quiet as he watched closely, wondering what he was doing. It was getting hard to ignore the shouting that was starting outside. So many voices were trying to convince the Magenta Tiger to give up and come outside.

Through all that, though, Sync could hear the faint sound of something tearing through the walls. It was eerie and the young man hoped it was something that Tacyturn was doing and not the people out to get him.

Sync watched closely as a line appeared in the corner of the room that was about six feet tall. There was a thin sheet of metal that had sliced through from the other side and was starting to form a small box in the corner behind a coat rack. Tacyturn's right eye was electronically crackling.

Sync quickly realized it was a piece of technology that Tacyturn's own tech had manipulated into coming through the wall from whatever building shared that wall. When he saw the tech flicker and become the exact same colour as the interior wall of the dance studio, Sync knew it was an enhanced window like the one in their apartment—but fancier.

It was one of the advanced ones that could extend along the walls to make the screen bigger—either just widescreen or transforming the entire room. The building next door was either a pricey apartment or an executive business suite. The old dance studio was probably abandoned because it was going to be phased out and replaced with something higher end.

It was clear that Tacyturn had forced the screen to extend beyond its assigned boundaries.

Just as Sync was going to say something, Tacyturn shoved him into the corner. The tech began to form around him.

Sync quickly realized that Tacyturn was not going to be in there with him. The young redhead anxiously grabbed his jacket sleeve.

"*What are you doing?*"

To avoid answering, Tacyturn quickly kissed Sync, forcing him into the corner again. He then closed him inside of the screen as he cried out to object.

Just as he did so, people upstairs had broken cautiously into the attic and those nearby broke down the front door in the entryway a level below him.

Tacyturn waited in the shadows until enough people filled the building. Then, using his gun on electroshock mode and exposing the electric arc, he set a nearby curtain on fire. Then he moved to a closet and lit up the costumes inside. The fire quickly consumed everything in its path, hungry for the dusty old wood they were surrounded with.

Very quickly, the main level was on fire, heading upwards at an alarming rate.

As the fire started to grow and rage, Tacyturn slid through the flames and killed each person who had now let their guard down to panic. He didn't hesitate and he didn't bother to keep tidy—the fire would take care of everything. Bones broke, blood splattered and bullets blew through flesh and matter. The mirror that filled an entire wall shattered as he threw a body into it.

Sync could hear nothing from inside of his screen shield. He hugged himself and prayed that the kiss that had been planted on him wasn't to say goodbye.

At first, he figured he was hidden away to keep him safe—but he also realized he was probably hidden away to keep from being a useless distraction and fucking something else up. If he had just shut up about his feelings, he was certain that Tacyturn would have been able to predict and avoid the situation they were in. They would have been several steps ahead.

Tacyturn kept an eye on Sync in the corner of the room the entire time. He knew that the superior technology was fireproof, being that it was part of the enhanced fireproof walls of the expensive building next door—but only to a certain degree. That degree was about 1,100 °C.

As flames started to lick the corner, Tacyturn headed upstairs to the attic, stepping over bodies—and pieces of bodies. There was one final person making their way up to escape.

Tacyturn pounced on him as he reached up to the open window. Just before cutting his throat, the driver's tech indicated that he was handling someone who was only just a boy—about thirteen years old.

Instead of aiming for his heart, the driver stabbed his knife through the boy's palm that was holding a gun. This caused him to cry out in pain and drop the weapon, no longer able to grasp it tightly.

The young boy stared into Tacyturn's red eye, terrified with tears streaming down his cheeks.

When he pulled his blade out, the boy swiped at Tacyturn who easily dodged and caught his wrist. Just as he raised his wounded hand to strike, Tacyturn pressed it hard against the wall beside his head. The boy grimaced with pain as pressure was applied to his bleeding palm.

When he tried to speak, Tacyturn shushed him by putting his now bloody hand on the boy's throat, squeezing tightly.

"This happened because you found me," Tacyturn darkly chided him.

Then he threw the boy through the glass of the burning attic window.

Grabbing the blanket that had been on the expensive piano, Tacyturn swiftly went downstairs, gracefully weaving through the flames which were now immense and would not be stopped easily—if at all. He went to the corner where Sync was and covered himself and the hidden screen compartment with the blanket.

After only twenty minutes, the unfought flames had consumed the entire building, fueled by old junk and flammable debris. The only thing that remained mostly untouched were pieces of the room attached to the fireproof building next door.

As the fire was investigated, the strange intact fireproof blanket hanging in the corner was yanked down, only to reveal a coat hanger in the corner. There was no sign of the Magenta Tiger or the young man he was with. All of the bodies were burned beyond recognition and no one had seen the Magenta Tiger leave the building.

As some tried to guess which blackened body was his, others were certain that he had escaped like the ghost he was.

Inside of the hidden corner piece behind the coat rack, Sync was pressed up against Tacyturn with his arms tightly around him, holding his breath. He focused on the driver's calm heartbeat.

The driver was hunched down in the small space with his forehead pressed up against the fake screen wall and his eyes closed, focusing entirely on scanning everything going on around their safe hidden corner. He kept his arms around the young man, tightly grasping the fabric of his suit, letting him know he was protected—but also quietly letting him know that he should not move until his grip relaxed.

He made sure no one was going to check the building with pare tech. Luckily, no one felt the need to—they were sure there was nowhere left to hide. Still, Tacyturn was ready to act the moment their corner became unsafe.

That moment never came. Once the police arrived, all of the hunters for the Magenta Tiger ran into the shadows. There was a quiet moment that Tacyturn saw an opening for them to leave and they quickly took it, resetting the digital screen and easily avoiding the police and anyone that he had tagged as they kept each other occupied. For the first time, Tacyturn grabbed one of the countless complimentary umbrellas around the rainy electric city to help them blend in.

Once in a safe place tucked beside a busy noodle bar, Tacyturn examined Sync to make sure that he wasn't hurt. He was entirely unscathed. Tacyturn was bloody and scorched, but otherwise unharmed—none of the blood was his.

They could tell that Bandit was sitting on a nearby awning and watching over them because of a familiar soft purple glow that enveloped them.

Sync decided not to ask what Tacyturn had done—but his heart still ached with curiosity.

He had a feeling in the pit of his stomach that was an unsmotherable desire to be just like him—someone he could depend on. He hated being a Thornwryght, but he wasn't sure if being like Tacyturn was any different from that.

Sync knew it had to be better than being himself, though. Tacyturn deserved better.

XVII.

"Das ist nur recht un billig."

TACYTURN SAT ON AN OLD deactivated rooftop HVAC unit and leaned against the apartment complex's neon sign. It was just after sunset and the rain was drizzling. He could tell it was about to pick up—the rain seemed programmed to pour at night. He mused to himself about God being a programmer and their world just being a program.

They had just finished practicing hand-to-hand combat and Sync was doing quite well with the freedom that they had with The Nineteen thinking that he was dead. It had been nearly two months since his suicide video was completed.

Tacyturn still didn't want to push it, though, so he often cut the training short to help Sync. There was a weight on Sync's shoulders that he couldn't shake. He had gone from doing nothing with his life to being forced to prove himself to an entire crime syndicate. He was expected to go from hiding in a cellar to assuming a throne.

When training ended, Sync always suggested that the driver go off on his own—he was concerned that being stuck with him must be draining. Tacyturn insisted that it wasn't, but Sync insisted that he still take a breather.

Even though Tacyturn never brought up the time that ended in fire, Sync would still reassure him that the night had been worth it. He had been able to get his tech fixed and accidentally faked his own death.

"Of course all the people you killed that night would disagree, but the night went well for you in the end! Now we're both dead!"

"Surpassing everyone else."

"Heh, yeah . . . surpassing everyone else." Sync bit his lip. "You too, right? You're not just gonna be watching from . . . beneath me, right?"

Sync could see that Tacyturn didn't want to talk about Heaven and Hell—and of the two where he belonged.

His thoughts were confirmed when Tacyturn responded. "I like to be beneath you."

The redhead covered his face with his hand and snorted. "Ignoring that you probably mean while fucking, I'm gonna have to point out the fact that you could also mean that you like being . . . assigned to me. All the more reason that you should go off on your own, okay? Get the fuck away from me because you can! . . . Can't you?"

The driver often declined his offer to go off alone, but that night he went to the rooftop.

Tacyturn's eyes were closed as he actively scanned the world around him. He ignored all of the bodies he could sense down through the apartment building and focused on Sync, making sure he was safe. He gave Sync privacy and kept an eye on just the perimeter of the apartment, only checking in every so often. When he last checked, the freckled young man was playing with his vidphone and laying upside down on the couch.

A little bit after 8:00PM, Tacyturn's vidphone rang. Checking in on Sync with his scanner, he saw that Sync was calling him. He answered with a video call.

Before even saying anything, Sync looked upward, now knowing exactly where the driver was. He recognized the neon sign.

"I was going to ask you when you were going to be back, but apparently you haven't even fucking left, have you?"

Sync rolled himself off of the couch and headed out of the apartment, able to get out without the *Blade Runner* vidkey.

"I'll be up there in just a second. Is it raining? Of course it's fucking raining. Are you sure you want to come with, Bandit?" Tacyturn heard a demanding meow. "Okay, then let's go. You know, I think you've got a bit of an attitude—" Then the call ended.

After Sync hung up, he appeared on the rooftop just a few minutes later. Bandit started running around in circles, playing with the raindrops.

The young heir approached Tacyturn, knowing exactly where he was hiding.

"I was waiting for you to come back with the vidkey so that I can go out without having to bother you to get back in." Sync pocketed his hands and slouched. ". . . Can I go out on my own?"

Tacyturn nodded.

"No, I mean . . . I mean, I know I'm *allowed* to." He moved closer to the driver and nervously shuffled his feet. "I mean, *can* I? Do you think it's something I should try doing? If anything went wrong, I think I've learned enough to be able to protect myself, but . . . maybe not? No amount of training can change who I am, as determined as I might be."

"You can do anything, Sync."

Sync had to laugh and couldn't help a bit of a sassy reply, "I can't deflect bullets."

Tacyturn looked at him, but said nothing. The look in his eyes made it seem like he was reiterating what he just said.

"I appreciate your confidence, but that's not gonna work." Sync nervously walked in a circle. "I've been told so many things in my life, but I need to do something to prove it to *myself*. How can I fight The Nineteen if I can't even walk alone in the city? I mean, I was alone when I was following you, but you were always within yelling-for-help range. And I was fucking following you, which isn't very . . . independent. I'll probably get shanked or end up in another burning building or something if I'm alone. I'm sure you're not the only monster in this city, but at least I don't have to worry about you because you probably are one of the scariest ones." He quickly looked back at Tacyturn, angrily reacting even though the driver had said nothing and looked indifferent as usual. "You damn well know I mean that as a compliment."

Then Sync sighed. "I'm doing alright fighting, though? Really? Good enough that I should be able to walk through the city?"

"You won't need to fight."

"How do you know?"

When Tacyturn said nothing more, Sync said, "Well, I won't go far, so you're probably right. I'll be right back." He turned away, then turned back. "Hopefully. I'll probably run back. I'm good at running. Will you be here? I shouldn't be gone long."

The driver nodded.

"Well, then I won't need the vidkey."

It felt awkward walking away from Tacyturn to go into the city alone, so he did it very slowly.

Sync walked to the door that led down through the apartment building and hesitated, wondering if Tacyturn was going to follow. The driver didn't move and just closed his eyes again.

The young heir was a little disappointed as he heard the door close behind him and never open again. He stood out of sight down the stairs for a long time, waiting. His chest started to ache as he wondered why he was letting himself be so dependent on Tacyturn.

Sync didn't know what he would do without him—but he was about to find out.

Just as Tacyturn saw his scan of Sync head through the lobby and out into the street, Tacyturn stood up and followed his path directly above him along the rooftops.

Wherever the young redhead went, Tacyturn copied him flawlessly on a much more complicated landscape. He leapt across buildings and slid down poles, sneaking effortlessly along shadowy paths he remembered taking years prior, though now they were more complete with all of the construction being finished.

Sync was unaware of his presence all the way to the coffee bar.

As Sync went inside, Tacyturn glided onto the rooftop and crossed his arms, leaning into the darkness behind a Japanese neon ad. With his technology, he kept track of the young man—and also Bandit, who had decided to follow Tacyturn along the rooftops, too. She sat nearby on a neon dragon's head, cleaning her cloud-like paws that were getting muddy.

Tacyturn decided he didn't need to listen, so he just watched and waited. Sync's emotional state was nervous, but soon relaxed as he started to banter with the barista. Tacyturn thought about joining him as a surprise after he had been alone for a sufficient amount of time.

Just as he was deciding whether or not he would, someone that Tacyturn had tagged in his tech system arrived at the coffee bar. It was someone he had wronged before—a modest balding middle-aged German man in round black glasses named Ulrich Vogel.

Ulrich was armed, but not seemingly looking for trouble—just for coffee. He had not been part of the mob at the dance studio or outside of the cyber bar. Tacyturn figured that he started carrying a gun after going through what the driver did to him. Tacyturn was certain now that it was best for him to stay out of sight—Sync would gain more confidence that way, anyway.

A moment later, Tacyturn saw that the tagged individual said something to Sync. Sync's reaction was confused and annoyed. Deciding to use his pare tech to watch and listen, Tacyturn observed more closely what was going on below his feet. He was immediately privy to the fact that the conversation was about him.

"—named your custom drink Magenta Tiger, didn't you?" Ulrich asked.

"Yeah? The fuck do you care? Didn't anyone teach you to mind your own fucking business? What if I just like the fucking colour and I'm a fan of big stripy pussies?"

The man seemed to rightly pick up on Sync's defensive tone. He moved closer to Sync, who was unable to back away due to the counter being right there. He couldn't escape to another part of the coffee shop. He was cornered. He thought about getting physically aggressive—but decided against it. He convinced himself he wasn't being a coward—he was just being polite in a public setting. He thought about the fact that Tacyturn only ever moved if he needed to and tried to channel some of his patience and calmness.

The stranger's concerned tone dropped, trying to keep their conversation as private as he could, "You must have crossed paths with him before. What are you, sixteen? You're a little young to have to deal with that. I know people who can help you."

"I still don't see how that would be any of your fucking business."

"So, you do know who I'm talking about. I just want to let you know that you're not alone, whatever he did to you or your family."

Sync was trying to suppress any amusement as he started to just respond with a bit of underlying cheekiness.

"I do hope I *am* alone in how we met," he responded, clearly reminiscing about their sexual escapades.

Ulrich still seemed more sympathetic to Sync than understanding his subtext. "Ah, yes. Understandable." He patted Sync's arm and the young man yanked himself away. "We all hope that those who hurt us don't hurt anyone else. What did he do to you?"

"You first," Sync demanded. "What the fuck did he do to *you?*"

The way Ulrich told his story made it clear he had told it many times before.

"He came inside my home and shot my wife and I. As I chased after him, he shot me again and burned the house down with my wife still inside."

Sync couldn't stop showing a sad expression, but he was annoyed with how nosy the man was and how eager he seemed for sympathy. He had already prepared himself to never be surprised by anything that Tacyturn had done—though it was easier when he just didn't know.

Growing up in the Thornwryght family had already desensitized him quite a bit, but Sync didn't lose his sense of sympathy entirely. He had always grown up with a sense of pity—normally directed at himself.

When Sync said nothing, Ulrich asked, "You?"

"He fucked me more times than I can count," Sync said.

"Oh, dear, I'm sorry. That's terrible."

"No, it's not."

Sync was now starting to stifle his sympathies by being mischievous. He was still, above all, annoyed with the man butting into his business. He was uncomfortable with the social interaction, but he decided to go about it in an amusing way, hoping it would fend him off. He wanted to make sure no one else would approach him, either.

"I'm sorry?"

"I don't think you understand what I mean. I mean that he has fucked my brains out. Repeatedly."

Sync kept his serious expression as the colour drained from the man's face. The redhead was going to make him regret prying.

"He leaves me wanting more and my body craves him fucking me every second that I'm awake and dreams of it every second that I'm asleep. His sexual mastery is unparalleled. He touches me in ways I never knew were possible. Even when I think I've just had the biggest orgasm I've ever had, the next time he makes me come it's even more amazing. He leaves my asshole raw, my dick quivering and my throat burning. He's fucking perfect and one day I hope he'll be my husband so that I don't ever have to share him with anyone else."

Ulrich had slowly backed away from Sync. Tacyturn's expression softened with amusement, but a little bit of concern with how much he was being truthful and how much he was just messing around with the nosy German.

There was an obvious silence in the coffee bar—even the barista was hesitant to call out Sync's drink order to let him know they were done.

"Remember how I said it wasn't any of your fucking business?" Sync added with a chuckle. "That was a warning, bitch."

It was clear that Ulrich felt completely disrespected and looked as though he wanted to get physical to put Sync's inappropriateness in its place—but something was holding him back.

Sync could tell and laughed. "What's the deal? If you want to hit me, hit me."

"I don't hit children."

"Ha! I was born in '63▶▶. You can do math, can't you? Or do you need an abacus?"

Sync could see that most of the people eavesdropping were now no longer looking horrified like they were tempted to summon the police. They were now mildly amused and shocked with Sync's openness about his sexual escapades.

Ulrich scowled. "You're never going to grow up with an attitude like that. Not to mention a baby face I can't take seriously. I'd sooner shove a shnoolie into your face than my fist."

"A fuckin' what?" Sync groaned. "I don't want anything from you in my face, thanks. Just came here for coffee in my face." He thought his statement was stupid—but not as stupid as this nosy person's threat.

Tacyturn detected the death threat that Sync didn't due to being distracted by not knowing what the German had said. The driver knew he was talking about a pacifier.

"The iced and hot Magenta Tigers," the barista awkwardly uttered, trying to quickly interject once coffee was mentioned and before anyone else started talking again.

Sync kept his devious, yet pleasant smile and grabbed the neon drinks, thrilled to see that the iced one was coloured magenta with lines of white chocolate and caramel syrup around the inner edges of the cup—it was a very tiger-like look.

The young redhead went to leave, but Ulrich didn't want to let him go. He did not want to let the young man leave with the confident smirk he showed the German as he pushed the doors open with his back.

"You know he's playing pretend, don't you?" the older man said as he grabbed his own coffee that had just been finished and followed Sync. "There's no way he's going to be able to stand you for much longer. He's going to do something to you eventually, if he hasn't already. He's a sadist!"

"How do you know that?" Sync responded, still holding onto his smirk even though the German man was now in his face again.

The German man hesitated for a noticeable amount of time, enough time for Sync's eyebrows to raise, showing his skepticism—and his impatience.

Ulrich then removed his scarf and pulled back his tweed jacket and undershirt and revealed a scar in the shape of a bite mark on the back of his shoulder. Sync knew a bite mark had to be serious and deep for it to cause scarring. He also saw that there was an obvious molar missing on the bottom right. He realized he wasn't sure if Tacyturn was missing a molar or not—he thought he knew his body pretty well by then.

"And?" Sync decided not to act like it was a big deal, even though it was making the wheels in his head turn. Tacyturn would never tell him what he wanted—but maybe this random man just did. "*I'm* not fucking stupid. He's not going to hurt me."

"Someone needs to."

The old Sync would have just left the conversation now that he wasn't trapped anymore, but he felt like he should do the opposite of what his instincts were. He already was and it was working out fine. He also felt like he should defend Tacyturn—and learn more about him on top of it.

Tacyturn was noticing that Sync had again missed another threat and wondered if he was distracted by what Ulrich had just revealed.

"Listen. I think you just need to take a fucking moment to think about what has happened. Yes, he was probably the one who shot you and your wife. He was probably the one who lit the fire that burned your house down. Okay, he bit you really fucking hard and, I'm just saying, it looks like you didn't take real good care of it while it was healing. But everyone keeps forgetting that he's a hitman. Hitmen are *hired*. They are told what to do and do it, usually for money. It's just a job. I think you and everyone else against the Magenta Tiger need to get your fucking heads out of your asses."

Sync took a few steps backwards, still working on making his escape.

Now Tacyturn knew that Sync had been distracting himself by thinking of the next thing he was going to say and missed the threat that way.

Sync continued, "Do you know what that means? That means he had to be fucking *hired* by someone. I think you should be looking for the mastermind behind the acts. Could be someone you know. It's probably someone you know and probably someone you're close to. Probably someone you fucking trust." Sync shrugged and turned away, gesturing dramatically with the drinks. "Of course, it could also be some random mother fucker like me."

Ulrich began staring suspicious daggers into the young redhead.

As he left, Sync had one last thing to say, "Next time you see him, you should probably just fucking ask him instead of trying to kill him." Realizing that he may have just accidentally thrown away Tacyturn's possible faked death in a fire, he clumsily added, "I heard he may have died in Hellfire a couple months ago, though, so I might need to find a new hitman husband."

Sync wanted to run, but maintained a casual walk.

Above the coffee bar, Tacyturn watched as Ulrich stared at the young redhead for a long time. Once the older man saw what direction Sync was going, he went to talk to people in a nearby car, telling them that he thought he found the mastermind of the Magenta Tiger and that if the Magenta Tiger really was dead, he was possibly planning on creating a new one.

After just a moment of whispering about torture and murder, they all stepped out of the car, clearly armed and planning to act. There were two men and one woman who now joined the German, who was the only one who seemed apprehensive.

The four individuals started to follow Sync and Tacyturn stayed above them, moving along the rooftops again. Bandit went off to directly follow Sync, enticed by the aroma of whipped cream.

Once far enough into the darkness of an alley, the man in the very back of the line pulled a knife out of his jacket, preparing to use it soon. Tacyturn's magenta eye turned red.

Tacyturn immediately slid down the crooked side of a building and swiftly ran by, cutting the man's throat as he twirled him around into the adjacent alley. He laid him down and ran the dead man's own blade through the wound in his neck, cutting it a bit deeper, and discarded it nearby.

None of the other men had noticed and Tacyturn climbed back up the next building along their path, washing the blood from his hands and blade in the rain.

The rest of them started to whisper about pulling their guns out, but kept glancing over to people sitting on their balconies nearby, oblivious to the fact that the driver was moving along the balconies, too. A flash of lightning had revealed where Tacyturn was, but they were still being terribly unobservant.

Tacyturn could see that Sync was close, but still walking eagerly back to the apartment without knowing what was going on behind him.

Then when the pursuers realized one of their own was missing, they decided to follow suit and split up, so Tacyturn had to move quickly before any of them caught up with Sync.

Dropping down to the closest one, Tacyturn pressed his gun to the back of his neck and fired a single muffled shot. The woman had heard the gunshot and was now on high alert, whirling around and pointing her own gun.

Moments later, Tacyturn emerged from the darkness, dragging the corpse with him. The woman gaped at him. She fumbled in her jacket and pulled out a bounty cube.

As she rolled it open, she confirmed what she saw and immediately fired at Tacyturn.

The driver artfully dodged them, using the corpse to deflect bullets as he ran headfirst into the woman. Tacyturn disarmed her with a blade deep through her wrist and flipped her onto her stomach, breaking her arm behind her back. He dropped her as she writhed around in pain, deeming her no longer a threat.

He stole the bounty cube from her jacket and put it into his own pocket.

Tacyturn then reached into the back of the dead man's neck and pulled the bullet out of the wound, pocketing it. The woman watched as Tacyturn took her gun and fired a few shots into the same hole.

Then the woman struggled as Tacyturn fired the gun under her chin. The driver put the gun in her lifeless hand and then left to catch up with Ulrich.

Ulrich waited behind a wall as Sync walked down the street, about to pass him. The young man had stopped to look around, having heard the gunshots. It just made Sync want to get back to the apartment faster and he moved more quickly down the street towards the hidden Ulrich.

Ulrich was slowly pulling his gun out of his jacket to prepare to shoot the young lover of the infamous Magenta Tiger. He fumbled with the gun as he trembled with uncertainty.

Just as Sync passed Ulrich, Tacyturn tugged the German behind the building and threw him hard onto the ground, disarming him at the same time. The maneuver had been so quick and silent, Sync heard nothing but his own footsteps and continued his trip back to the apartment.

Ulrich gaped up at Tacyturn in horror, staring fearfully at his burning red eye.

"I-It's *you*! You're alive! He does work with you!" he gasped. "Is he your mastermind?"

Tacyturn didn't react. He only stared at Ulrich as he slowly stumbled to his feet.

Angrily thinking about his dead wife, Ulrich attacked Tacyturn with his fists. They had a fist fight, but not for long. The German man managed to punch Tacyturn in the face, but his eyes were already bruised, anyway. The driver hardly reacted to it. He allowed it to happen.

Ulrich knew he would lose to a direct brawl with Tacyturn and instead scooped up his fallen gun after the successful punch and tried to catch up to Sync, knowing that he had a chance to at least try to shoot someone clearly important to the Magenta Tiger. Sync looked like an easy and fragile target.

Tacyturn didn't let him get far, following him closely through the streets. He knew exactly where Sync was and Ulrich didn't. The German man was scrambling to catch sight of the young redhead. He was also terrified because he lost sight of Tacyturn.

Trying to see if he could spot Sync again, Ulrich climbed up onto a nearby building via a fire escape. As he turned wildly around, he caught sight of the young redhead through an alley, now with a cat across his shoulders licking cream off of his coffee straw.

As Ulrich hopped off the building and walked across a sunken structure, he heard a gunshot, felt a bullet zip by, and then heard the sound of glass shattering. Just as he was taking a step onto a glass sunroof above an indoor garden, it blew to pieces and he fell hard through it and landed into what felt like a jungle.

Landing gracefully next to him was Tacyturn. The driver effortlessly picked Ulrich up and threw him hard against the wall, pointing his gun right at his heart.

Ulrich held his breath, but the driver didn't shoot. He was waiting for his next move. His eye had also calmed and turned grey. Ulrich thought about the advice that Sync had given him.

"Who hired you to kill my wife and I?" he desperately inquired before the hitman could kill him.

"Your wife and her lover," Tacyturn responded in a German accent.

Tacyturn didn't want to tell Ulrich anything, but he thought he should. He wanted to reward him for taking Sync's bold advice, just in case it one day caught up to Sync in his favour.

"What?" Ulrich's face twisted up into disbelieving shock.

While he was stunned, Tacyturn yanked Ulrich forward and pulled back his jacket to see the bite mark—he wanted to see what Sync had seen. It was a bad scar. His eye briefly pixelated to white.

"Did my wife make you do *that*?" Ulrich's sarcastic tone made it clear he was grasping on to a bit of hope that Tacyturn might be lying.

The driver pushed him back up against the wall. "It was a permanent reminder of your loss and guilt."

"What do I have to be guilty about?" Ulrich barked.

Tacyturn said nothing—but his stare made the German's angry demeanor crumble. He had nothing to hide from the man who had been there for all of it.

"I know I should have never cheated on her," he defeatedly uttered. "You showed up when I thought I was already at rock bottom." His tone turned venomous. "Then you dug me a hole."

"I handed you the shovel, but I did not make you dig."

Ulrich bit his lip, knowing he was right. "Is she still alive?"

"I never shot her."

"But the f-fire! You must have killed her in the fire you started!"

"I didn't start the fire."

Ulrich's expression turned blank and he went limp, staring into nothing. Tacyturn let go of him and he sagged.

"I will kill you if you even look at him again," Tacyturn threatened, his right eye becoming red once more.

The old man snapped out of his stupor. "I swear I won't touch the Winzling."

Tacyturn put his scarred hand around his throat and squeezed, forcing him to his knees.

Ulrich coughed, struggling to correct the mistake he thought he made.

"Ack! I swear I won't hire anyone like you to touch the Winzling, either!" The hand squeezed harder. "I won't look at him! I won't even think about him! Please stop!"

Tacyturn shoved him onto the floor covered in broken glass. He wet his hands in the rain that poured in through the broken glass roof, then wiped the watered-down blood onto the man's jacket. He turned to leave, pressing the bloody bullet from his pocket deep into the dirt of a nearby potted plant.

"But the bounty on you is still too good to give up on, isn't it?" Ulrich mumbled as he watched Tacyturn leaving, thankful to still be alive and not be abused any more than he already was.

He knew how lucky he was—Tacyturn had just revealed he was still alive. Perhaps he hoped no one would believe a sad aging geezer.

The driver paused and turned to look back at Ulrich, revealing his eye was grey again.

"*Das ist nur recht un billig,*" Tacyturn said.

Just as Ulrich pulled out his gun to shoot Tacyturn, the driver disappeared and the bullet hit the vine-covered wall.

Tacyturn made his way back up to the roof of the apartment just as Sync was making his way through the building. The young man had snuck in behind someone else who had used their access disc to get inside.

The driver sat in exactly the same way he had been when Sync left just as the young heir appeared again.

Sync shook his head, comically disappointed. He clicked his tongue. "Ah, right where I fucking left you. I know you say you don't do anything if you're not told what to do, but this is just fucking lazy, you know? Just calling it like I fucking see it. I think you need a hobby."

The young redhead offered Tacyturn a hot coffee. Tacyturn opened his magenta and blue eyes and looked at it. He seemed apprehensive.

"What the fuck is wrong? Have you never had your own coffee before?"

Tacyturn shook his head.

"Ah, I guess my father did make it into a privilege one earns. No one knows what needs to be done to earn it from him. I think only our mothers were ever given coffee, so maybe you have to suck his dick to get it?" He shrugged. "Don't want to think too hard about that, do we? Well, this one's for you because you've more than fucking earned it," Sync said as he shoved it into Tacyturn's hands. "And not because you—I mean—ah, I don't think you ever? Don't answer that. But you did—I mean to me—I was there, so—I mean, that's not what this coffee is for. Not that your skill wasn't prize worthy—"

He awkwardly turned away, pinching the bridge of his nose, forcing his brain to stop floundering.

The young man flatly stated, "I didn't know what kind of coffee you liked, so I asked them to invent one that tasted like a spiced biscuit and to make the same thing for me, but with ice."

Sync pressed the cold drink against his hot and embarrassed cheek. When he looked back at the driver, his face bore the same calmness as always.

"Let's just say the coffee is for your unparalleled patience for me running my mouth."

Tacyturn sipped his coffee, pleased with the warmth that enveloped him. Even though he knew coffees really were just frivolous treats, he still could not entirely subdue the feeling of veneration by being served one by a Thornwryght.

Sync eventually relaxed—just in time to be angry about the temperature.

"Jesus, it's *fucking cold*," Sync grumbled as he blinked up at the rain, trying to find a spot that was covered to stand.

Bandit had already curled up under a vent, licking at the raindrops that dropped from the edge of the metal.

The driver looked at Sync as he was sipping his iced coffee, pointing out the obvious with minimal expression. He offered up his hot coffee.

"I wanted an iced fucking coffee, stop looking at me like that! Shut up!" he huffed. "I don't like waiting for hot coffees to cool the fuck down and then in, like, three minutes they're already fucking gross and lukewarm and taste like they've been sitting out all night in the sun. I mean, sitting out all night . . . on a hot night. Obviously, there would be no fucking sun. My father's favourite drink is always iced, isn't it? And I never hear shit from that even though it's always been fucking raining when I've gotten one. Granted, I'm in a heated car when I get them, but . . . what was I saying? Shut the fuck up!"

Once Sync stopped talking, Tacyturn expectantly opened his jacket up.

Without another word—and still looking angry—Sync climbed up on the HVAC and huddled up into Tacyturn's warm body as he wrapped his jacket around him. They sat for a moment in silence, watching the rain and admiring the city's lights.

"Are you ever afraid?" Sync asked him out of nowhere.

Tacyturn didn't respond, so he further explained.

"I mean, are you afraid of going back out there as often as you'd like? Because of all of those people who want to hurt you? I met one at the coffee shop. He was really fucking annoying, but I gave him shit to think about."

Sync avoided mentioning that the German stranger had also given the heir a lot to think about.

Tacyturn reached into his jacket and pulled out the bounty cube. Sync took it and opened it up. It revealed all the known information about Tacyturn—very little.

"Holy shit! You're worth a ton! Good thing I'm already rich or this might be tempting as fuck! This is fucking new, isn't it? They put this out back in August?"

"Just this past week."

"But what's the point? People think you're dead, don't they?"

"Not until they see a body."

Sync had to chuckle. "Well, good fucking luck. You're not going to be taken down by anyone. You're too wicked cool."

"The bounty will bring on professionals that I don't have tagged."

"You're still too wicked cool to let anyone get you. But I understand now. You're not afraid, you're just being smart about it. You'd have to kill everyone who tried to kill you." Then Sync realized, "Shit, I would have one of these, wouldn't I? If they had seen my face? Or at least I would be a part of yours."

Sync flipped the cube around, revealing more information as he folded it in different ways. It had a photo of Tacyturn from when he was eighteen. It had his right eye constantly changing colours, figuring they were unsure of what the real colour was.

"Looks like this bounty is in Hollywood only. You won't have to worry about it when we leave, right? You just won't come back here. It would be stupid. You wouldn't walk into a room full of people who want to kill you, right?"

Sync sipped his coffee as he had a thought.

"Like I'm going to do. I mean, a peninsula full of people, but . . . is that really what I'm going to do?" he asked. "Will that work? And even if it does work, what's going to happen when everything goes to plan? At least with the outcome where I get shot dead, I know what the future holds. But what if I become the next in line officially? What then?"

Sync felt Tacyturn hold him tighter.

"Whatever your father wants."

"You'll go back to being his bodyguard? You'll never be around!" he whined. "Father goes off on trips around the world all the fucking time. He'll probably still hate me. Who knows what he'll make you do. I don't like that."

"I'm supposed to work for him until one of us dies."

"I hope he dies first," Sync mumbled, darkly.

He had been secretly hoping one of The Nineteen was going to kill Ephraym to try to take his place, then Sync would just have to show up and maybe fight one person for the throne, taking it the same way they did.

"If I lose my credibility, trust in me will fade away."

Sync burst dramatically out of Tacyturn's jacket and climbed into his lap, straddling him.

"Then you'll just have to find a new fucking career!" Sync thought he saw a skeptical look in his eyes. "You don't have to waste your talents. You can just go back to being a stunt person! Just try not to lose anymore teeth doing that, okay?"

Sync paused to see what Tacyturn's reaction would be. The driver didn't react—he already knew how Sync knew. The young heir didn't ask how he lost it, so he didn't correct his assumption.

Moving along the conversation, Sync hummed in thought. "This fucking bounty will make it hard to come back here, though. You might have to change your look." Sync leaned in and pulled the tie out of his hair, releasing his magenta pony tail. "Ugh, that would be a fucking shame, though. You look so fucking good. With your forever black eyes, it just looks so wicked cool!"

Sync peered closer, thinking one of Tacyturn's eyes looked redder than it had just before he left to get coffee. Then the young redhead gently ran his fingers through his hair on both sides of his head, admiring his face.

"You should be *on screen* with close-ups. You would play badass characters with little dialogue and all action. We could remake *Blade Runner* and look like geniuses, although I suppose that's sort of abusing our power like my father fucking does. Maybe when I take over, I'll turn the syndicate into a legit filmmaking company. The peninsula is big enough for tons of sets. The mansion, too. We could rent some of the sets out to other filmmakers and make money that way on the side. Instead of fucking up our world's timeline, we'll create our own fictional alternate universes!"

Sync came back from his distracted thoughts to see that Tacyturn was enjoying the affection he was getting. He could tell Tacyturn was trying to hide it, though.

"Or you could just retire early and get pampered for the rest of your life. I don't think anyone has ever coddled you. I'm definitely not very fucking good at it, but I can learn. You seem to like your hair being touched. This is good fucking news because I like touching it! Is there anything else you like?" He leaned in close to Tacyturn, fumbling nervously with the driver's jacket. "You'll let me know if there's ever anything I can do for *you*, right?"

"You'll know."

Sync had to laugh. "Really? All this time you've been trying to tell me how important it is that I need to fucking tell people what I want and you're just not gonna do that yourself?"

"I am not an important person," he said.

"You don't think it's important for me to know what you want?" Sync asked.

Tacyturn shook his head.

The young heir hummed in thought. "Maybe what you want will match what I want."

"Be in sync, you mean?"

Sync laughed again as he stared off into the rain that was picking up. "Ha, yeah! Maybe we'll be in sync." He added softly with a yearning purr, "You'll definitely be."

Sync watched the droplets of rain falling from the sky and landing into puddles, becoming one with the other raindrops. The redhead climbed off of the HVAC and walked into the heavier downpour, suddenly having a desire to be enveloped by it.

"I feel like it might be possible that we want the same thing. I mean, you're up here in a place that I always fantasize about being. On a rooftop at night . . . in a neon city . . . in the rain . . ." Sync walked closer to the edge of the building to look over. "It's why I had always thought about it being a good place for me to . . . take my final step."

Instantly after finishing the last word, Sync felt a hand tenderly grip his wrist. The young man smiled and looked up at Tacyturn.

"Not anymore, though. I already did that, remember? We've got it on video. Besides, I want to see what the fuck happens next. I absolutely don't want to miss the next cool thing you do."

Tacyturn gently let go and Sync sighed dreamily and looked around.

"I still love being up here, though. You must like it, too, because you picked it as your place to hang out. Or did you pick it for me? You don't have to do everything for me, you know."

Tacyturn said nothing.

"Now I fantasize about better things in a location like this. It would be the perfect place for a first kiss, but we're well beyond that, aren't we?" Sync pointed out with a chuckle. "We've been more than kissing for almost two *months*, but it feels like a whirlwind amount of time."

Sync wasn't sure why he was in such a good mood, but he didn't fight it or doubt it. He just felt like he was where he was meant to be—or maybe the caffeine was kicking in.

He continued, still sounding like he was on cloud nine, "It would also be a fucking amazing place to get proposed to." Then, he snorted, "Or a good place to fuck."

When he turned around to look at Tacyturn, he was down on one knee. Sync felt his chest go hot and his freckled cheeks flushed. He stared at the driver, unsure of how to react.

Then, after a second, Tacyturn started to undo Sync's belt.

Sync laughed and playfully shoved him away—which really just pushed himself backwards. Tacyturn's actions showed some mischievousness, even though he had virtually the same expression he always did.

"You mother fucker!" Sync breathed. "You are getting better at being funny, though. You really got me good!" He grasped his chest and sighed heavily. "I clearly set myself up for that."

Tacyturn stood up and gently put his hand under Sync's chin, examining his wet face. Deciding Sync was getting too soaked, Tacyturn put Sync's hood up and led him back to the area where the rain wasn't as heavy.

Sync was still feeling the lingering effects of having been so stunned.

"Were you serious about doing it up here?" Sync asked, trying to amuse himself to stop feeling shaken. "You know, be *in Sync*." He took a moment to chuckle awkwardly. "Or did you just choose that one for the good timing?"

"I don't have a ring, but you will," Tacyturn responded.

Sync paused as he fumbled with fixing his belt—he was unable to decipher the driver's latent emotion that time.

". . . O-Oh?"

"The Thornwryght signet ring will be yours."

". . . Oh."

XVIII.

"Suddenly we have no time at all."

SYNC WAS CONTINUING TO DO well learning to fight, now doing even better after his walk in the city and their conversation on the rainy neon rooftop—he was still riding on cloud nine.

He was proud of himself for going out into the night to get a couple of coffees without getting into any sort of trouble—or needing a babysitter. It added to his main motivation, his growing enthusiasm to become a hero that Tacyturn could depend on if he ever needed it again. He had stood up for Tacyturn and he was proud of it.

That idea was still strange to the driver, but he was touched. Tacyturn tried to disregard that feeling, though, because he thought that it was dangerous for Sync to care too much about one person—especially a disposable person like a crime syndicate bodyguard.

The only thing that Sync was against was learning to attack if he wasn't the one being being provoked. He wanted to learn how to defend.

When it was time to go back to claim his empire, Sync refused to attack anyone unless they attacked him first. Tacyturn thought that was respectable, but knew he had to train Sync to be able to dodge whatever came first.

Sync also said he wouldn't attack anyone unless they attacked Tacyturn first, too. The driver wasn't so keen on that. He didn't know how to get Sync to care less about Tacyturn's well-being. Being worried about someone else could cause distractions.

Tacyturn had also offered to teach Sync how to drive like a stunt driver, but he dismissed it.

"I don't even know how to *drive*. Tobyas used to tell me that if I ever got behind the wheel, the car would probably end up going over a cliff. There are a lot of cliffs on the peninsula."

Sync also figured he would probably not need to drive—but using a gun would be useful.

Learning to use a gun eventually caught on as Sync tried his damnedest to mimic his teacher. They practiced with the light burst setting on the prop gun that burned whatever it hit. His aim became very precise and he no longer reacted to kickback. His arms felt stronger because of it and it pleased him—they still looked like noodles, so he wasn't as pleased as he wanted to be.

The driver did his best to train Sync the way he wanted to be trained, applying it to situations with guns. He didn't want to learn how to find weaknesses and openings and fire the moment he saw them—he only wanted to be able to fire back first with the same amount of threat that was aimed at him.

"If someone points a gun at you, you must point one back."

"What if it's an accident that they point one at me?" Sync had asked.

"You must shoot first and ask questions later."

"Is that . . . really the way to fucking do that? I guess that's the way the syndicate does it, is it?"

"They should have been more careful."

"But they haven't even shot me yet!"

"Just pointing a gun at someone is very dangerous."

"Let's say that I wanted to only shoot someone if I knew that they were actually going to shoot me . . . Is there a way to tell?"

Tacyturn explained that Sync should keep an eye on the trigger finger and where it was—if it's in position to fire, the person is serious or stupid.

Both were dangerous.

If they just wanted to scare him, they would likely keep it off of the actual trigger to keep it from accidentally firing. He also explained how to know when certain guns were loaded and that the safety was off.

He explained further that Sync should see if they're aligning the front and back sights, looking down the gun with possibly one eye—if they're doing it right. Sync should check to see if they are bracing themselves with their stance, ready for kickback.

Then there was the final tell that should make Sync act within a fraction of a second—if they take in a sharp and focused breath, they are likely about to fire upon the next exhale. At this point, Sync would definitely have to shoot the person—not a warning shot, but shoot them somewhere that would kill them fast. He pointed out every place on his own body.

Sync watched as Tacyturn acted out everything he should look for and took note, even though he would jest sometimes.

"What if the person pointing a gun at me is super fucking handsome? That would be a problem, wouldn't it?" Sync had teased once.

"The barrel of the gun will be the bigger problem."

"What if there's more than one gun?"

"Always look for the biggest threat and handle them first."

Tacyturn was not blind to noticing that they were acting more and more domestic in the underground apartment. Every night they slept together and every morning they woke up together. Sync liked Tacyturn's warm and protective hands on his body, especially putting a hand on his throat, just resting there and getting hot. The driver never did it himself—Sync would place it there. Sync wasn't sure when he had discovered this, but there was something comforting to Sync about it now, like his hand being there shielded him from anything else at his throat. Tacyturn moved it as soon as the young man was asleep.

Bandit was even snuggling up around Sync's neck some nights. She also liked to lean up against the large scar on Tacyturn's head and purr—he wondered if she thought the mechanical whirring was his own purr and was responding to it.

They were getting into a routine and it was feeling strange for the both of them, but they appreciated the predictability in their own ways. They weren't worried about the unexpected.

Sync was getting as comfortable as he used to be in solitude—but now he wasn't alone.

Tacyturn's life was predictable for the first time—but his instinct told him to fight it.

Every time Sync wanted to thank Tacyturn, he would gently touch the back of Tacyturn's head—the first gesture of affection he had ever given him back in the cabin. Tacyturn never did it back.

The only thing that was unexpected was when the young man revealed a side of himself in the bedroom that Tacyturn hadn't been ready for—and didn't think he ever would be. But he had an idea what had sparked it—meeting Ulrich and hearing the shit he had to say about the Magenta Tiger.

When Sync tried to get Tacyturn to choke him while they were fooling around, he refused. He had then tried to get Tacyturn to bite him and

Tacyturn wouldn't.

"I will never hurt you," he said, firmly.

Because he had to explain himself, Sync was suddenly very flustered. "What if it's something that I w—that I *like?*"

When the driver said nothing, it triggered Sync's anger to hide his embarrassment.

"What the fuck is wrong with that? I . . . like the idea of being bitten or having my hair pulled. Something about getting choked or getting slapped on the ass, or—" Sync's face went bright red. "But not just by anyone. You. I wouldn't trust anyone else. I don't know why this is how I am. I fucking deserve it, for sure, if that helps."

"I could never do any of that to you."

"Why, because I'm a Thornwryght? Don't fucking give me that!" Sync barked, pulling Tacyturn by his tie to keep him from getting off of him. "You're a violent person, Tac. I saw you choke that woman in the cyber bar!"

Sync bit his lip, realizing that he had revealed that he had followed him in there.

"I was far enough away that I couldn't hear anything and then I left after I saw it. I didn't know what else you were going to do to her and I didn't want to see it. I thought it was because it scared me, but I think a part of me was . . . jealous. I realized it's not really that weird to want to be . . . manhandled, is it? I didn't even think about it being something I shouldn't be embarrassed by enjoying until—"

Sync stopped, not wanting to tell Tacyturn that the German had told him that he was a sadist, which he discovered would be a perfect match for his own personal desires that he had previously been afraid to explore. He was just realizing at that moment that it may not have been true.

The bite was real, but it may have just been part of an act he was told to do. It was too late to take back what he was saying, though. But he wanted to be honest.

"I just never knew the right person to make me . . . crave it, not fear it."

Sync could see Tacyturn was torn between thoughts. He knew the driver was violent, but he hid it from the young man unless it was necessary to protect him. He allowed Tacyturn to climb off of him and sit at the edge of the bed.

Sync thought he was preparing to answer, but he said nothing.

"I don't understand why you won't show me a little bit of the other side of you. I know you're a monster, Tac."

Tacyturn's eyes met his—he couldn't tell if he was troubled by what he said.

"Maybe it's the Thornwryght blood in me, but I'm really fucking turned on by the fact that you're a cold-blooded professional killer. I'm so into it that you're with *me*, even though I'm clearly not worthy. I'm not made of the same stuff as you to be that cool, but I really admire that you are. You don't need to hide any part of you from me. You're so talented at being wicked and I just would like it if you weren't afraid to get your hands dirty with *me*."

Tacyturn turned away and looked down at his scarred hands. Still, he said nothing.

Sync gently touched his hands. "I know you won't really hurt me, because I *am* fucking afraid of getting hurt . . . but I'm not afraid of getting rough. I'd be honoured to take part in what you do best. I bet you could really rock my fucking world. I mean, more than you already do."

Annoyed with the driver's usual silence, Sync grabbed the rope around his neck and tightened it to show he was serious.

"I bet you'd do it if I was bulletproof!"

Tacyturn gently loosened the rope. "I would gladly let you do whatever you wanted to me."

Sync huffed and turned away. "This is fucking stupid. I don't know why I don't just keep my fucking mouth shut. I keep on fucking talking and I thought I was doing a really decent job for once, but I never find that magic word that clinches what I'm trying to say."

Tacyturn was surprised that Sync was ignoring his actual magic words for getting Tacyturn to do what he wanted him to do. The driver was waiting for him to drop a command to force him to do it, but he never did it. He figured the only reason must be that he wasn't as serious about it as he was making it seem—or he was testing him.

Tacyturn was used to being constantly tested.

Then Sync got an idea. "Wait, what if we have a magic word? A safe word? You know about that, right?"

Tacyturn was familiar—he had always been instructed to ignore them.

"We'll pick a random and uncommon word that I can say if you're going to hurt me in a way that I don't like." Sync scooted back over to him.

"So, you don't have to be worried about actually hurting me."

The driver looked at him, clearly inquiring about what the word might be.

Sync hummed in thought, then said the first word that came to his head.

"Chauffeur?"

The young man wasn't certain he saw it, but it seemed like Tacyturn flinched.

Without another word, the driver stood up and left the room.

"Wait, what the fuck is wrong with you?" Sync asked as Tacyturn he disappeared. "I—! That's—!" He stumbled over his words. "You're not just a fucking driver to me!" he called out. "That's not what I fucking meant! It's just a word that I would never say while we're—ah, FUCK!"

Sync fell out of the bed as he tried to scramble quickly out of it.

He stared at the ceiling. "Are you fucking kidding me?"

Knowing that he had already screwed up the previous conversation, Sync sighed. Tacyturn had a right to not be into the same thing as him— but it puzzled him because it seemed like something he would be into with how vicious he was. It was the only reason that Sync had even felt confident enough to ask.

Then Sync realized that maybe that's not how Tacyturn was at all— maybe that was all enforced by others.

Maybe Sync was the only one seeing the true Tacyturn.

He took a moment to stare at the neon stars on the ceiling before getting up and finding Tacyturn.

When Sync emerged from the bedroom, the driver was leaning up against the frame of the digital window. Tacyturn was staring out at a street market.

The young man approached him and leaned against the wall a few feet behind him.

"How much of you is who you are and how much is who other people made you become?" Sync asked. "Who is the Magenta Tiger and who is Tacyturn?"

He was not expecting a response to a tough question, but he wanted Tacyturn to think about it—and know that he was thinking about it, too.

"I heard some of those fuckers before the fire. They called you Magenta

Tiger. It was also on your bounty cube. I guess I just wanted to say that that's a pretty wicked cool name. Maybe I'll make that the syndicate's new logo since the current one is shit and it already looks like a tiger when you squint at it. I already made it into a new coffee beverage. Maybe it'll catch on. Maybe my new signet ring."

Tacyturn's expression softened, but he said nothing.

"What if I don't want my father's throne, though?" Sync asked. "Maybe you and I can just live here in Hollywood . . . or just somewhere else and we can use the name. It's a much nicer name than Thornwryght. But fuck those 'Y's, right? We can't take your last name because apparently you don't have one, do you? Did my father take it from you?" Sync didn't even wait to see if the driver would answer. "Then I guess we'll be Tacyturn and Synclare Holliwood."

He glanced over at Tacyturn whose back was still towards him.

"It'll be a last name that's not attached to my family's corruption!" Then, he sighed. "Not that changing a last name will just magically erase the corruption my family caused. Especially to you . . ."

Tacyturn knew that Sync not only wanted their interactions to be on an equal level, but that Sync also wanted their future together to be mutual. Sync, again, was avoiding the words that would force the driver to give him exactly what he wanted. Tacyturn was stunned by this, but also moved by it. But he wasn't sure what the future was.

He was destined to be killed by Synclare, according to Ephraym. He was merely avoiding it in his borrowed time.

Wanting to fill the awkward silence, Sync continued, "Sometimes I want to see what 1983 would be like if my family hadn't meddled. Did we do something amazing or hellacious?" He sighed. "I don't know if I can live with that constant tension of duality."

Tacyturn spoke, but didn't turn around. "Your father's legacy is your right, but what you want to do with it may differ from his vision."

"What I want has nothing to do with the syndicate," Sync said.

Tacyturn waited for him to continue.

After a long pause, the redhead added, "I don't want anything if you're not there with me."

"I will do whatever you want me to do, but I don't want to be your weakness, Sync."

"What do you mean?"

"If you care about someone, their fate decides yours."

Sync gestured angrily. "Stop talking in fucking riddles, Tac!"

"If anyone found out about us, we'd be at their mercy."

Sync grabbed Tacyturn's shoulder to get him to turn around. He did.

"What *about* us?"

The driver shook his head. "I advise you not to give it a name."

The young man was starting to look upset. "I *do* have a name for it," he said, defiantly.

Tacyturn gently put his fingertips on the young man's lips to keep him from saying anything further. "What if you had to prove yourself by killing someone under that name?"

Sync slapped his hand away. "I wouldn't fucking do it!" He paused, then asked, "Would you?"

"I would make sure not to have anyone that met the requirement."

The young heir hugged himself and turned away.

Nearby, Tacyturn's vidphone cube lit up. He ignored it.

"What are we doing, Tac?" His voice cracked.

"We're working on getting you home."

"Things don't always go to fucking plan," Sync growled, not happy with the response. "Because of fucking weaknesses . . . like me."

Tacyturn sighed. It was enough to get Sync's attention and he looked back at him. "If I let you be my weakness, I might fail you."

"You could never fail me!"

"I'm here to fight for you."

"You don't have to fight *everything*," Sync said. "If you're actively fighting off something in your own heart, you'll also fail, you know."

"I can only do what I'm told, Sync."

Sync stared at Tacyturn for a long moment as he felt his heart drop into his stomach.

"Is that all this is? Like every other time with everyone else? With so many other fucking people, I'm just . . . another one," Sync whimpered. "You're just . . . fucking me because I want you to fuck me? You're just playing house with me? You're only affectionate when I want you to be? You never initiate anything, I always have to come to you. Do you tease everyone like you one day plan to tie the knot? But that's not the fucking kind of knot you tie, is it?"

Then Sync suddenly realized something.

"I've never even seen you smile. I don't even fucking make you smile," he said pitifully.

"You could."

"I don't mean LIKE THAT!" Sync shouted. "It's not the same if I just fucking TELL you to do it! Why don't you ever smile? Did my father tell you to never let yourself be happy? Or does it fucking hurt to smile somehow? Did getting shot in the head make you forget how to?"

Tacyturn's silence only angered Sync more.

"You're only stuck with me because my father is making you . . . Did he ask you to pretend to like me to make me trust you?" Sync grabbed his own head and turned away. "This is just how my whole fucking life is! Why have I been purposely blinding myself from the obvious truth? My father made someone sacrifice himself for a fucking stupid family sacrament, my father paid whores to take my virginity away because I was so pathetic, and now, NOW—!"

Sync whirled back around, clenching his fists. "My father sent you here just to make me PLAY PRETEND! He wanted to see what I'd do having control over one person before he'd ever let me control an ENTIRE FUCKING ORGANIZATION!" He sobbed, "LOOKS LIKE I'D JUST BLINDLY FUCK EVERYONE AND THINK THAT I WAS IN LOVE WITH THEM ALL!"

He slid down the wall and sat on the ground as he added, softly, "And I'd truly believe that they were all in love with me, too." Sync put his face into the cradle his arms made and cried. "Why did I fall so fucking hard?"

Tacyturn remained quiet and still and stared at nothing.

After a long moment, Sync lifted his wet eyes from his arms, but did not look up at the driver. He was teetering between sad and angry.

The young redhead took on an accusing tone. "Why did YOU make it SO FUCKING EASY?"

From Tacyturn's expression, it seemed he wasn't sure what Sync meant, but he still wasn't speaking. So Sync let himself continue. "The first time I asked you to fuck me, you didn't have to kiss me so much and so sweetly . . . but you DID. You didn't have to take me on my back, staring into my eyes, but YOU DID! You didn't have to put your hands in mine, BUT YOU

DID!" He looked desperately up at Tacyturn. "YOU DID! WERE THOSE PART OF JUST DOING WHAT YOU'RE TOLD?"

Tacyturn could tell Sync was still reaching for an answer he wanted to hear. Sync could tell by the look in his eyes that the answer was not going to be what he wanted to hear. Sync choked up, wishing he would just stop talking—but he wasn't done yet.

"What exactly did my father tell you to do? With me?"

Tacyturn said nothing.

"I—" Sync took in a deep breath and let it out slowly. "I *want* you to tell me what my father wanted you to do with me."

Tacyturn turned away from him and Sync thought, for a moment, he was showing a brief moment of refusal. But then the young man heard and saw his father out of the corner of his eye. His chest felt momentarily twisted up in fear that his father had arrived at the apartment.

When he turned to look, the large projected screen had turned on and a life-sized image of Ephraym Thornwryght was floating before him. He was standing in his office, where he usually made his video calls. It was clearly from a vidcall that he had with Tacyturn. By checking the timestamp, he knew it was when they were already together in the cabin.

His father's video image was jumping through the same four repeated lines.

"I want you to keep him unharmed."

"I want you to stay by his side."

"I want you to do whatever is necessary to toughen that little shit up."

"I want you to do what you can to gain his trust."

Sync slowly stood up and stared at the screen, moving closer to it. Just when he thought his heart couldn't crumble a little bit more, it did.

"I knew I should have just shut the fuck up for once," Sync mewled.

Then, very suddenly, Sync began throwing angry fists at the image of his father. It only frustrated him more when he hit nothing but air. He was nearly toppling over from the force of the aggression and it was just pissing him off further. He angrily yelled.

He then whipped around towards Tacyturn like he was going to hit him, but stopped. He stared at the driver who continued to have the same expression he always did.

Sync really wanted to hit him, but he didn't have a solid reason—his father was the one who was making Tacyturn do everything he did. But Sync wondered why Tacyturn went as far as he did to follow all of his Thornwryght orders.

They could have just become friends and Sync would have trusted him and cared deeply about him. Sync trusted him and cared about him before they had ever had sex—it was what made Sync want it in the first place. He had also been developing a schoolboy-ish crush, which did help, but Sync had crushes on many different people he deemed cool—mostly out-of-reach celebrities.

If Tacyturn had tried seducing him at the cabin, it may have gone differently—he wouldn't have been into it then.

"I want . . ."

The young redhead nearly backed out of what he was going to ask, but then it seemed like Tacyturn was willing to do anything for him at that moment. Sync wasn't sure why he felt that, but he could see it in Tacyturn's eyes. Sync forced himself to be confident in his demand.

"I want you to stand where my father is."

Without hesitation, Tacyturn walked into the image of Ephraym Thornwryght and lined himself up exactly with his face and chest.

Sync approached and stared at them. He wasn't sure what he was looking to see or feel, but he was waiting to feel something. He wanted to see who he would lock onto—Ephraym, Tacyturn or both.

Then Sync threw a punch as hard as he could into their merged faces. The floating screen flickered and disappeared, malfunctioning due to the strike the tech had just taken.

Tacyturn didn't react like an average person would have, but it did cause him to take a step to the side to catch his stance. Sync couldn't tell if he had done that on purpose, or if his strike had just been that good due to the driver's training—it was just another moment of uncertainty when it came to Tacyturn's intentions.

Sync had ultimately pretended that he was hitting his father, so he did get a little bit of satisfaction from that. He was using Tacyturn to get that satisfaction, though, so he also hated himself a little bit more. He had a deep feeling in his Thornwryght gut that he was doing exactly what he was expected to.

A still of his father cut through Tacyturn again—Ephraym's expression looked proud, like he knew Sync had just done what he was supposed to do as a Thornwryght.

Sync grabbed Tacyturn's shirt and pulled him forward out of the image of his father, hiding it.

"I want you to get rid of my father," Sync sternly said.

Tacyturn wrapped his head around all of the layers that statement offered. There was something familiar about the words, but he couldn't pinpoint why. He went with the obvious meaning as the still of Ephraym dissipated behind him. A still darkness enveloped them both again.

"So, I *am* just another fucking job?" Sync suddenly sounded very calm, but his voice was still brittle. "You've been dealing with my father's shit for seven years. Why did I think I would be any fucking different than anything else you've ever been told to do?"

He stared at the Thornwryght logo on Tacyturn's tie.

"If you had been sent to save Brayd, what would have happened to me? Would my father have even bothered to have you pick me up on the way out?"

"I was sent to save Brayd, but I was too late, so your father sent me to you."

The truth was like a fresh cigarette burn to Sync's already shattered heart. He continued to stare at the crime syndicate logo like it was laughing at him.

". . . Ah, fuck. It's my fucking fault because I still keep fucking talking." Sync let go of the driver's shirt and turned away, pulling on his red hair. "Just like that, huh? You failed to save the better choice, so you were stuck with me. I wonder if you would have just ended up fucking her, too. I'm sure she wouldn't have been able to resist. She always liked your look."

Now thoroughly depressed on top of being heartbroken, Sync was feeling—and sounding—like he was emotionally dead.

"You must be so tired of having to play pretend. I'll make it easy for you from now on. I'll fix whatever I've fucked up. I'll learn what I'm supposed to learn. I won't be distracted anymore. Don't worry, I'm sure there's plenty of time."

Tacyturn's vidphone lit up again. He wanted to continue ignoring it, but then Sync's vidphone also lit up.

Curious, they both retrieved their vidphones from opposite sides of the bedroom and found invitations from Ephraym Thornwryght for a party—a party for the Thornwryght heir to be chosen.

It was set to happen in three days on November 19th—barely enough time to get back to the peninsula.

"Ah, fuck," Sync breathed. "Suddenly we have no time at all."

Without another word, Sync immediately went to bed once he saw how late it was. He had put on his green sweater, clearly not expecting to have any company with him in bed that night to help keep him warm.

Tacyturn quietly went back to the digital window and leaned his head against it.

He remained there for several minutes, quietly reflecting. His scanner was picking up Sync's inability to sleep because of his soft weeping. He saw the outline of Bandit going to comfort him. Sync had expected her and appreciated her, but when he felt her on the bed, he had hoped it was someone else.

The driver promptly rammed the right side of his head into the window, fracturing the screen into shards of mismatched flickering scenes. At the same time, his right eye fragmentally tessellated through several colours at once.

XIX.

"I wish he was here."

THE RIDE BACK TO THE Thornwryght peninsula was long and quiet. Sync sometimes pouted in the back seat and slept and sometimes he pouted in the front seat and stared out the window. From both places, he controlled the music that was playing so that they didn't feel tempted to confront the awkward silence.

They had wanted to leave Bandit in their nice apartment, but they were worried about what would happen to her if something happened to the two of them. Much to her chagrin, the poor dilute calico cat had to endure another long car ride.

Tacyturn was speeding as much as he could so that they would have plenty of time to prepare before making their entrance into the mansion.

The first night, Tacyturn drove through the night and avoided sleeping while Sync slept.

The second night, they stopped at a gym to bathe and then parked the car in a remote area so that they both could sleep and Bandit could wander around freely.

Tacyturn couldn't even pretend to sleep, though he desperately wanted to. Bandit spent most of the night staring at him through the windshield, looking displeased.

Sync wanted to get a hotel room, but Tacyturn warned that getting too comfortable might distract them.

"Comfortable doing what, exactly? The only thing I'd be doing is fucking jerking *myself* off. I want to be jerked off by you, but such is fucking life," Sync had grumbled, tired and agitated—and still heartbroken.

The next morning, Tacyturn had driven to a small breakfast café to pick up something for them to eat. He went inside alone while Sync remained in the car. Bandit was asleep in the front seat.

Sync fidgeted around uncomfortably in his solitude as he was left to think about how much he wanted to be touched. Sync had been getting so much attention from Tacyturn and now he wasn't. His body was used to it—and craving it. The constant ache was starting to wear him out.

Tacyturn was always nearby and scanning him, so he knew there was no way he'd ever be able to get away with touching himself. Now that Tacyturn was in a shop, he thought he'd finally give in. Sync felt dirty just unzipping his pants under the blanket, but he didn't care.

Just as he was shyly getting started, the car door opened and Sync inwardly flipped out. He thought Tacyturn was returning to the driver's seat, but suddenly Tacyturn was sliding up right next to him.

Without saying a word, Tacyturn reached under the blanket to help him out. Sync didn't object. He wanted to move closer to the driver, but instead pressed himself against the door.

Once he finished, Tacyturn licked the edge of his fist and promptly left the backseat, going back into the café.

Sync was left confused, but satisfied.

Then he remembered what he had said the night before about what he was going to do if they were in a hotel—and what he *wanted* Tacyturn to do to him.

He hit his head on the window, disappointed in himself. He had accidentally abused the words that Tacyturn was conditioned to obey. The driver had managed to do it swiftly and without making a scene, respecting Sync's desire to distance himself.

The young redhead couldn't decide whether or not he was disappointed by that.

He felt like a piece of shit that wasn't worthy of having the power of bossing people around. He retreated further into his shell for the rest of the trip.

On the third evening, they arrived at the Thornwryght peninsula at just the time when the party was about to start. On the outskirts of the property, they changed their outfits.

Before they had fought, they had agreed that it would be a power move to dress differently than everyone else when they returned to the peninsula. This would make them stand out, but it was like having a bulls-eye on their back—and still having the confidence to show up.

Because everyone on the peninsula was forced to always wear suits, Sync and Tacyturn adjusted their outfits to make them far more casual. It was going to be ironic to go to a party and dress down while everyone else was in a suit—or dress, which were allowed in a party setting only.

Just before leaving Hollywood, Tacyturn had disabled the alarm and backed the Whisperunner through the wall of the Electric Reel costume warehouse.

Grabbing whatever looked good, they quickly stashed a bunch of items from sections of their sizes into the trunk and drove off. They went through it later and pieced together their outfits.

Tacyturn had decided to wear dark denim skinny jeans and a magenta T-shirt that happened to have a graphic of a pistol and stars. He kept his same black penny loafers and wore his tie as a belt instead because the waist of the jeans were loose on him.

There had been a lot of items in the warehouse that were his signature hair colour and the driver knew Ellenoir was inspired by him.

Tacyturn confirmed this when he saw the design on the back of a navy-blue bomber jacket that had a magenta lining. There was a large embroidered patch of a magenta tiger surrounded by guns and tires. The tiger had raccoon markings around its heterochromatic eyes. The right eye was just a tiny mirror that had been sewn in. The jacket also had Japanese lettering that said "Magenta Tiger." He had mixed feelings about wearing it, but he just wanted to find something to conceal his gun.

Sync hadn't been as lucky with his finds, but he was still pleased. He kept his neon checkered shoes—he liked them way too much. He was pleased when he found pants that fit him—torn black leather pants. He liked that the length of them showed off his fluro orange socks. He had even found a tattered kilt to wear that he thought looked badass, having always admired the punk style adapting it. It was a middle finger to the norm—and he respected that.

He did find a checkered T-shirt that he was pleased with. He also found a fluro windbreaker that matched him—it was mostly green and orange like his hair and eyes, but with a few zig-zags of black and white checkers. He then topped his outfit off with all of his pins on his jacket, kept his mother's black diamond earrings on, his rope around his neck and the fedora he already had. He tied the end of the rope to his prop gun and tucked it into his pants, fearful of someone ever disarming him.

"I think we look pretty fucking cool," Sync said, peeling off green sunglasses, having put them on just for the sake of what he was saying. "It looks like we just don't give a fuck." Then he tossed the sunglasses away. "I wish I had that checkered star hat, but *somebody* fucking lost it."

After letting Bandit free to roam the peninsula, Sync and Tacyturn abandoned the Whisperunner just before reaching the mansion's gate. On foot, they headed in.

Immediately they came upon several security guards in suits.

Tacyturn tugged Sync aside before they were spotted. Just before Tacyturn leapt into action, it was Sync's turn to tug him back.

"This won't fucking work if we have to do this all the way to the mansion. As cool as it would be to watch you tear-ass through there, we really shouldn't do it like that. It's really fucking far and we know the place is swarming because of the party. *You* would be part of the swarm, at the heart of it."

Without saying anything further, he indicated to Tacyturn that he wanted to climb the tree they were under.

Tacyturn easily lifted him up and watched him scale the tall tree. Sync checked the nearby sunken laboratory and infirmary building and could see that the lights were off and there was no security. It was locked and closed.

Sync allowed himself to drop, still trusting Tacyturn to do his job protecting him. The driver caught him easily and set him down.

"Looks like they closed down the lab for today, so no one is there guarding it. I bet all of the medics and scientists were invited to the party, that's fucking nice. We just need to get in there and then I think we can find help." He saw Tacyturn's curious expression. "Yeah, fucking help. You'll fucking see if you can just get us in there."

Thinking about what he knew about the laboratory and infirmary, Tacyturn considered all his options. The security system was too complex for him to intercept with his technology from a distance, but all he needed to do was get someone with a code to open it—for a good reason.

Without much more thought, Tacyturn and Sync wandered stealthily as the driver scanned all of the men and women around, looking for a particular individual. His scanner let him know of all of their heart rates and how they were feeling emotionally.

"What are you looking for?" Sync asked.

"The chink in the armour."

He focused on the one guard who had an elevated heart rate—and was clearly tweaking out on something. His scanner picked up the drug paraphernalia in his trench coat pocket.

Tacyturn also knew him personally—he was the asshole that claimed to have murdered Sync's mother. Tacyturn had heard all about it from him, even though it had happened about eighteen years prior. He had never liked the man, but Ephraym had repeatedly suggested that he let Lothan be. Eventually, Tacyturn figured it out on his own.

Knowing how Ephraym operated, Lothan definitely wanted the credit for destroying such a beautiful, peaceful woman to get immunity from the wrath of the Thornwryghts for his out-of-control drug use.

Ephraym wanted a disposable person to take the fall for that woman's death—but Tacyturn knew that Ephraym expected his death to come because she was Brayden's mother, not because she was Synclare's.

His drug addiction was encouraged by Ephraym so that he remained easy to take out when the truth came to light.

Wasting no time, Tacyturn took aim and shot three of the guards in his group in strategic ways that would hurt enough to drop them and disorient them, but not threaten their life.

As they fell over in confusion, Tacyturn ran behind the asshole guard and ripped his large trench coat off. He then turned Lothan's gun on himself, suggesting a paranoid drug-induced attack and suicide.

Tacyturn quickly re-hid beside Sync with the coat and they waited.

Not long after, the men who were injured were taken to the infirmary where Yenvieve and other medics arrived in their suits and dresses to unlock it and tend to the wounded.

They moved as close as they could to the building before the next step would be within view of another human. Tacyturn put on the large trench coat and then stabbed himself in the arm. Sync objected too late and was saddened to see him do harm to himself. Tacyturn wrapped it with a handkerchief.

The driver then grabbed Sync and removed his fedora, putting it on his own head. He pulled him under his jacket. He removed his injured arm from the sleeve and picked the young man up and held him close to his body. Sync clung to him.

He now looked about the same weight as the man he had just killed.

"Good thing I'm fucking tiny, I guess," Sync mumbled from under the coat. "And good thing you smell fucking amazing. Also, I bet we look fucking ridiculous."

Then, walking like he was supposed to be where he was, Tacyturn waltzed into the infirmary.

Just as Sync was starting to slip, Tacyturn stood patiently off to the side behind a desk to let the young man's feet comfortably touch the floor. They waited for those who were hurt worse to get healed first.

"Yenvieve, we want her," Sync said.

He pointed a finger out of the jacket towards the medic with the long black hair pulled up into a bow made of her own hair. She had just recently added a pale blue streak to her raven locks, using it to artistically create the knot of the bow.

Luckily, all of the other medics left first while Yenvieve finished with the man who had been injured the worst.

Once the injured man insisted he was fine enough to go inside for the open bar, Yenvieve excused him.

She walked gracefully up to the desk with a little bit of a sway in her blue floral dress—she had clearly already been partaking in the free drinks, herself.

"What can I help you with?" she asked.

Tacyturn quietly showed her his arm.

"That is very easy. Sit down here." She pointed to a chair.

"I prefer to stand."

Yenvieve shrugged indifferently. "*Pas de problème.* These heels were my fault, anyway."

They spent a long moment in silence as Yenvieve stitched up his arm.

Then Tacyturn said, "I'm sorry Synclare never loved you back."

Tacyturn felt a hard nudge into his ribs.

The young woman looked up at Tacyturn in tipsy confusion. She recognized him and didn't seem to be bothered by his presence. "Oh, you're back. But, what do you know about Synclare and I?"

Tacyturn was purposely vague to let her move the conversation along. "It's because he loves someone like me."

Sync didn't react that time.

"Someone like . . . oh!" She hummed in thought. "Why wouldn't he just tell me that? I would have much preferred knowing that than just being completely avoided like I was a disgusting leper." Yenvieve sadly sighed. "I've heard a rumour that he killed himself. I only ever wanted the best for him. I want to talk to him. I wish he was here."

"*Voilà*," Tacyturn said as he dramatically opened his coat and presented the very shocked Sync to the very shocked Yenvieve.

The young redhead managed a crooked smile and a tiny wave.

"Oh, *la vache!*" she exclaimed, then grabbed him by the front of his shirt, pulling him closer to her. "What are you doing sneaking around? I thought you were dead! Everyone says you are dead! Are you dead?"

"Ah, no?" Sync was too nervous to look her in the eyes. She had a beautifully intense blue stare. "Not yet, anyway. Depends on what you fucking do next, I guess, Vie?"

The medic loosened her grasp. "What do you mean?"

"Depends on whether or not you notify everyone that I'm here."

"Why would that matter? Everyone knows that you're the only child Monsieur Thornwryght has left alive. I mean, they think you're dead, but clearly you're not. This party is supposed to pick one of those other bloodsuckers, but now Monsieur Thornwryght doesn't have to! You've got to get yourself to that party! I should be announcing that you are here!"

Sync nodded slowly, but stopped when he saw Yenvieve wasn't getting it.

"And whose blood do you think they'd want to suck if I waltz back in alive to take their fucking power?" Sync slowly asked.

The young woman thought for a moment, then understood.

"Ohhh!" she gasped. "You've been hiding from them because they're trying to kill you, haven't you?" Then something clicked and she said, "You both stole that Whisperunner, didn't you?"

"We . . . borrowed it?"

Yenvieve huffed. "Sucks to crawl out of an upside-down car." She shoved Tacyturn before working on his arm again, finishing up the stitches. "Thanks for that!"

"Could have been worse," the driver said.

"Ugh, yes. Yes, I know. I have healed the damage you have done before, Tacyturn. You're very messy," she chided him. "But good experience for me."

Tacyturn concurred with a head cocked nod.

"So, Synclare, what are you going to do?" Yenvieve asked while cleaning up. "You're going to need me if you're here to claim your throne."

"Well, yeah, I fucking know! That's why I—"

The young woman walked up close to him and leaned in, crossing her arms behind her back. "You're going to need to prove you can do that by providing a woman to make babies with!"

Sync's eyes widened in confusion and distress. He backed into Tacyturn, hiding underneath the trench coat again.

Yenvieve tittered. "It's true, though. You can't control a family-owned business without being able to make more family. It'll be very impressive to rule the syndicate with a sexy and strong man at your side, but there's not much you two can do together about *making* children. You know the rules, *oui?*"

She peeled back one side of the jacket to reveal half of his panicked expression. He had been worried enough about just surviving this ordeal, he had forgotten all about the fact that he would need to continue the bloodline as the last Thornwryght.

"I'm just saying, I'm offering to do that for you so that you succeed today. It will be no problem, I assure you! It would be my pleasure." She looked up at Tacyturn, clearly pleased with the way he looked. "I could make heirs for both of you! As many as you want! Every night could be a ménage à trois!"

Sync reached up and snatched his fedora from Tacyturn's head, using it to hide his own face.

Yenvieve chuckled and nudged the driver with her hip. "Your *petite chouchou* is adorable, isn't he?"

Angrily, Sync burst out of the jacket. "I'M NOT HIS—his fucking WHAT?" He calmed himself by focusing on brushing himself off when he didn't even need to. He put his hat back on. "I don't remember what that one means. Anyway, this needs to fucking stop. We need your help getting into the mansion, Vie."

"I can be your escort, of course!" She twirled in her vintage blue dress. "I'd love to be linked between two important and handsome men as I walk into a very important party! I will be the most popular girl there!"

Sync stopped her from twirling by grabbing her shoulders. "No, we need to sneak in."

Yenvieve pouted. "You're going to ruin my first fancy party ever, aren't you?"

"I plan on ruining it for at least nineteen fucking people, yeah. But you're not one of them, Vie." Sync's voice dropped to a regretful whisper. "I've ruined your life enough as it is."

"Aw, Synclare!" She gently cuffed his chin. "I was heartbroken, but my life was not over."

"Great, good for you. But it's not your fucking life I'm talking about."

"But you said—"

"Just forget it," he grumbled, aware of his lack of consistency.

X X .

"My loyalty never went away."

YENVIEVE HAD PROMISED NOT TO say anything about their presence once she had finished helping them. She wanted to stay with them, but Sync insisted that she enjoy the party.

She was also still very tipsy and hyper—they didn't want her to give them away. She was very attractive and gained instant attention—attention they didn't want yet.

The medic had taken them down to the bottom level of the laboratory and unlocked access to the secret passage that connected to the basement of the mansion. Sync had known it was there only because he was quite familiar with the basement—it was where his own secret room was nestled.

Sync was annoyed when he found out that Tacyturn's wristband had access through the door they needed to get to, even the lab's front doors. Yenvieve had to explain why it wouldn't have worked.

"It notifies security whose badge is used. You don't know who is monitoring that right now. Could be someone loyal to someone who wants you dead, right? They know Tacyturn was with you last, I'm sure they'd at least come investigate. For me? I use this passage all the time. It leads right to my room in the mansion." Then she had pinched his freckled cheeks. "Besides, I know you wanted to see me! We've got to make up for lost time! I want to hear all about you and *votre grand petit ami rose.*"

Sync tried his best to ignore her as she rambled in a bubbly manner the entire time. He wished Tacyturn would say something about their broken relationship to ruin her mood. Sync wondered if he was enjoying pretending that their fight never happened.

Sync realized then that he also wasn't eager to correct Vie—maybe for that very same reason. Life had made more sense before they fought.

Once Yenvieve had left them, it was very quiet. Sync was following Tacyturn, but only because it looked like he knew exactly where he wanted to go. Sync didn't know what Tacyturn was up to because he knew where the party was being held and they were moving along the array of rooms where the servants lived instead.

They arrived at a specific room, but it was locked. Sync thought he was going to watch Tacyturn break it down, but he unlocked it with an unenhanced key from his wristband.

Upon going inside, both of them could tell that the tiny room had not been entered in many years. It was mostly empty.

"Whose room is this?" Sync asked, looking at motorbike trinkets on a shelf.

"Mine."

"Yours?" Sync picked up an old 1-euro coin off of the ground. "I thought you stayed in a room near my father's?"

"This was before that."

"Oh?" Sync uttered, confused. He looked up to see a camera in the corner of the room. "Oh, awkward." Then he whirled around to Tacyturn. "Wait, before? What did you do before being my father's bodyguard and before going to Hollywood?"

From under the mattress, Tacyturn removed a magenta knitted cap. It was torn on the right side and stained with blood. Sync immediately knew when he must have last worn it—and it looked familiar.

Tacyturn thought for a long moment as he felt the fabric between his fingers. He glanced up at the camera in the corner of the room.

While Sync was looking away, Tacyturn injected some of the illegal drug he had confiscated from Lothan into his own neck. Even when Sync looked back at him, Tacyturn acted as if nothing was shifting the chemicals in his brain to allow him to be able to do what he wanted to do.

"What the fuck are we doing in here, Tac? We've got a fucking party to crash, don't we?"

Sync was only pretending he was eager to get a move on.

Once Tacyturn felt his brain sever everything that held him down, Tacyturn dropped the hat and pushed himself against Sync. He peeled the fedora from Sync's head and grasped his face, kissing him. Sync dropped the coin, startled.

Sync shoved him away. "Don't you fucking dare! You don't need to do that anymore! I don't want you to do that anymore! *We don't have time for this!*"

Ignoring him, Tacyturn tossed the fedora and grabbed him again, lifting Sync up and pushing him up against the wall. It was more forceful than Sync had expected and it knocked the air out of his lungs. Once he caught his breath, he shoved the taller man away again.

Sync growled, "This shit is over between us, Tac. I thought I made that pretty fucking clear. We're just here to get me home and—"

Tacyturn picked him up and threw him onto the bed. Sync put his foot against the driver's chest and kept him a leg's length away.

"FUCKING STOP, TAC! I WANT YOU TO STOP!"

The young redhead relaxed and laid back in a dramatically limp manner after he said his command—but Tacyturn didn't stop. He leaned over Sync and continued to kiss him, tearing the kilt off of him. Sync was confused.

"What the fuck?" he gasped and pulled away. He rolled off of the bed and stumbled to his feet. "Tac, you're supposed to STOP! . . . Right?"

"I don't want to be Tacyturn anymore," he said, his accent now different.

"Wha—?" Sync took an apprehensive step back. "Who do you want to be, then? And why the fuck are you suddenly talking like Vie? Sure, it's super fucking cute when she does it and—" He nervously bit his nail. "—super fucking cute when you do it, too."

Tacyturn calmed his advances and approached Sync. He leaned down and gently kissed him. The kiss lasted a long time due to the moment that Sync allowed himself to be charmed by his French accent.

When their lips parted, Tacyturn said, "I want to be Kovous Jaecar Chauffeur again."

Sync was shocked, but then clearly upset. "That's not fucking funny, Tac. You must have known he had an accent when I told you he was Vie's brother. I don't remember telling you his full name, though. I don't . . . even know if I remembered what his middle name was, myself, so I don't know how *you* could have known it . . ."

He pushed him away, his heart hurting for so many different reasons at once.

"I don't fucking like this. This is a whole new level of fucking with me. Why are you doing this? Is father still putting you up to making me pissed enough to hurt someone? Am I supposed to drag your dead body into the party? BECAUSE THAT'S NOT GOING TO FUCKING HAPPEN! NO FUCKING W—!"

The driver grabbed the rope around his neck and pulled him closer, stifling his shouting. "I know why you wear this rope, Sync." He grasped the knot and slid it closer to Sync's throat. "I tied this knot myself."

Sync's jaw dropped. He had told no one about where the rope came from.

The young redhead choked up. ". . . Vous?"

Tacyturn nodded.

"B-But I killed you!" Sync mewled in distress as he looked at the bullet wound in his head in a way he never had before—he had done it. He ran his hand across it, remembering it when it was fresh. His heart ached with guilt.

"You did, but now I want to come back," he purred as he amorously grabbed Sync again, untying the prop gun from the rope and tossing it aside.

"W-Wait!" Sync cried out, feeling conflicted by his happy tears and Tacyturn's romantic gestures.

Tacyturn removed his own jacket, then peeled off Sync's between eager kisses. He cast his own gun aside. His hands wandered up his checkered shirt, untucking it from his pants.

"I—ah! I want to talk to you!" Sync breathed. "There's so much more to say—!"

"We'll get to that, *mon amour*," he whispered sweetly against his lips. He knew that he only had a small window of time to act before the drugs he took wore off and his boldness would be lost again.

He suddenly forgot how to breathe as it made him melt into a pure moment of bliss—like a dream coming true.

Sync always wished Kovous never died, but he never imagined in all those mature years that he was praying for a miracle that he would be with him intimately—especially without even knowing about it as it was happening.

The driver then gracefully swept Sync off of his feet and spun him onto a shelf he deftly cleared, making the younger man slightly taller than him. He then used his tech to trigger the torchlight on his vidphone that had been cast aside. He turned on Sync's shoes and removed them, tossing one under the bed and the other hitting the light switch and landing in a corner.

When the light turned off, Sync could see that his vidphone was casting stars onto the ceiling and walls and his shoes were emitting just enough light to feel like there were neon signs nearby.

Tacyturn then triggered the sprinkler system with his tech causing it to rain down on them.

"I wanted to take you to a rainy neon rooftop. This is the best I can do with what I have."

"You're too wicked cool, Vous," Sync whispered through his own happy laughter, amused and impressed with their makeshift romantic setting.

The love making that followed had been the best and most pure that they had ever had.

The driver was rougher than usual, but careful and Sync was in submissive heaven.

Tacyturn—as Kovous—felt free. He was especially pleased when Sync sometimes pretended he wanted him to stop. He didn't hear the safe word—his surname—so he knew he really didn't want him to. He didn't have to obey, even though it was spoken out loud by a Thornwryght.

The driver was able to act like an equal to Sync—and Sync was able to escape from being important to simply be a slave to pleasures of the flesh. It was an escape for both of them—an escape they could only achieve together.

Tacyturn was able to reprogram his mind for the two of them. He hoped he could keep it up, but he wasn't certain. But he didn't care—Sync was all that mattered to him and all of his focus went on pleasing him.

The driver felt lucky that he had found a relaxing drug in the trench coat that they stole from Lothan—it helped immensely. He only used a small portion of it, but it was enough to take the edge off of being his damaged self.

Afterwards, they laid together in the bed which was wet with water and sweat. They were in an embrace that they never wanted to get out of. The sprinkler had long since stopped, but the stars and the neon glow remained. Tacyturn had wanted to take him almost anywhere else that wasn't a dingy old servant's room—but the place was swarming with enemies and guests of enemies.

Sync looked at the light bite mark on his shoulder flecked with droplets of water. "Look at that, you *are* missing a molar!" he pointed out. "Please don't tell me that was something you had to do yourself."

Tacyturn said, "I won't."

Sync sighed angrily. "I'm not much of a killer like you are, but if I had a list of all of the people who ever made you hurt yourself . . . I would probably not kill them myself, but hand them over to you on a silver platter and watch. Killing is not my thing, even though I—" Then he had a thought that suddenly changed him from angry to pleased. "Wait a second. You're still alive, aren't you?"

Tacyturn nodded as if the question had actually been as serious as it sounded. He knew he was headed to a life-changing realization.

With a giddy gasp, Sync exclaimed, "I've actually never killed anyone, have I? What a relief!"

"Do not go telling everyone," Tacyturn chided him.

"I won't, I won't."

Sync leaned back against Tacyturn, feeling a weight lift from his shoulders.

He threw himself back forward when an obvious connection hit him.

"It was the Rilangs, wasn't it?" Sync asked as he pointed to Tacyturn's bite mark again. He didn't even wait for Tacyturn to confirm it. He knew. "That's why they didn't retaliate to what you did to them. They knew they fucking deserved it. No wonder I didn't feel bad. I somehow knew they deserved it, too. I thought my acting was just that amazing."

"You were not acting."

"Wasn't I?"

"That was just you with confidence."

"That was just me . . . with *you*," Sync purred and leaned into the driver again.

He looked around quietly for a moment before speaking up again. He tried fixing his wet and tousled red hair.

"I remember this room, now. I barely ever came to visit you here because we both agreed that this room was a shit hole," Sync said with a laugh. "My room was huge and full of fun and expensive things." He grabbed the noose hanging from the bedpost. "That's why you used this rope to climb up and visit all the time, right?"

Able to form more words in his alleviated brain, Tacyturn had a lot to say and was able to say most of it. He had to put in extra effort to remain focused—which was an unsettling feeling he kept to himself.

"I couldn't stay away from the adorable little Synclare Thornwryght. He was always following me around and telling me how cool I was. I was just the mechanic's son. You reminded me of Tintin. You still do." He gently ran the tip of his fingers through Sync's overgrown quiff of ginger hair. It stubbornly remained even though his hair was wet. "With Haddock's temperament, though," he added, fondly.

"Of what with who?"

"Comic book characters I grew up loving. They are all over Belgium."

"Are they cool?"

"Wicked cool."

Sync was pleased with the comparison, making a note to find out more about the characters.

The young redhead pointed to the bloody knitted cap. "I gave you that, didn't I?"

"It was your favourite hat because it was your favourite colour. Then you told me that I looked so cool in magenta that you had to give me your favourite hat and favourite colour and it was now *my* favourite hat and favourite colour."

The young redhead had to laugh—he had no idea he had that much of an influence on him.

But then Sync grew somber as he finally asked the question he didn't want to ask, but he had to know. He tried to block out the coming-of-age Thornwryght sacrament that required him to kill someone before he reached puberty or he would be killed himself—and he had especially tried to block out that Kovous had offered himself as a sacrifice to keep Sync alive. He always hated himself for accepting.

"How did you survive, Vous?"

Tacyturn explained what had happened several years ago in more words than he ever used at once—but still the minimal amount he could.

"You remember what happened just before you left me to die."

Sync whimpered, "Don't say it like that . . . even though it's true. God. I do remember." He rubbed his head. "It's easier to remember now that I know it turned out . . . better."

Kovous gave him a moment to think about it and have the situation fresh in his mind. They had been in the Thornwryght garage. Sync had tried stabbing him several times first, but failed to do anything life-threatening. Kovous had then convinced him to make it quick and shoot him. After he had shot him in the head, he used a vintage instant-print camera to take a picture of the "corpse" as proof to his father. He didn't leave right away to deliver it, though. He spent several minutes sobbing next to his best friend's body.

"I only pretended to be dead. Once you left, I dragged myself to the closest car in the garage."

"Which one?" he asked, trying to divert from the more depressing details.

"The brand new fluro orange 1975►► Drofton Aphotic Coupé."

Sync was shocked to hear it and showed it by sitting up to look at Tacyturn in the face.

"I thought maybe it would look like you drove me somewhere to bury me yourself."

"By stealing my father's newest car?" He was impressed. "You were always ballsy, weren't you?"

"The idea was that I wanted you to look ballsy, but also prudent. I had used a rain poncho and driving gloves from the glovie to keep myself from bleeding all over it."

"He would have noticed the tiniest drop and let everyone know about it. I heard nothing, so you must have kept the car pristine." Sync leaned into him, whimpering as he pictured it and trying to focus on how impressed he was. "Where did you go?"

"I drove myself to the hospital."

"Thank God."

"I barely made it. In fact, I didn't really make it on my own. The only reason I survived is because your father showed up."

Sync was stunned and gently touched his cheek. Tacyturn reassuringly kissed his hand.

"He had watched everything on the security cameras. While you looked for your father, he was looking for me to make sure I died. He wanted me to die for your sacrament and to die for stealing his car."

The redhead huffed, "Probably for the car the most, though."

"But, when he found the car in perfect condition and learned of how fast I got there without getting pulled over or scraping even a curb, he was impressed. He was even more impressed when he saw how close to death I was."

"As he should be."

"He had also been intrigued with my loyalty to you. My loyalty never went away."

The driver sat up and kissed the young redhead gently, wanting to take a break from talking.

Sync never wanted the kiss to end.

When it finally did, Tacyturn continued to explain, "Your father ordered the emergency surgery to save my life, but I had to agree to do everything he wanted me to do for the rest of my life. He wanted the same loyalty for himself that had put me in the position I was in for you."

"And you agreed," the redhead said with a sigh that was mixed with so many emotions. He was relieved that he had survived, but to become a disposable Thornwryght servant could be considered worse than dying.

"He also took the opportunity to put the experimental technology in my head."

"To make you super wicked cool!"

Tacyturn's expression softened. "The most important thing was that he counted me as a kill for you and you were safe because of it. You had no more time to kill anyone else. Your voice had already started to change."

"I remember my father told me that he took care of your body. I even overheard him tell Vie and your father that you were dead."

"He took me to Hollywood to make my transformation into someone new since Kovous was now dead. I went in as nothing and came out still alive as Tacyturn the Magenta Tiger. It was enough to impress your father and he gave me the honour of being his bodyguard."

There were suspicions that Kovous' father, Jarman Chauffeur, tried to do something to Sync in retaliation for his son's death because, by the time Tacyturn came back to the peninsula, the Belgian mechanic had disappeared. Yenvieve conveniently had forgotten anything that might make her loyalty sway. He knew now what may have done that.

Tacyturn still had no idea where his own father was, though—either alive or dead. He wasn't even just a jar of ashes in the basement.

"I don't know why he didn't make me forget you. Maybe he was afraid of erasing that loyalty he wanted for himself. Or he wanted to torture me or test me, letting me see you but not letting me talk to you. Even just recently he had directed me to see you getting burned with cigarettes again, but I wasn't allowed to intervene. Maybe he wanted to remind me of what happened when we were younger."

"What happened when we were younger?"

The driver gently touched the burn mark on the back of Sync's arm. "I saw them sneak up on you. I had never been around for them before. I think you were coming to visit me. I threatened them with a tire iron, allowing you to run off. I spent almost three days in the trunk of the Peugot Furet I was working on."

Sync sighed with relief, but then quickly added, "I mean, not that that's a good thing, but it could have been way fucking worse!"

Tacyturn's silent stare was telling.

This made Sync's expression turn worrisome. "It was worse, wasn't it?"

"They tossed in whatever cigarettes they had on them and a half-full matchbook before they closed me in. They said they were going to burn you several times with each cigarette left unsmoked by the time they opened it up again. They said they were going to take your green eyes when they ran out of freckles."

"What the fuck?" Sync was stunned, but not surprised. "How many cigarettes did they throw in?"

"Each one of them had a pack. There were five of them."

"How many cigarettes are in a pack?"

"Twenty."

Sync jumped up, grabbing Tacyturn's arm. "How many of them did you smoke?"

"All of them."

The young redhead's jaw dropped and he hugged the driver tightly, pressing his face into his chest.

"Why did you do that for me?" he whimpered. "It could have killed you!"

"I was born to protect you, Sync," Tacyturn said, holding him tight. "That was when I knew. My only regret is that I couldn't get them to stop forever . . . until you killed me." He touched the most recent scars on his hands. "But even that didn't last."

"Well, I'm not killing you again just for another several fucking years of being alive and not being burned," Sync huffed. "I'd rather burn every minute for the rest of my life."

"That wouldn't happen. I would burn whoever was doing it . . . and I would only need to do it once."

The driver's voice was heroically dark and it gave Sync chills—he had a feeling there was something Magenta Tiger about it.

Tacyturn could then feel the minuscule amount of the drug he had taken wearing off, letting his experiences affect his mortal body. Forming sentences in his head and sending them to his lips was getting harder again. He was glad he had been able to tell Sync things he had wanted to tell him for years.

The driver wished that he could be on these drugs all of the time, but it affected how he worked and ruined his focus. It muddled his brain tech and he knew he was nothing without it. He also did not want a weakness like addiction—and he could see himself getting addicted. It was also why he never drank alcohol. His job was to be unbreakable and in crystal clear condition.

Sync shook his head, dizzy from the weight of everything he was being told. He wanted to cry and he wanted to laugh—he wanted to scream at The Nineteen and his father. He wanted to set the mansion on fire.

"This is the most I've ever heard you speak, like . . . ever," Sync said to try to make himself laugh. He only cracked a smile.

"I've spoken to you more than I've ever spoken in the last seven years. Right after I was shot, I never spoke. It was . . . harder. That's why your father named me Tacyturn after just a few months of calling me Nothing To as a name."

Because it sounded unclear, Tacyturn explained that his full name for the first few months was Nothing To Chauffeur. It was a sort of bon mot that Ephraym had labeled him with as a challenge to make the hidden message obsolete and untrue. Once he proved that one of his strengths was being obedient and keeping his mouth shut, he became Tacyturn with the 'I' removed—for a reason different from the Thornwryghts themselves. It was symbolic of the driver losing his individuality.

Tacyturn had also lost his vision in one eye, which the technology had fixed—but Ephraym thought his name should lose one, too.

Sync scrunched his nose up once he caught on to the wordplay. "Sounds like the typical dumb thing my father would come up with, yeah. I think it's a way to let people know he's actually insulting their intelligence, not actually thinking he's clever. Or he's challenging someone to roll their eyes to give him an excuse to execute them."

"Being around you helped me say more, but I never said enough, did I?"

"Definitely fucking not!" Sync playfully scolded him and nuzzled against him.

Sync was able to pinpoint most of the faded scars that he had given to Kovous several years ago and it saddened him. He sighed.

"But everything happens for a reason, doesn't it?"

"Yes it does, *mon amour*." Tacyturn glanced up at the security camera in the room.

After a long moment of enjoying the company of one another, they realized it was time to get back to what they were doing.

The party had already been going on for hours and midnight was when the announcement was going to be made—that was hardly two hours away.

Yenvieve had even messaged Sync wondering where they were.

"How am I going to show up at this party?" Sync asked as he dressed himself in his clothes again, thankful for the fact that Tacyturn had covered their clothes with a blanket and kicked them under the bed to keep them from getting too wet. "I've got to look really fucking cool somehow. I don't know how I'm going to do that. I have nothing to show for myself."

The young redhead's eyes wandered around the room, seeking inspiration. They landed on the bloody hat on the wet floor.

A lightbulb clicked on in his head.

"I want The Nineteen to be happy to see me and there's only one way to do that!"

Tacyturn curiously tilted his head. Sync tapped on his own temple.

"You came back from the dead, Vous, so now it's my turn! This shit's gonna be like a movie! We're good at that, aren't we?"

The driver gently kissed the back of his hand. "Especially if the genre is romance."

Sync hummed dreamily as Tacyturn tied the gun to his rope and tucked it into the hem of his pants for him.

Then the young redhead had to chuckle. "I fucking hate romance movies, though."

"Then our genre can be pornographic."

Sync playfully—and sordidly—laughed. "Now that's more like it!"

XXI.

"Eye for an eye."

WHILE GETTING THEMSELVES ON THE move again, Sync sent a long message to Yenvieve requesting more of her help.

First, she had to go to where they left the Whisperunner and retrieve a bullet from the cup holder. If security asked, she was following a stray cat because she wanted to pet it. She was drunk and cute and they were sure they'd be fine with it—and maybe even help her by keeping an eye out. If luck would have it, Bandit might be at the car and she could take a picture with her as proof.

Then, she had to take whatever makeup she had and meet them in the canning room—a room that was likely to be empty for the night. They had first considered the classroom, but realized that was probably where the babysitter was watching the young children.

Yenvieve was suspicious of the weird requests and, as Sync was trying to figure out what to say to her, something clicked.

"Oh my God! Vie's your fucking sister!" He stumbled down from sitting on a stack of crates. The driver caught his arm to steady him. "You *have* to tell her! She'll be so happy you're alive! And she'll stop . . . eye-fucking you! I mean, hopefully? Can't let that poor girl keep doing that to her own brother."

Tacyturn was scanning the hundreds of jars along the shelves.

"Maybe I should wait until she's not intoxicated."

Sync could tell he was nervous about it. He turned him away from pretending to look at the jars by tugging on his jacket.

"She offered to have your babies, for fuck's sake! You definitely *have* to tell her while she's already had too much to drink!"

Sync then turned away from him and began typing a message to Vie, leaning back against the driver.

"I'll tell her that we have a surprise for her in return. A really big one!"

"I've got to stay Tacyturn until this is over with."

Sync understood. If anyone happened to remember anything about the mechanic's son, they'll realize that he had not actually killed Kovous Chauffeur and missing a sacrament would mean that he could not take over. He doubted any of The Nineteen would remember, though—the son of a mechanic was no one to remember. They didn't even care about Tacyturn's existence and he was probably responsible for most of the syndicate's success for the past five years.

Whilst they waited for the medic, Tacyturn and Sync had broken into some jars, leaving a mess as they sampled.

Throughout the time that Sync was snacking, the driver kept wanting to kiss him.

Sync laughed and playfully shoved him away as he stole a half of a peach right from his mouth.

"You're acting like you haven't already kissed me like nine hundred fucking times before, Vous."

"It's because I haven't." There was something desperate about his tone.

"You haven't?"

"Not with this accent."

Charmed by this, Sync gave in to a lengthy make out session. The young redhead couldn't tell if they were trying to make up for lost time—or if they were running out of time.

An hour went by before Yenvieve finally skipped into the canning room. She looked around the mess until she saw the two men in the corner of the room.

Sync pushed himself away from Tacyturn, pretending they hadn't just been kissing. The driver's subtly dazed expression and messy hair gave it all away, anyway.

Yenvieve skipped over and leaned in, taking a deep breath of both of them.

"Oooooh, booooys? What have you been up to? Care to tell Mademoiselle Chauffeur all about it?"

Sync zoned out for a long moment as if he was preparing to, then tersely said, "No."

"Oof, you tease!" She huffed and crossed her arms. "Thanks for sending me off on a long walk in the cold dark while you guys had all the fun." She dropped the bloody bullet onto the nearby table. "Did you know that you also have some teeth in your cup holder? Oh! I did find your kitty, though!" She pulled out her vidphone and showed them the photo of her cheek-to-cheek with Bandit. "*Elle est si adorable*! I am going to steal her."

"Did you bring makeup?"

"I did," Vie said as she dropped her purse down on a crate with a heavy thud. "What do you want me to do?"

Sync straddled another crate right in front of her and pointed to his head in the same angle he had shot himself in his suicide video.

"I need you to make it look like I was shot in the head right here."

Yenvieve fanned herself. "Oh, my! That's quite the task that I should be able to do very easily. You picked the right lady. I know gore and I know makeup!" she gleefully exclaimed. "Do I get my special surprise after?"

Sync looked back at Tacyturn. The driver thought for a moment, then nodded.

The young redhead dismounted the crate and walked over behind Tacyturn, blocking his face with a crate lid after doing a fancy spin with it. The driver ever-so-slightly raised an eyebrow at him from behind the lid.

Then he pulled it away and exclaimed, "*Voilà*!"

She stared at the two of them, unamused with her hands on her hips.

"Your brother!" he then added.

Immediately her brow furrowed and her lips parted in confusion. "Pardon?"

"I bring you Kovous Chauffeur back from the dead!"

She still didn't react. Her stare hardened like she was hearing a tasteless joke.

Tacyturn approached her as she stared at him.

"*Mon petite olivier*," he said.

She softly gasped. "Vous?"

The driver nodded.

"I . . . I don't understand?"

"My father reprogrammed him into a new person. Vous died and Tacyturn was born." The guilt weighed on Sync. "I'm sorry about that."

"So, you're seriously telling me that I get my childhood sweetheart and my brother back from the dead in the same night?"

Then she screeched with excitement and jumped into Tacyturn's arms, hugging him tightly, tears streaming down her cheeks.

"*C'EST INCROYABLE!* THIS IS THE BEST NIGHT EVER!"

"It really fucking is," the young redhead said softly. "I hope it stays that way."

He watched and listened as Vie and Vous spoke to each other in French. When they kept side-eyeing him, he was a little nervous and his freckled cheeks went red, wondering what they were talking about.

They both had something bizarre in common—being intimate with him.

After a moment, Sync coughed to get their attention.

"Hey, can we get back to putting the fucking bullet hole in my head?"

Yenvieve wiped the happy tears from below her eyes, trying not to mess up her makeup.

"Yes, of course. I'm going to be needing more of this makeup, too, I must look a mess! My eyeliner is making me look like *him!*" She pointed to her brother's bruised eyes. She then saw just how much concealer was on her hand. "*Oh non*, my birthmark is showing."

Yenvieve had a café au lait spot from the corner of her left eye that curled underneath her eye in a half moon shape. A smaller bit was separate near the very tip and looked like a heart. She had more of the birthmarks on her body that clothes easily hid, but she had to use makeup to hide the one on her face—Ephraym wanted her to.

Sync knew this and grabbed her hand to get her to stop hiding it. "You don't need makeup to hide who you are, Vie. Just use it how you want."

She smiled fondly at him. "Suppose I should just toss my makeup, then?" she asked, lifting up her purse and acting like she was going to throw it.

"If . . . you *want*. But, I need you to use it on me first! Or have you forgotten?" Sync huffed and grabbed the purse—then fell forward because of the sheer weight of it.

After getting everything prepared, she began using what she had to make a very believable bullet wound in Sync's head. The only thing she had been unsure of were the shades of red that she had. Tacyturn offered to re-open his wound to use his blood and Yenvieve objected, pointing out her perfect stitching job.

Sync had then taken his "OUT RAGE OUS" pin and cut himself on his head, right into her makeup gore. He bled and both Yenvieve and

Tacyturn were upset by it.

"Why did you do that?" Yenvieve huffed, then delicately used it for her work on Sync.

"Because Vous wouldn't shoot me in the head?" Sync responded, sarcastically. "He should be able to, anyway. Eye for an eye. Brain damage for brain damage." When he saw her serious blue stare, he added, "Down to every last detail, you know? If for some reason someone needed to test this blood, I want them to confirm it is actually mine." He flipped the pin around in his hand. "Might have a little bit of Vous', too, though."

The medic shook her head, but then stopped when she realized what he had said.

"What did you mean about eye for an eye?"

Sync bit his lip and shifted just his eyes to look over at Tacyturn who tilted his head at him, making it clear that he was now curious as to what he was going to respond with.

"Oh. I, uh . . . may have been the one that . . . shot your brother in the head?"

Sync braced himself, but then saw that she was completely frozen. Concerned, he slid the crate back a foot away from her, wondering what was going to happen.

Sync added, "For a Thornwryght s-sacrament?"

When she still didn't respond, he cautiously scooted back even further.

Then Yenvieve slowly stood up. She looked calmly over at her brother and he nodded.

Walking up to Sync, she said, "I know you were born into the fate of being a little Thornwryght brat, but *how dare you*! I have known Tacyturn for a while and he's *nothing* like my brother! Everyone always talked about the damage to his brain and what was wrong with him. He became a robot that never acknowledged any of the rest of us unless he was told to! He's broken and *you* did that to him! I don't know why he's sweet on you if he knows that!"

She looked at Tacyturn who had stood up, but showed no emotion otherwise.

"And it looks like he'll still protect you over his own sister. What twisted way did you break him to get him to be at your mercy? I know what Thornwryghts are like, but I always thought you were different, Synclare

Tymotheos."

Sync was surprised with how calm she was, but he was not liking what she was saying.

Standing up, Sync raised his voice louder than hers. "HE'S NOT FUCKING BROKEN! NOTHING IS WRONG WITH HIM!" He assertively stepped towards her as she stepped backwards. "HE'S ACTUALLY REALLY WICKED COOL AND HE'S ALWAYS BEEN REALLY WICKED COOL!"

Yenvieve crossed her arms. She respected the fact that Sync was passionately defending Tacyturn over anything negative she had said about Sync himself.

"You think being 'wicked cool' is really important?"

"Yes, I do. You know what else is fucking important? You keeping your opinions *to yourself*."

Tacyturn walked between them and touched both of their shoulders. They both softened, but continued to scowl at each other. He pressed their hands together and planted a gentle kiss on them.

Then he slid the crate forward with his foot and sat Sync back onto it. He directed Vie back into position where she was leaning over him on her taller crate. He handed Sync the mirror and handed Vie the makeup tool she had been using last.

Then, Tacyturn sat down away from them and against the wall of jars, keeping an eye on the mansion around them.

Quietly, Yenvieve finished giving Sync a remarkably realistic looking gunshot wound to the head.

He admired it in the mirror as she sighed and leaned back against the shelves behind her, feeling extremely sober.

"This looks wicked! Like for a movie! I won't be able to wear my hat anymore, but that's okay." He looked over to see she was purposely not listening. She was using a liquid eyebrow pen on the bullet that was to be pushed into his fake wound next. "What are you doing?"

The medic gave an exaggerated shrug and said nothing.

"Are you still mad at me?" Sync asked.

Yenvieve still said nothing, pinching her lips together.

"Oh. You can share your opinions again."

"Oh, thank you, Monsieur Thornwryght," she said, purposely sounding extra sweet. She showed the bullet to Sync—she had done a doodle of a cat face.

Sync scrunched up his nose. "Uh. Why? No one's going to see it . . . hopefully."

"Because it looks too real even for me, cher. But I can smile knowing there will be this silly little kitty in that terribly convincing mess I made on your head."

Even though what she said showed she truly cared for him, she still sounded huffy.

Sync was going to let it go, but then she none-too-gently shoved the bullet into the make-up gore on his head.

The redhead gently tended to it and remarked, "You didn't say if you were still mad at me, but I think I know the answer now."

She sighed, sitting down and crossing her legs and arms. "How can I be mad at you? My brother clearly isn't and he's the one who is in love with the same boy who shot him in the head. Who am I to say what he's feeling is wrong? I think it is, but *c'est la vie*."

"La Vie," her brother added without missing a beat.

She chuckled and looked back at Tacyturn. "You've always been the odd one. Look at your hair!"

"Hey, his hair is wicked cool!" Sync barked.

"There you go again with that." She jumped to her feet and prodded him in the chest with her fingers. "Is that all you ever say?"

"No, sometimes I tell bitches to keep their opinions to themselves!"

"Is *that* all, then?"

". . . Yeah, maybe?" His voice cracked into an inquisitive tone, not able to think of anything else to say.

"Oof, we've got to work on your verbal swordplay if you're going to be the next boss, *cher*."

Sync huffed. "I prefer gunplay." It sounded confident, but in his head he was thinking about the fact that it was a long-range weapon one can use a fair distance from danger.

"Shooting blanks, clearly."

The redhead mumbled in a frustrated manner as Yenvieve comforted him by patting his shoulder.

Tacyturn couldn't stop his expression from fondly softening.

XXII.

"I want you to give him his last sacrament."

YENVIEVE RAN SCREAMING INTO THE Thornwryght party just before midnight.

Everyone in the ballroom turned and looked towards her as she ran into one of her medic friends, grasping her arm. Then all of their eyes cast up to where she had run from, fearful about what was to follow.

Tacyturn emerged from the hallway on the second level, holding Sync's limp body in his arms. Everyone at the party gasped and gawked at the driver and the body of Synclare Thornwryght. He was looking dead in just the same way he had in the video.

"Is that Synclare?"

"Holy shit, he brought his body back to us!"

"What the fuck are they wearing?"

"Maybe he didn't want to be buried in a suit."

"Figures that freak wouldn't mind taking the clothes off of a dead body."

Ephraym shoved past partygoers to see what was happening. He was angry—he knew it had to be another stunt.

Once Tacyturn was at the top of the stairs, Ephraym climbed up the grand staircase on the opposite side of the room and pointed dramatically at the driver and his son's "corpse."

Ephraym's voice boomed. "Whoever gets the bullet from inside of Synclare's skull gets to be the next leader of this syndicate!"

Tacyturn wasn't surprised—he expected such a request from his boss. Ephraym was tired of what they were doing and wanted to blow it wide open, ruining whatever they had planned.

Fortunately, it fit right in with what they had planned.

The driver watched as The Nineteen emerged from the crowd and everyone else fell back. A lot of people fled the room, trying to get their vidphones back from where they were locked up. Because guns were also not allowed in a party setting, Tacyturn only had to worry about physical contact and close-contact weapons.

As they ran up the stairs towards him, Tacyturn rolled over the banister and landed sitting on a divan. Sync's only job was to remain completely still, completely trusting Tacyturn—and he did.

The driver artfully dodged and fought off anyone who got close to him. This only angered Ephraym more—his son wasn't doing anything at all.

"TACYTURN!" Ephraym howled.

The chandelier shook from the intensity of his voice. The Nineteen stopped, getting out of the way so that Ephraym could look directly at his bodyguard as he spoke. Tacyturn obediently turned towards him.

The crime boss' voice lowered, but still reached across the room. "I want you to drop him. Drop him where he belongs," he growled.

Ephraym was appalled as he watched the driver carry Synclare to the elevated decorative throne at the end of the ballroom that was designated for Thornwryght leaders. The bodyguard sat him in it and Sync remained limp, but stayed upright.

Ephraym Thornwryght glared at them when he realised that Tacyturn was not disobeying him—he was being cheeky, though, and interpreting his command in a way that put Synclare in a better light. After a tense moment, The Nineteen charged at the throne.

Just as they started up the stairs, Sync smiled. The few of The Nineteen at the very front saw this and abruptly stopped. The others stumbled into them, puzzled.

Then Sync chuckled and sat up. A few gasps were heard.

The young man then picked himself up and stood on the throne.

Reaching deep into the fake wound in his head, Sync pulled the bullet out and held it up.

"Now I've done more than any other heir has ever fucking done. I have the blood. I captured proof of me killing the owner of that Thornwryght blood." He flicked the bullet and caught it. "Now I've retrieved the bullet from my own skull."

Sync stared hard down at The Nineteen, then looked at his father.

The young redhead laughed. "What more do you fucking want?" he challenged.

Tacyturn couldn't help staring at Sync with admiration. When Sync glanced back to see this, he smiled.

After a long moment of quiet murmurs, his ex-brother Tobyas took an assertive step forward towards Sync. "I'm going to shove that fucking bullet BACK into your skull AND FUCKING TAKE IT!"

Inspired by Tobyas, the other eighteen decided they wanted in on it, too. All of them moved towards Sync to try to grab him.

Sync's chest tightened and Tacyturn stepped forward, protectively. Sync pushed him back, reassuringly. They were attacking first—it was his time to defend himself and show Tacyturn that all of his time was not wasted to try to make him a stronger person.

Just like the driver taught him, Sync dodged and struck whenever necessary. Because he was so much smaller than The Nineteen, he seemed far more nimble. Sync twisted a few knives back towards the owner of the knife—or into someone else nearby.

Sync was lucky that The Nineteen were not actually decent fighters. They had always had hitmen do their dirty work, but now Ephraym was making them have to act alone. Sync thought the video game simulations were far more challenging. It was making him feel cocksure.

Tacyturn watched intently. He was extremely proud of Sync, but he was still terrified of something happening to him. There were a lot of people to fight at once, even if they were not skilled. He moved closer to the fight, wanting to be within a certain distance to step in if he needed to. Keeping up with nineteen people through his scanner was a challenge.

As Tacyturn moved towards the scuffle, he heard a voice in his head.

"You know what I'm going to do next, don't you?"

It was Ephraym. Tacyturn didn't know he could speak to him through his brain tech, but he also found himself not surprised.

Tacyturn stopped and glanced up to where his boss had been—he was no longer there.

"It's a little fucked up that you finally told him who you were," Ephraym continued, trying to stifle his annoyed tone. "That makes your sacrifice even greater, though. Is that what you wanted? You want him to know just how fucking loyal you are to him? I have to say, I would have been proud of him if he had been fucking you like the servant you are, not the other way around."

Tacyturn listened intently, but never took his eyes off of Sync. He flinched when he saw Sync hit the floor hard on his shoulder. He started to move in to save him.

"I can detonate you, Kovous."

The driver stopped. Tacyturn's lips parted, but he kept his face emotionless. His right eye went white with shock—a little bit of purple dusted across it.

He was relieved when he saw Sync get himself back onto his feet just fine.

"If you try to run away with him, I will detonate you. If you both run away, even in different directions, I will detonate you. He will be hunted and alone and lost for the rest of his life. He'll die out there. Or maybe I'll let you both run away and set it up so that you will both blow up if he ever touches you again. You'll be the bigger man and stay away from him until one day he'll find you and take your hand in the middle of a crowded street, hoping to surprise you."

Ephraym paused to let the scene sink in.

"If he refuses to do what he's supposed to do, I will detonate you and leave him to The Nineteen. Or maybe he'll be just close enough to you to fill two needs with one deed . . ."

Tacyturn used the pare tech in his scanner to try to peel away the mansion and find Ephraym from the corner of his eye, still focusing on Sync. Somehow, Ephraym could tell. He could also tell that the driver's eye was starting to turn red—his tell when he planned to maim or kill.

Ephraym laughed. "If you kill me, it won't matter. While you were busy fucking my son, I did a little bit of programming on you. You were within range of a recording device, so I was able to. Bit of a rookie mistake, wouldn't you say? Why didn't you damage the camera? Now I've made it so that everything is already set to happen if your heart doesn't stop beating soon, even if my heart stops beating. Killing me will not work. You will detonate anywhere near my son for the rest of your life. The explosive is powered by the fucking blood pumping through your veins."

Tacyturn found Ephraym in the nearby security room and his boss looked right at him.

"If he kills you, he gets to live like a king and be surrounded by a kingdom. He'll be protected by so many people that will protect him better than you ever did. He'll have more money than he will ever need. Every wish of his will be granted. He'll finally be 'wicked cool' as he wants to be, as he admires you to be. He will be free to roam the world without ever being afraid again. No more hiding. No more being burned. What do you think should happen, Kovous? Let's see if you did your job. I kept you alive just for this moment. I want you to give him his last sacrament."

The driver watched as Ephraym returned to the ballroom at the top of the closest set of stairs. He was grinning.

"ENOUGH!" Ephraym called out.

The Nineteen stopped and backed away from Sync who was looking tired, but proud of himself. He still gripped the bullet in his fist—no one was able to pry it from his hand. He panted, out of breath. He had several wounds, varying from bruises to bloody cuts.

"The Nineteen have failed. It is now midnight and the heir is rightfully Synclare Tymotheos Thornwryght. He is The One." He applauded, slowly and firmly.

The partygoers around the edges of the ballroom also started to clap. The Nineteen and their families were fuming, especially Tobyas. They wanted to keep fighting, but Ephraym's security began showing up around the perimeter of the room, threatening anyone who wanted to do anything that Ephraym didn't allow.

Sync wasn't sure how to feel. He was afraid to feel relieved—it felt like it was still far from over.

"It's time for Synclare to take the leader's sacrament. I will allow him to do this sacrament early to ensure his place."

Sync took on a puzzled expression as he stopped checking to see if his lip was bleeding. He looked up at his father.

"Like me and everyone before me, the sacrament must be complete. The final sacrament just for you, Synclare." Ephraym paused for dramatic effect, enjoying Sync's nervous stare. "You have to kill someone of my choosing."

The young redhead clenched his fists and took a step back. *"Are you fucking kidding me?"*

"And the person I choose . . ." Ephraym coyly grinned. "I want you to kill the person that you love most in this world."

Sync's eyes widened and he immediately looked at Tacyturn—but then was suddenly aware that he shouldn't have. He nervously glanced away, but then shot the driver an accusing look, wondering if he knew about it.

Tacyturn's expression remained as it always was.

The redhead took a few steps forward and shook his head at the crime syndicate boss.

"NO FUCKING WAY!" he barked, throwing the bloody bullet at his father, who caught it. "FUCK YOU!"

Sync then heard gasps and murmurs. He looked around, wondering if it was because of what he had said to Ephraym Thornwryght.

Then he saw Tacyturn was standing closer, pointing a gun at him.

"Wh—?" Sync gasped. "What are you doing?"

Tacyturn's accent had returned to a modulated southern drawl. His right eye was flickering between magenta and blue.

"My heart is yours to do with as you please, even if it means to put a hole in it."

"Oh no . . ." Sync mewled.

"You are a force to be reckoned with, Synclare, so prove it."

Sync remembered his training from Tacyturn—he was supposed to pull his gun on anyone who pointed one at him. He ran his hand down the rope around his neck and onto the gun in his jacket, realizing what might be going on. Still, he was confused.

Tacyturn's accent then returned to his native one.

"I'm sorry, Sync. You're going to have to kill me."

Sync's insides twisted up. They were the exact same words that a sixteen-year-old Kovous Chauffeur had said to him just before he had killed him the first time. He saw that his eyes now matched each other—they were Kovous' electric denim eyes again.

"I could never do that," Sync said, trying to sound firm.

Tacyturn's voice raised slightly. "You already did."

"YOU LET ME!" Sync cried out.

The young heir looked around, trying to seek a way out of what was going on. Everyone was expectantly watching him as if he was lucky to get such an easy task after everything he had gone through.

Then the moment he looked back at Tacyturn, he saw the driver draw in a sharp breath—he was about to breathe out to fire.

Hoping that Tacyturn had a plan, Sync did exactly what he wanted him to do. He went by his advice—shoot to kill and ask questions later. He had even told him where to shoot him.

In a flash, Sync pulled out his gun, aimed and fired it at Tacyturn. The speed and force with which he yanked on the rope attached to the gun caused it to untie the ten-year-old knot around his neck.

The instant the gun went off, Sync knew something was wrong. The way the gun fired and the way the gun felt was all wrong.

When he looked at the gun in his hand, he saw it was not the prop gun—it was Tacyturn's real gun.

When he looked at Tacyturn, he hoped to see that he missed—but he knew he didn't.

Blood started to pour from the wound on his chest. His eye had uncontrollably ruptured into a piercing red.

Everything inside Sync and around him became muted and distorted—he heard Vie scream and his father laugh triumphantly. He limply let Tacyturn's gun fall to the ballroom floor.

At that moment, Sync knew that Tacyturn had switched their guns. All that time, Tacyturn had the prop gun and trusted Sync to be able to protect himself with the real one. That was the only reason that Tacyturn had even dared to point a gun at Sync.

Tacyturn didn't grasp his chest. He slowly got himself down on one knee, the prop gun suddenly feeling as though it were now too heavy for him, dragging his arm down until the barrel hit the floor.

He pressed his thigh up against his wound—just until Sync came to him.

Sync ran to him as fast as he could, stumbling onto his knees in front of the driver. He sobbed at the sight of Tacyturn's bleeding chest, trying to apply pressure to it with his hands. Tacyturn gently pushed his hands away.

When Sync looked desperately over at Yenvieve to come and help, he saw that she was being firmly restrained by one of the Thornwryght mansion guards. She was weeping into her hands.

Sync wanted to be angry, but he couldn't suffocate his tears long enough. He continued to try to apply pressure to his bleeding heart, but Tacyturn continued to patiently push his hands away.

"When I come back, I'll be ready to die for you again," Tacyturn softly said before his body grew too weak to speak.

When Sync looked directly into his eyes, Tacyturn could see that all hope was lost from his emerald ocean eyes. Sync saw that Tacyturn's right eye had returned magenta.

"I don't want you to die for me anymore!" Sync wept. "I want you to be with me forever!" He shook Tacyturn when his eyes started to dim. "Do you hear what I'm saying? *I want you to be with me forever!*"

Unable to get out any more words, Tacyturn felt himself going into shock as he leaned forward against the young man. Sync held him tightly, not knowing what else to do or say.

Sync wasn't aware of anything going on around the two of them. There was nothing else but the feeling of a bitter cold glow surrounding them as Sync desperately tried to harbour the small amount of warmth that was left at the heart of it between them.

Tacyturn was starting to feel heavier and heavier. Just before he blacked out completely, Sync felt him gently touch the back of his head, weakly gripping his hair. Sync wasn't sure what he was thanking him for—there was nothing he could do to save him. Sync squeezed him tightly, focusing on his heartbeat until he couldn't feel it anymore.

Sync felt the exact moment that Tacyturn died.

For a long moment, Sync refused to believe it. He held him tightly, not certain he would ever be able to let him go—if he stopped, he would fall apart at the seams. He was forgetting how to breathe—he still held in the breath he had taken in when Tacyturn was still alive. It felt like he was holding in a bit of Tacyturn's life's essence.

When he finally laid Tacyturn down and looked into his face, he couldn't contain it anymore. He felt lost and stripped bare without him. It made him feel impuissant seeing him the same way, fallen like a puppet with broken strings.

Sync bellowed in pure despair. The angry and heart wrenching sound filled the mansion, shaking everyone who heard it.

The young redhead wished that someone would put him out of his misery and shoot him in the heart, too. His heart being torn apart by a bullet would feel like relief from the heartbreak he was feeling. Even having a knife stabbed into him and twisted would alleviate his suffering.

Then he heard a gunshot. He braced himself, but no pain came. He began to wonder if he was killed too quickly to notice, hoping that Tacyturn would suddenly wake up and they'd both be trapped in the afterlife together.

Sync heard the room go into disarray. Above all the sounds, he heard the soft clinking of something rolling down the stairs. It came to rest near him. When he nudged it with his shoe, it rolled to reveal the smudged cat doodle—it was the bullet that had been in his father's fist.

When Sync looked up through his wet green eyes, he saw that Tobyas had shot Ephraym Thornwryght dead and was slowly ascending the stairs to stand above the body.

"There, see? I, too, can shoot the person I love most in this world!" Tobyas called out to the onlookers huddling against the walls and behind the tables. He reached down and took the signet ring off of Ephraym's finger, grinning as he put it on himself.

When Tobyas caught sight of his wife's offended look as he went back down the stairs, he turned and shot Teena between the eyes.

"Even better, I shot the *two* people I loved most in this world!" Tobyas ran his fingers through his black mullet. "And I'm taking it far better than that little brat is! He only killed some servant whose *job* was to die. Whoopity-doo!"

Tobyas stalked the room with well-bred dominance, clearly enjoying the spotlight.

"I think we can all agree on who would be the better crime syndicate leader. A small crying baby or a brilliant man who just did a heartless double homicide?"

When Sync saw that Tobyas had Tacyturn's gun, he felt rage flaring up inside of him. He jumped up and grabbed the rope still attached to it, yanking it hard out of his grasp.

Tobyas looked down his nose at Sync's tear-streaked face.

"I don't need it to kill *you*," Tobyas said, wrinkling his nose with disdain. "Do I still need to kill you or are you going to step down?"

"I'd have to take more than a step to get down to you, as far fucking beneath me that you are," Sync growled, trying hard to stifle his quivering voice.

Tobyas scowled, but then smiled. "I'm going to enjoy this," he said as he reached into his jacket pocket.

"No fucking guns," Sync demanded. The oldest of The Nineteen pulled out a cigarette and a lighter, greatly amused with Sync's fear.

Tobyas tittered, "*You're* the one who brought the illicit guns in and made quite a spectacle of yourself."

Sync untied Tacyturn's gun and set it down close beside the driver's hands. When he turned to look back at Tobyas, he saw that he had been waiting for him to look back so that he could watch him light his cigarette.

"Besides, I don't need one. I can even kill you without my cigarette going out," Tobyas proudly stated. "I won't even drop it." Then, he let out a smoky laugh, "*You* certainly won't be able to take it from me."

As Sync felt all of his twenty cigarette burns go red hot with fear, he watched as Tobyas waltzed over to the guest book and plucked the glass pen from the pedestal. He then went over to the bar and poured two glasses of whiskey. He broke the pen and drained all of the ink into the one closest to Sync.

He affably smiled as he tapped the now blackened whiskey with his cigarette, topping it with a dusting of ash.

"Just a little something for you to drink to toast my victory when I win."

Sync felt sick thinking about how he was poisoned as a baby. Tobyas took the opportunity he had made to lunge at him. The young redhead snapped out of his daze just in time and timorously threw the rope at him. It happened to go around his neck like a backwards scarf.

Just as Tobyas was trying to figure out his stupid maneuver, Sync went behind him and yanked hard holding both ends.

Tobyas choked and, before he could turn around and grab Sync, the young heir lost his grip on one end. Sync tugged hard as he moved out of range, causing rope burn on his throat. It pissed Tobyas off.

Tobyas continued to aggressively come at him, but Sync was quicker—most of the time.

Sync used whatever he could against the oldest of The Nineteen—plates, mugs, silverware, candlesticks and even someone's abandoned stiletto heel that Sync had quickly snapped off and stabbed into Tobyas' ribs as he climbed around a sushi cart to pounce.

Tobyas got a bit of revenge when Sync ended up with a blade in his leg, but Sync was able to twist and buck it off with a kick from his other leg. He then slid it across the room, far away from both of them.

At one point, Sync thought he saw Bandit. He was momentarily distracted by trying to find where she went and he didn't see Tobyas arm himself with one of the guns laying near Tacyturn.

Bandit had shown up and hissed at Tobyas as he reached for the gun the first time, cutting his hand with her claws. He growled and stomped at her and grabbed the other gun that was near the driver, instead.

The next time they clashed close together, Sync reached for the cigarette in Tobyas' mouth, unable to resist the chance of snatching it from his smug face. As he tried, Sync was met with the barrel of a gun pressed into the side of his head.

Without any time to react, the gun fired and Sync grasped his cheekbone and fell to the cold marble floor.

Tobyas flared up with pride and looked to the shocked crowd, hoping to see that they were pleasantly shocked and not disappointed.

Suddenly, they were all taken aback—but with awe and bewilderment.

"FUCK!" Sync yelled out in annoyance. "That fucking hurt fucking worse than any fucking cigarette burn! Jesus FUCKING Christ!"

The young redhead pushed himself to a seated position, showing off his scorched cheek as he checked the blood on his hand. It looked like a bullet had met with his flesh—then had just disintegrated.

There were many murmurs of confusion.

Tobyas' jaw dropped. "You should be FUCKING DEAD, you little bitch!"

Wordlessly, Sync got to his feet and slowly walked towards Tobyas. He kept firing at Sync, but what resulted was always just his scorched flesh, burning holes through his clothes. Sync flinched at the first few, but then braved through the rest.

Just before Sync was close enough to touch him, Bandit appeared and walked right behind Tobyas' legs. As he backed up in alarm, he tripped over the barn cat and landed hard on his back and elbows.

Bandit jumped up on a nearby winged fox statue and Sync appreciatively pet her.

Sync leaned in to Tobyas and plucked the cigarette from his lips. He took a long drag of it himself and blew it in his ex-brother's face.

"I fucking win," Sync said with a smoky breath.

Then Sync plunged the cigarette into Tobyas' eye, burning him blind. He screamed. The room hushed and waited to see if Sync would blind his other eye, too Surprisingly, he did not—he cast the rest of the cigarette aside.

[213]

The young boss took the prop gun from Tobyas.

When Sync straightened himself up, he finally looked around and saw the way everyone was looking at him—like he was now their leader. But he didn't care. He also didn't care that he was disheveled and wounded, his clothes covered in holes and blood.

Sync quietly went back over to Tacyturn's body and sat down. He took his scarred hand and pressed the back of it to his burned cheek. Bandit wandered over and pressed her nose against the scar on the side of the driver's head, purring against it like she was trying to jumpstart Tacyturn's tech.

As people started to rush Synclare Thornwryght, the syndicate security stepped in. The new boss was now their hot new priority.

There were so many voices overlapping, saying so many different things.

They talked about Sync's nine lives, like a cat—a spirit guide that showed up to help, that he must have summoned. They talked about bulletproof Sync and how impressive that was, what they had just witnessed.

All of them couldn't believe that this was the same Synclare Thornwryght that they knew—the small, angry and pathetic person that he always had been.

But all of what they were saying were just sounds. The only thing he wanted to hear again was Tacyturn's heartbeat.

"You have been chosen, Synclare," one of the oldest, Benjamyn, said. "You are The One. Tell us what you want."

Sync looked up to see that most of The Nineteen had approached him and they were kneeling respectfully. They were seeking retribution and guidance.

The young boss couldn't stand that they were crowding around him and the dead body of his loved one. He closed his eyes and took in a deep, calming breath.

Then, after he took that long moment, Sync said, "After you leave, I am not going to hunt you down, but I will kill you if I see any of you again."

"What are you saying?" they all asked in their own ways at once.

"I'm saying GET THE FUCK OUT OF HERE!" Sync howled. "YOU ARE NO LONGER WELCOME HERE! YOU ARE NOT THORNWRYGHTS, BUT—" He stopped and sighed. "I don't want to be either. The name means nothing to me."

Sync looked down at Tacyturn, remembering exactly what he had died for.

"But I have to be. The rest of you will take the surnames of your mothers. You can keep your fucking 'Y's, but just know that will make it easier for me to notice you. If you talk about our secret, I will try much harder to notice you and I won't have to try very hard at all to find a way to end you."

The young boss quickly commanded that security kick out his ex-siblings and get everyone else headed home. He made sure to tell the eighteen of them that whoever took care of Tobyas' children would gain a free favour—he was disgusted that he had to clarify that he didn't mean kill them, but adopt them as their own.

Sync looked up at Yenvieve, hoping she understood what had happened. The moment he did, he saw her get snatched by Tobyas and dragged out of the ballroom at knife point. Sync was surprised that security didn't notice. Though, until just moments before, Thornwryght security was loyal to Tobyas and likely turned a blind eye—a wry, but dutiful gesture. Knowing that they might not actually pursue Tobyas if he asked, the new boss decided to handle it himself.

Sync went after them, getting an idea of where they were headed—Yenvieve scolding him along the way in French helped him know where they were at all times as he ran ahead of them.

"I can't heal you while you're dragging me around like this! You want me to try to save your eye, don't you? If we just go to the infirmary, I'll be able to—"

Tobyas shook her. "Who are you to them?"

"Pardon?"

"I saw the way you reacted when the driver was shot. You're still fucking crying."

Yenvieve choked up, but kept a defiant glare. Tobyas continued dragging her down into the garage.

"That's what I fucking thought. If you meant something to him, I bet you mean something to Synclare. You were trying to court him a while ago, I remember that. Turns out he just didn't have a taste for tits."

Tobyas reached out and fondled her chest.

Yenvieve backhanded him across the face and he raged. He threw her down on the ground and she continued to kick and fight him, screaming obscenities in French.

When he realized that she was trying to delay him by wasting his time spewing French to piss him off, he roughly picked her back up again and headed to the midnight purple 1965►► Joßerand Tinqkov prototype car. She fought the entire way, making it take twice as long.

She was surprisingly strong—she would be stronger than Tobyas if she were sober.

He opened the driver's side door and threw Yenvieve inside, instructing her to get into the passenger seat. Then he sat down in the driver's seat and started the car.

Just before he could shift any gears, a rope appeared around his neck and tightened.

Tobyas gasped and sputtered as Sync choked him from the backseat with the noose he had re-tied while lying in wait.

"Get out, Vie!" Sync demanded.

As she scrambled out of the car—after first thumping Tobyas in the crotch—Sync dragged Tobyas into the passenger seat by his throat. He pulled as hard as he could on the rope as he stepped out of the car, then closed the rope into the rear car door. Now Tobyas was being awkwardly forced to hold himself up so that he wouldn't black out.

Sync leaned in to console Yenvieve, putting his hand around her waist. "Are you okay?"

"*Oui*, my dear boss." She nervously bit her lip, then asked, with tears in her eyes, "You didn't mean to kill Vous, did you?"

"That was the last thing I ever wanted to do," Sync replied, feeling void of emotion at that point so that Tobyas wouldn't see his sadness. "I would have killed myself first."

He slowly pulled the ribbons off of her dress and she didn't object to it or question it—he was the boss and allowed to do what he wanted.

Sync continued, "Vous thought the same way about me . . . and he got *his* way. That son of a bitch." Then, he sighed. "No offense to your mother," Sync dejectedly added, not able to properly convey that he was joking.

The young boss then opened the passenger door and wrapped one of the ribbons from Yenvieve's dress around his ankles while the medic helped. They closed the knotted ribbon into the door, keeping his legs pinned.

[216]

Then Sync went around to the other side of the car and slipped into the backseat again. Using the second ribbon, he pulled Tobyas' hands behind his head and tied them to the headrest. Sync noticed the signet ring on his finger and reached out to snatch it—but then let it be.

The older man laughed the entire time, clearly not taking Sync seriously in the slightest.

"Please go watch after Vous," Sync told Yenvieve, then got into the driver's seat.

The young boss then took the car out of the garage and headed out onto the peninsula.

Tobyas just laughed an extra throaty and breathless laugh once he saw the moon.

"So, what, you're going to show me more of what your pink boyfriend taught you? I know that's how you learned anything. You were so pathetic before he saved your life. Those were my men I sent in to get you first. I mean, after first getting the more important target."

Tobyas paused to watch Sync blow up with emotion in the way that he was known for—but he remained calm. His hands subtly tightened around the steering wheel.

"He had to try to teach you to be more like him so that he wasn't ashamed to be with you, huh? He taught you to drive real 'wicked cool', right?"

"Oh, no. No," Sync responded, sounding amused. "He didn't teach me to drive at all. This is my first time behind the wheel. This car will probably end up going over a fucking cliff," he said in a sure-fire tone.

Tobyas turned to nervously look out the window through his one good eye, lapsing into silence—he knew how many cliffs were out there.

"Don't worry about me, though," the young boss reassuringly added, seeing his ex-brother's fearful expression.

Then Synclare Thornwryght floored the gas pedal.

"I'm fucking bulletproof."

X X I I I .

"All I do is talk to you in my own mind."

THE MORE I TRIED TO find ways to be with you, the more I found out about what you left behind."

Synclare Thornwryght was in the middle of the Old Market in Brussels, Belgium. He was sitting on someone's flea market table, avoiding the rain and the people by being perched under a canopy.

In front of him in the crowd was Tacyturn standing there in the glow of the neon umbrellas that constantly went by, the only lights in the darkness of the night. He did not move or speak, even as people bumped into him. His eyes were on the Tintin trinkets Sync was sitting amongst.

"I visited Hollywood to find traces of you. You left behind a lot . . . and most of it wasn't good. I was attacked a few times when I accidentally gave away how much you meant to me. I almost didn't get away from some alive. I was foolish to go alone, but I felt you there.

"I went and threatened to burn down Electric Reel until they told me more about you. Do you know that they still hadn't found their pay? Well, they'll still never get it because I burned down the warehouse anyway. After hearing about what they did to you, I fucking had to. I used REW\Lync on them. I gave them their teeth back, too. I tried to put them back in their mouths, but I sort of missed and shoved them down their throats instead." Sync dryly chuckled. "My bad."

Tacyturn said nothing, but Sync knew he would ask a question if he could.

"Why didn't I kill them? I don't know." Sync shrugged. "I had just killed *you* . . . I wasn't looking to kill again. I don't like killing. But, from those fuckwits, I found out that you were a virtual object at Journeymind Escape. Money is no issue, so I bought you from Visard Lum to take home. She is not allowed to use you again. You were very expensive and totally worth it."

The redhead snorted. "Also, she wanted me to thank you for the broken eye socket."

The driver had no reaction.

"She had also modified your virtual scan to look more like you. She dialed your appearance forward so that you were twenty-three and not eighteen. She made sure you were the right height and had all your scars. She could refer to them with her pare tech security camera program when you had visited. She also overlapped the programming that made your bruises heal so that they never healed. I also requested a mode that made sure that you never smiled. I didn't want to see it that way. It didn't feel right. It wouldn't have been you, right?"

Sync stifled a laugh and shushed Tacyturn, even though he wasn't about to speak.

"I know. Don't ruin it. I need this. I don't want to mess up."

The redhead looked around the flea market, immediately returning to what he was saying—he had thought about it a lot.

"Every night since I found the virtual you, I spent time with you in a simulated world. You even sounded like you. You must have recorded your voice. Somehow, I could choose the accent. That must be where you used your talent the Rilangs forced on you. I chose to listen to the accent I knew best, the one I fell in love with. I fell in love with them all, though. The German one is pretty sexy. Also, the Irish one . . . and the Australian one, the Russian one, the British one and . . . Okay, yeah, all of them.

"I would have gone mad and stayed in the simulations forever, but your sister was there for me and kept me from indefinitely leaving myself plugged in until I fried myself in your arms. I was in the infirmary for a short period of time recovering from one night I nearly did just that. I decided to start looking into my father's work to distract me.

"As I took over what my father left behind, I learned more about your tech. Two years after you were gone, I found someone who was an expert at brain technology. I mean, we already knew someone but I wanted the help of a brain tech genius who also didn't want to kill you. Her name is Telsa. I learned that all of your memories, everything about who you are, was stored in your tech. According to the notes stored in there, the technology in your brain was a piece of a prototype for an android brain . . . an android brain that makes and stores memories and experiences to make them who they are, to make them human. It was also for someone to wear and load memories into it, then give it to an android to make them think they were human. Familiar, right?"

Sync looked over to a nearby café's digital window playing the faded visual memory of *Blade Runner*.

"It was like finding out you were alive. That was an amazing fucking night. I hadn't cried with happiness in a long, long time. And, much to the dismay of people around me, I stopped trying to move on. I knew I had to pursue what my father was doing."

His green eyes were on Tacyturn again. Sync paused to figure out what he wanted to talk about next, distracted by the syndicate logo on Tacyturn's tie.

"Remember when I wanted to make the syndicate a filmmaking company? I was serious about that after we talked about it. Maybe make the logo for it a gun, stars and a tiger. I already changed the syndicate logo to something cooler! You'll like it when you see it.

"I wanted to change the way my father was running the syndicate, but once I found out about your stored memories, I knew I had to keep pursuing the same path. I had to keep on his research and find the right brain that had the future memories of creating the perfect android. I couldn't wait for it to be invented on its own.

"I couldn't ask anyone to volunteer. Like DEL\Lync, you can't use any of the serums on people who are aware of it. It just doesn't work. The brain fights it off, closing its legs like a prude churchgoing bitch. So, I continued to kidnap children and administer the FFWD\Lync serum. I would then give them DEL\Lync and send them home, unharmed. I don't like it, but I needed to do what I can to bring you back to me."

Sync paused as he watched a child run by swinging a neon kendama.

"Two years after discovering your intact memories, we found the right child. She is the daughter of a fisherman in Japan. I wasn't even going to bother, but she was easy to kidnap. One of my men threw her toy into the water and the father went down to get it for her, thinking she had accidentally done it herself. When he surfaced, she was gone. We returned her a week later. I repeatedly sent letters assuring him that she was all right, but I doubt it helped much.

"Quietly in our own lab, we got to work. I don't care about selling the secret until I get to use it first. Maybe androids will be our thing, or maybe that's just too much to handle. If I was my father, I could create android hitmen and send them off into the world. But you and I know how sending androids out into the world goes. Once I'm done with the technology, I'll just sell the knowledge to someone else—and it'll be their problem.

"They'll probably hire us to retire them. I think we'd do pretty good. That sounds like something my father would have done, right? Throw a problem into the wild and then charge people to let us fix it."

Tacyturn picked up a pin of a red and white rocket.

Sync continued, "There are so many things I want to ask you. I've had some moments where I have doubted you. But I was thinking about our fight we had and then when you told me who you were. Did you tell me that you were Vous and call me your love just so that you could get me to put down my guard so you could switch our guns? You gave me everything I wanted and that was plenty to distract me. I was thinking maybe because you still never smiled. I've still never seen it. Why would you smile when you were just setting me up for what I did?

"I mean, I wouldn't blame you if you were just telling me what I wanted to hear all the time we were together. We didn't know each other long enough to fall in love, did we? I mean, we did . . . but we were really young when we met and not thinking about shit like that yet. I fell in love like a fucking school girl losing her virginity to a bad boy, but I don't think I was very emotionally sensible at twenty. I think you can agree with that. I don't even think I am now, frankly. But now I have become six years older without you and I still feel love for you."

Sync sighed.

"I told you I fell really fucking hard, Vous. I just wish I knew for sure if you fell at all."

Lightning flashed in the sky finally—he thought he had requested for more.

"Just like I have doubt, I do have hope that I meant as much to you as you made me feel like I did. In my father's program that he used to control you, he had a log that was keeping track of your emotions. Your eye colour. You didn't show emotion, but you did feel it and he implanted that code so he could make sure that you were not ever just putting on an act. It was probably easier to manipulate you, as well.

"Even though I thought that magenta was your default colour, it wasn't. Your default colour was your natural electric denim eye colour . . . which is a super wicked cool name for your eye colour, by the way. Magenta was just the colour your eye always was when you were around *me* . . ."

Sync leaned down to catch Tacyturn's eyes to see their colour. He smiled when he confirmed that one was magenta.

"He also gave you the authorization to revert your eye's colour to your default if you needed to hide your emotions. You hardly used it, though. So, what did you do to make your eye stay magenta? Were you thinking about me? Have you been able to think about me for six years after I lost you? Or has it only been like you were sleeping?"

There was now much more lightning flashing and thunder rumbling. He was amused as he watched the crowd get startled by this—not Tacyturn, though. His eyes were still undeviatingly on the contents of the table.

Sync sighed wistfully and stared into the sky. "I can't wait to tell you that I also found a letter from my father. He was killed moments after you died. Father knew he was going to die and the letter states that he knew he was dead by the time I was reading it, but he wasn't sure by whom. He addressed it to both of us.

"He used FFWD\Lync on you when you were very small and didn't speak any English. He stole important information from you that he almost didn't bother to translate. Your alternate future was responsible for most of the wicked cool car technology we have right now. Isn't that perfect? That's why you drive so well. You were supposed to be the father of that technology.

"He apologized for stealing it from you and has dared you to one-up yourself and make them fly now. Like I did. It made me remember seeing you tinkering with cars with your father and I asked you if you could make the car fly. You told me you would work on that. I was ten then. That's when you used the rope to climb into my window, claiming you flew up there in a flying car. I believed you for . . . a minute, but it was an amazing minute! So, where are my fucking flying cars?" He playfully punched Tacyturn's shoulder.

"I've been able to look at you for real. I can't wait until you're actually looking at me. You'll see that I have more scars now. They look just like the cigarette burns . . . but bigger. I can't wait to tell you about how the syndicate thinks I'm bulletproof because Tobyas shot me up with the prop gun on its highest setting. They were super fucking painful, but now I'm not afraid of cigarettes anymore.

"I'm scared of less things now . . . I'm more confident. That's all because of you. You're in for a treat if—*when* you get back. I've been bottled up for six fucking years. Crime syndicate bosses don't need that kind of pressure. I need to let it out. I think I'm doing my job all right, but I think I could do it better with you.

"I'll be way more wickedly cool with you by my side again. I can't wait until I no longer have to think about everything I want to say to you. I don't have to say everything I want to say to you in a simulation. I don't have to dream about what I'm going to say to you while I'm asleep. All I do is talk to you in my own mind. So much research over the years and nothing to show for it until now. I'm tired of unspoken words and I just want you to look back at me. I can't wait to—"

From the corner of his eye, an alert materialized. He covered Tacyturn with an overlay of the call as he accepted it.

"What is it?" Sync tersely asked.

A woman's cautiously tender voice spoke. "I am sorry to bother you, Mister Thornwryght. You wanted to be *here* the moment he was ready. He's almost ready. So, by the time you—"

Sync didn't need to hear anymore. He looked apologetically at Tacyturn as he tore his headset off and the simulation abruptly disconnected, rattling his brain.

He dipped out of the pod of simulated rain and tore out of the mansion into the real rain. The boss eagerly stumbled across the property and none-to-gracefully made his way into the secret level of the laboratory until he was face-to-face with the android that looked like his childhood friend. His head was ringing from not properly disconnecting from the simulation and he couldn't stand up straight or get his eyes to focus.

"Everything is ready."

Synclare Thornwryght looked at Yenvieve who gently touched his nervous cheek and helped steady him by linking her arm into his.

Noticing he was surprised by her statement, she chuckled. "I had people run from all of your favourite corners of the mansion and time it. Then I insisted that Telsa call you when that amount of time was left."

Sync looked appreciative—but trepidatious. Yenvieve could feel him trembling.

"Don't worry," she said with a calm smile. "Your world is about to make sense again, *mon chéri*."

"What about yours?" he asked.

Yenvieve was going to lose her place next to Sync—in bed and everywhere else. She was prepared for that. He loved her—but not the same way he loved her brother.

She began straightening up his outfit which looked a little disheveled after he scrambled unsteadily to the laboratory. He was in a soaked and wrinkled green jumpsuit—not how he wanted to present himself for that moment, but he forgot to care.

"My world has always made sense. I'm perfectly prepared to fight my brother for your attention and to fight you for his attention," she teased as she brushed his longer wet red hair out of his emerald eyes. "Besides, every night can be a ménage à trois!"

His freckled cheeks went red and he furrowed his brow. "*What?*"

Vie tenderly chuckled. "I tease. I just wanted to put some colour in your cheeks, Sync."

She kissed him on his lips and left the room, ordering everyone else to, as well. In six years, she had learned to know exactly what Sync wanted without him having to say it. He bottled himself up as he waited for the day when he didn't have to anymore—that day had, hopefully, arrived.

Sync waited for everyone to leave. Everything was uploaded into the lifeless android body and he no longer needed anyone else in the laboratory.

Bandit jumped up and laid across his shoulders—she seemed to have a snooty expression because she was the only one allowed to stay.

The syndicate boss stared at the body that was being held upright in a glass pod by a single tube into the back of his neck.

Nearby, there was a table of important items ready to go back to their original owner. Sync approached the table and removed the gun from his holster and placed it on the table where it belonged.

He then went to a control panel and turned on the walls. Each wall was rigged with electric tapestries to make it look like they were standing on top of a neon rooftop in the middle of the night. The ceiling was made of glass to help with the atmosphere—without actually letting rain in to ruin all of their expensive technology.

All that needed to be done was wake him up and he could do that alone—he wanted to do it alone. He had so many things to say that he didn't want anyone to hear. He disabled the sound recording for the room. He was afraid to speak until the android could listen, but his thoughts still raced with everything he was dying to tell him.

I'm about to talk to you. This is going to work.

I don't think I'm going to even be able to contain myself.

I've been wanting to talk to you for six fucking years.

The moment you look at me, I think it's going to just overflow out of my lips.

You know how I can fucking get.

I hope you're prepared for that.

Taking in a deep breath, Sync approached the pod. Lightning flashed, bleeding in through the glass ceiling, lighting up the android's handsome features. It just looked like he was sleeping.

Eager to wake him up, Sync pulled the life lever. The boss heard a crackle of electricity and spasmodic thrumming.

The pod shuddered, unexpectedly cracking the glass ceiling above. Rain showered into the laboratory in a zig-zagging line from the pod to Sync.

Avoiding the water, Bandit jumped off of his shoulders and onto the nearby camera, blocking it with her fluffy tail—everyone who was secretly watching even with the sound disabled could now see nothing. Yenvieve crossed her arms and huffed because she had wanted to witness such a momentous moment. She was still over the moon for the two of them, though, and crossed her fingers.

Then the pronged tube detached from the back of the android's neck and he gasped, catching himself with one hand onto the glass and the other grasping his chest. The textured glass cracked and then shattered in thousands of tiny cubes. Without the support of the glass, the neon pod just fell apart all around him.

Vapours rose from every part of bare flesh the android body had exposed.

The android looked down at his hand and his chest. His memories flooded back. The colours in his heterochromatic eyes returned pixel by pixel.

Then Kovous J. Chauffeur looked up at Sync and smiled.

It took Sync's breath away.

THE END